Lone Star Homecoming

Lone Star Homecoming

A Texas Justice Romance

Justine Davis

TULE
PUBLISHING

Lone Star Homecoming
Copyright© 2020 Justine Davis
Tule Publishing First Printing, June 2020

The Tule Publishing, Inc.

ALL RIGHTS RESERVED

First Publication by Tule Publishing 2020

Cover design by Lee Hyat Designs

No part of this book may be used or reproduced in any manner whatsoever without written permission except in the case of brief quotations embodied in critical articles and reviews.

This is a work of fiction. Names, characters, places, and incidents are products of the author's imagination or are used fictitiously. Any resemblance to actual events, locales, organizations, or persons, living or dead, is entirely coincidental.

ISBN: 978-1-952560-33-0

Chapter One

THE MAN KNOWN lately as Kane Travis stood staring at a sight he'd never thought to see. The green waves of the Northern Lights rippled in amazing motion across the dark sky. He could still see some stars through the green, as if it were nothing more than a veil, some thin curtain blowing in the wind. Except there was no wind—it was dead calm, which made it all the more eerie.

He'd never thought to see any stars that could rival those over Texas, but he was thinking Alaska might give them a run.

And he *wasn't* going to start thinking about Texas again. He'd had thirteen years now to break that habit, and he was beyond disgusted at himself for how easy it was to slide back into it, back to those early days when it had been a deep, solid, ever-present ache inside him.

Why Alaska?

I've always wanted to see the Northern Lights. And it's as far away as I can get from Texas.

He hadn't said that last sentence aloud to the captain of the fishing boat *Kenai King*, not when he was essentially begging a ride from him. When the man had asked him if he was running from something, his answer had been, "Just myself." He hadn't wanted the man to think he was a criminal on the lam.

Of course, there was still and always the distinct possibility he was exactly that. For all he knew he was on a wanted poster back in Last Stand. He'd run checks, when he could be reasonably certain of not being tracked, and had never found anything indicating he—or anyone—was wanted in the death of Police Chief Steven Highwater. Of course it had been thirteen years, but he doubted the very public death of a police chief would ever be forgotten.

He no longer had the instinctive, cringing reaction he'd once had when he thought of it, a sort of internal cry of "I didn't mean it!"

Because he was no longer sure he hadn't.

He was no longer sure of much of anything about the first sixteen years of his life.

He stared up at the light show above him, and focused on how even knowing how and why it happened didn't take away any of the magic of it. As he looked, the back of his neck started to itch. He reached up, tugged off the heavy, woolen knit cap, and rammed a hand through his tangled hair. The hat served its purpose in keeping him warm, but he hated the feel of it. He'd grown up wearing cowboy hats, and anything else still felt strange.

And there he was, mentally back in Texas yet again. He tried to corral his thoughts by grabbing a handful of the hair that reached down past his ears and giving it a yank.

You need to borrow a pair of scissors somewhere and whack

this off. Or just do it with the knife.

He pulled the hat back on. Summer was nearing, but last night they'd had a cold snap—unusual, or so Jay at the coffee shop said—and it had dropped back down into the twenties. Of course the average daytime highs here in the summer were cool even for nighttime in Texas.

Stop it.

He watched until the light show faded, watched his breath swirl out into the cold air for a while, thinking about the vastness of this place he'd only seen the barest edge of.

Guess I should be glad climbing Denali wasn't on the list.

But he wasn't glad. Because this was the last stop. The end of that list, or at least all he'd set out to do. He'd accomplished it all, seen all the places except the one he couldn't; it was in no way feasible, so the beaches of Honolulu would not see him. So in essence, it was done. Thirteen years of hand-to-mouth living, skating by, always looking over his shoulder. When he went back to the tiny storeroom above the general store where he was sleeping these days, he would get out that now tattered and worn list, and cross off that last item. The list of a lifetime, written by a man who hadn't had that lifetime to see it through.

Thanks to you.

But it was done. He was done with the task he'd never really expected to finish.

And now he had no idea what he was going to do.

LARK LECLAIR SAT up groggily, so sleepy she wasn't even awake enough to get angry about the double attack that had awakened her on the one morning she'd planned to sleep in. Yet.

The rhythmic thumps from her right told her Jimmy Alvarez was wide awake and bouncing his soccer ball in the apartment again. The more uneven thumps against the wall to her left told her Lena had brought another one home last night; the woman seemed to think by sleeping with as many men as her ex-husband had women she was somehow evening the score.

Lark rose hastily and headed for her bathroom before she had to listen to screaming from both sides: Anita, Jimmy's sweet mom yelling at him to stop, and Lena at the man of the moment to keep going. She should have gone to her parents' house in Austin last night instead of waiting until today. At least she would have had some peace.

She seriously considered decamping to the living room, but it wouldn't be any quieter there, where the noise from an awakening Last Stand would be rising. Maybe she should just curl up on the floor here in the bathroom and try to grab another hour. But she knew if she did she'd only feel worse than she felt now. It would take her until noon to really wake up. What she wouldn't give to move to a place where the only noise was the wind in the trees or the occasional bawl of a cow. She was going to have to put that higher on the list. Maybe at the top, now that she was finally financially even.

Serves you right, trying to be everyone's savior and spending yourself into a hole doing it.

She sighed as the tired old self-lecture went through her head again. Tired because she knew she was incapable of having done it any differently. When her job had been kids at risk, she didn't just go to the extent of her authority with Child Protective Services to help them; she had all too often delved into her own pocket to help them more, even if it was only a small toy or stuffed animal to truly call their own. Or given them one of the picture books she'd written and had printed, at her own expense, with a story that often gave them hope.

But it had also cost her so much more, darn near including her health. As she'd been told three years ago.

You cannot keep this up, Lark. It's eating you alive because you can't save them all. You're only twenty-eight, but you are a wreck. For someone your age, you're a disaster, to put it bluntly.

But they need someone who honestly cares, who will fight for them.

Yes. But you keep this up and you won't be fighting for anyone.

Lark knew Doc McBride had been right, and that she'd had to leave. And she couldn't deny she was much happier, healthier, and almost out of debt now that she'd been working for *Building Families*. The job at the private adoption agency had saved her.

Between yawns as she turned on the shower and grabbed a clean towel she spared yet another moment of thanks for Last Stand Police Chief—and her friend—Shane Highwater, who had recommended she talk to them when he'd encountered her sobbing openly after her last case, the case that had broken her, of a little boy she'd been ordered to return to the mother's custody. An order that had resulted in the boy's death three months later. Had it not been for his wise counsel that night...

She was still pondering the turn her life had taken as she walked the short distance to Java Time, wondering if there was enough caffeine in the world to get her going this morning. And nearly collided with a man headed for the same place.

"Sorry," they said simultaneously, and both laughed. And laughed again when they realized they knew each other.

"Scott!" she exclaimed.

He looked a little surprised. What, he hadn't expected her to remember him? The guy who had made one of her dearest friends so happy it almost hurt to be around her?

"Lark," he acknowledged, holding the door and gestured her in rather gallantly.

"Hi, Lark," Mike said from behind the counter. "The usual?"

"Hold the whipped cream and add a shot of espresso," she said ruefully. "I need the caffeine."

Mike laughed and turned to make the drink. Lark turned back to the man behind her. "How's Sage? It's been a couple of weeks since I've talked to her, and I've been working on a complex case and haven't seen her in over a month."

But when she had seen the youngest Highwater sibling, she'd looked happier than Lark had ever seen her. And Lark knew it was thanks to this man, one-time Last Stand bad boy

Scott Parrish, home from his stint in the Marines.

"She's good." His smile broadened, and changed, and Lark guessed he was the big reason her friend had been otherwise occupied. And she could guess doing what; Scott Parrish was a thoroughly sexy guy.

She took the cup Mike held out, stepped back and waited until he made a quick order of plain black coffee. Scott took it, paid, took a sip and then looked over the rim of his cup at her. "You're coming with us to Oklahoma City, right?"

She knew he meant the NRHA Derby, the big reining competition that Sage's beloved Poke was entered in. Sage had high hopes, and although she didn't know that much about it, Lark loved horses and thought the sweet dun was wonderful. She'd watched Sage work him a couple of times, and what she got out of that horse was, to her eyes, remarkable.

"I'd planned on it," she said.

"Good. I want everybody who'll go there to cheer them on."

"And console her if it doesn't go well?" she guessed.

"That, too," he agreed. "But I think it'll be fine. They're an amazing team."

She nodded. "They are. And she's so happy I think Poke has caught her mood."

This time he grinned. "I hope so."

"Now that you're back, if they could just find her brother I think her world would be complete again. At least, as complete as it can be." She knew the Highwaters would forever feel the loss of their father, the man all of Last Stand had looked up to and respected. Although his eldest son, who had eventually stepped into those police chief boots, was doing a fine job of gaining that same kind of standing, and no one knew that better than her.

"Sage and I got closer than we've ever been to finding him," he said.

"What you found out in Seattle? Sage told me there'd been great progress, but we didn't get into detail before my work got complicated. Not to mention she's been a little...distracted," she teased.

"So have I," he admitted with an endearing smile. "But what happened was, someone there recognized a picture of him."

She blinked. A picture? "From when he was...what, sixteen?" That didn't seem likely, since he'd be twenty-nine now.

Scott smiled. "No," he said, pulling out his phone. "A picture Sean had aged up. Now we know it's pretty accurate."

He held it out for her to see, and her breath caught. Kane had been two years behind her in school, but every girl there could pick out the youngest Highwater boy. There was just something about him. All the Highwaters were almost unfairly attractive, but Kane Highwater had been—and apparently still was—wildly beautiful. The near-perfect features, the dark hair that had always been a bit too long, and those striking hazel eyes that had sometimes looked green, sometimes gold, sometimes light brown.

"I'd think he'd be pretty unforgettable," she said quietly.

"That's what the volunteer at the pop culture museum said," Scott answered with a crooked smile. "But now we know where he was less than four months ago. We're getting closer."

Lark smiled back at him. She liked the way he kept saying "we." To her it meant the Highwaters had accepted him completely, in a way Sage had told her his own blood family never had. And when they said goodbye, her sending with him a promise to call Sage and finalize their plans, the smile lingered.

Good for them. They deserve the fine reputation they have in Last Stand.

But did Kane Highwater deserve it, too? You couldn't have been in Last Stand at the time of former Chief Highwater's death and not have heard the rumors. She discounted 90 percent of what she heard generally, but suspicions in such a high-profile incident were long-lived. Kane had always had a reputation for being a bit tempestuous anyway, and when coupled with the circumstances of what had happened, it was easy for people who generally assumed the worst anyway to assume it had been more than a tragic accident.

But if Lark had learned anything in her five years with CPS it was to never assume you knew all of the truth based on what people said had happened. Especially when dealing with kids—and Kane had still been one at the time—the why sometimes far outweighed the what.

The image of that photograph, of what he looked like now, lingered in her mind all the way to Austin.

And her tender heart ached for the boy he'd been.

Chapter Two

THIS WAS INSANE. He was going to regret it. He was so going to regret it. He'd known he would and he'd done it anyway.

Hell, he'd probably been doomed from the moment he'd found out—entirely by accident and because of a television show his boss, the owner of the hardware store, happened to be watching. A show about, of all things, champion reining horses and trainers. And how the sport had grown, with big prizes at shows all over the country. Which had, inevitably, gotten him thinking about Sage. Because reaching that level had been a dream of hers from childhood.

But then he started down a rabbit hole like Sean used to do. Wondering if she was still set on that dream. If she'd ever found a horse that could take her there. Which got him looking up the Derby in Oklahoma City, the only big competition he specifically knew about. Which got him remembering the time they'd all gone, when he'd been twelve and Sage ten.

It had been the last big trek with all of them, because Shane was heading off to college that September. He remembered Sage reading aloud from the program she'd looked up. *The National Reining Horse Association's Derby showcases the best four- to six-year-old reining horses and their riders.* She'd been so excited she'd about driven them all crazy on the nearly eight-hour drive. And had about killed herself so they didn't have to make too many restroom stops for her, slowing them down.

And then he'd gotten to poking around on the computer Mr. Lindsay let him use after hours, as long as he didn't go hunting down porn, the man had told him sternly.

"Not a problem," he'd answered rather sourly.

He'd never found that kind of thing particularly satisfying. He preferred reality when it came to sex. Oddly, he'd found the longer he went without—the last time being a woman he'd met in a small Northern California town about eight months ago, when he'd had to stop and find a few days' work at a lumber yard to pay for gas and a little food to make it to Seattle—the less he missed it. It was as if the sexual aspect of his nature had somehow gone to sleep. Which was probably for the best, given his life.

Of course then the truck had blown up on him, and he'd been back to hitching again. Damn thing had had a full tank, too, and that money would have fed him for at least four days, if he'd been careful.

But all thoughts of that had been blasted out of his head when he came across a blog with a list of the current entrants for the NRHA Derby in Oklahoma City in June. And his gaze locked on one, single line.

Highwater's Hot Poco, ridden and trained by Sage Highwater, Last Stand, Texas. Entered in all eligible Non-Pro Levels.

He'd scrupulously avoided doing any online searches for any of the Highwaters, even Sage, knowing how much whatever he found would hurt. Yet there he'd ended up, staring at the string of words, frozen in place as surely as if he were sitting outside in the dead of winter here in Ketchikan. Somehow seeing proof that she was alive and obviously well only intensified the ache.

And now here he was, sitting almost as frozen, on a plane about to touch down in Oklahoma City. He was only on a plane at all because, when he'd been looking at bus tickets from Seattle Mr. Lindsay had looked over his shoulder—probably checking for that porn—and remarked for twenty bucks more he could fly. And when he'd said he didn't have it to spare, not if he was going to eat and find a place to sleep when he got there, the man had stunned him by pulling out a twenty and handing it to him.

"Go home, son. Do what my boy never did. Whatever you left behind, go back and fix it."

It was the first and only time Mr. Lindsay had ever mentioned he even had a son. But Kane thought he knew now why the man had taken a chance and hired him at the store, without knowing anything about him except what Kane had told him. He hadn't lied about work he'd done, but he'd had no way to prove it, either. The kind of jobs he'd had weren't the type to write recommendation letters.

But he wasn't really going home. He probably could have flown into Dallas even cheaper, but he'd sworn he'd never set foot in Texas again and he'd meant it. Oklahoma was close enough. Too damned close, in fact.

He still wasn't sure what on earth he was doing. It wasn't like he was going to find Sage, walk up to her and say hello. Hell, she'd probably shoot him on sight. And he wouldn't blame her a bit.

But he needed to see her. He just needed to see her, know she was all right. That she'd turned out okay. Not that he really had any doubts. Even after what he'd done, she'd have been okay. Shane would have seen to that. He might have lost his faith in most everything else, but he knew Shane Highwater would do what had to be done. It was in his DNA, just as it had been in his father's.

And then the plane halted at the gate, and Kane wished more than anything that he could turn around and go back. That he'd never had this crazy, insane, ludicrous idea. He'd half expected it to blow up on him when he tried to board the plane, but the ID he'd acquired in California had held up. And here he was, just him and the small backpack that held everything he owned. So what came after this? What would he do?

Time, probably.

He was only half-joking, knowing there could well be jail if not prison in his future, that maybe he'd just missed finding the data online. But right now, now that he'd finished that list that had been his focus for the last thirteen years, he wasn't sure that might not be for the best. At least he wouldn't have to think about it constantly, to live with the possibility hanging over his head. Nor would he be worrying about food, or a roof.

Maybe he should go home. Maybe he should just go

back to Last Stand and march himself into Steven Highwater's old office and turn himself in to whoever was wearing the chief's stars now. He could just imagine how that would go.

Hi, I'm the guy formerly known as Kane Highwater. I killed the guy who used to have this office.

He could almost feel the heavy metal of the handcuffs on his wrists. And wondered again if maybe it wouldn't be for the best. Because he was tired. At only twenty-nine, he was almightily tired. Being in so many places, even places he'd liked, but always knowing it was temporary. That he'd be moving on. In fact, he'd gotten to the point where starting to feel comfortable in a place had been his signal to move on. Because he didn't deserve to feel comfortable.

His head fell forward, his forehead resting against the heavy glass of the porthole window.

God, he was tired of running.

LARK STOOD IN the middle of the Highwater cheering section, grinning. As they all were. Because Sage and the brilliant Poke were doing amazing things out in that arena. She knew because Sage's best friend and fellow horsewoman, Jessie McBride, was practically delirious with excitement, and her boyfriend, Asher Chapman, was grinning at her.

Lark was glad she had Scott beside her to explain, because while she could thoroughly appreciate the flash and fire of the powerful, agile horse and the skill of his rider, she didn't understand the finer points of what she was seeing. But Scott had thrown himself into learning every bit of it, and was more than willing to point things out, like the way Poke's planted hind leg never moved in those amazing spins, and how he never hopped in those incredible sliding stops. She liked the way the horse seemed to dance when they changed directions in the big circles, something Scott told her was a flying change of lead, which made perfect sense once he'd explained it to her.

"She's freaking going to take it all," he yelped when her score was announced, from which Lark deduced a two-twenty-seven was very, very good.

"They," Shane Highwater corrected mildly, and with a smile.

"Yes, sir," Scott said, and with amusement Lark saw he'd flushed slightly at his own words.

"We'll break you of that 'sir,' eventually," Sean, standing beside his beautiful Elena, said cheerfully.

When the excitement had ebbed a little, Lark excused herself with a smile, trying to reorient herself and find the restrooms. This place, grandly named the Jim Norick Coliseum after a former mayor of the city, was huge. The Highwaters had all been here for a couple of days, making it a big family outing, the family having doubled in size in the last year. In a very good way.

She was so glad she'd come yesterday—it had been worth it for this final triumph. She wasn't looking forward to the seven-hour drive back home, but there was no point in her staying when they planned to hit the road as soon as they could, even though it would be almost all a nighttime drive. They wanted to go home, and she completely understood that.

As she walked past the various vendors, trying to spot the sign for the facilities, she laughingly thought she should leave a trail of breadcrumbs to find her way back to the location they had staked out right next to the arena fence.

An idea stirred. Something like that might make a useful story. And might help teach younger kids to pay attention to their surroundings more, to mark a trail in some way, so if they got lost they just might be able to find their way home. She could make it about how a little boy or girl hadn't had breadcrumbs, but was able to bend a plant here, leave a mark in the dirt there, maybe even an arrow pointing the way.

She slowed her pace, her mind starting to race, and only aware enough to keep out of people's way. She hadn't written a book since the Murphy story, three years ago. The tale of the pinto pony who always wore a leprechaun hat had been something she'd used to help calm distressed children, all too often after they'd witnessed something horrible. Somehow escaping into the tale of a magical pony who could make everything right—once he figured out what right was—seemed to often do the trick. Well enough that even now that she was gone, she knew CPS still kept copies of the book at hand for just such situations. And the Last Stand library had some copies; in fact she knew assistant librarian Joey Douglas had used one to calm a lost child not long ago. She kept them handy herself even now that she was dealing with much happier situations, to give to the new parents of a child she'd helped them add to their lives, as a personal gift of sorts.

She was probably prouder of that book than anything she'd ever done, outside of her work, and she often wondered why she'd never tried to write another. But until this moment, another idea hadn't grabbed her enough. And she didn't want to have to go through that awful mess with the illustrator again. The woman had been talented, yes, but she'd also kind of lost track of whose story it was, taking off and drawing scenes that not only weren't in the story, but weren't even representative of the story. And she hadn't seemed to get that that was important for children of the age Murphy was aimed at, that they wanted the visual story to match the words, and that was critical to their language and reading development as well.

That's what she'd gotten for taking a chance on a new artist, apparently. Courtney had felt all those details impinged on her artistic freedom. Lark had reminded her she was getting paid, and it had gone downhill from there. But it had come out all right in the end, and once they'd discovered it was useful CPS had reimbursed her for some of her costs to put it all together, so she tried to write that part off as a lesson learned not to go with someone just because they were talented.

She kept thinking as she utilized the facilities, a little startled at how that little idea—one of those breadcrumbs, as it were—had sparked this tumble of imagination. By the time she dried her hands and headed out, she had almost the whole idea set in her mind. As she threaded her way back through the crowd, she began planning. She would start as soon as she got home, she promised herself as she dodged a family headed the other direction. Someone else dodging them bumped her, an older man who looked as if he'd walked out of the old west, with battered cowboy boots and a hat to match. But he touched the brim of that hat to her in apology, and she smiled and nodded back at him. She did like cowboys who had that old-world manner.

Maybe all she'd needed was to get away for a bit, spend some time in a completely different place and environment like this. She should remember this, in case she wanted to—

Whoa!

She stumbled as the word—so appropriate to the setting—shot into her mind. *That* guy had had an entirely different effect on her than the old hand. She blinked. Searched the knot of people standing to her right, looking for the man she'd just glimpsed, in the green shirt and jeans, carrying a small backpack, the man with the dark hair and eyes who seemed to spark gold even from ten feet away. The man who moved like some kind of big cat, quick, lithe; the man who was turning more than one female head with his wild beauty...

Wild beauty. Those words...she laughed at herself when she realized.

Your imagination really did kick into overdrive.

She knew it had to be that. Her imagination had already been fired up with that book idea, coupled with having just seen that photo the other day. Because there was no way she could have really seen what she thought she'd seen.

There was no way Kane Highwater could really be here.

Chapter Three

"KANE!"

He froze. His breath slammed to a halt in his chest.

Don't turn, don't turn, don't turn.

It rang in his head like a mantra that could save him.

It wasn't Sage. That was all he knew for sure, because she and her horse had just finished that blistering run that had garnered a score that had the entire arena audience, which was no small number, roaring with approval and excitement. He'd been a little surprised at how much he remembered, as he'd watched her put the horse through his paces.

But he also knew there'd been a contingent from Last Stand there cheering her on. He guessed that from the loudest cheers that had come from a spot halfway down the arena.

He hadn't looked. Didn't want to look. He wasn't here to see anyone else; he only wanted to see Sage for himself. Which he had. And he'd seen that not only was she excited about her horse's great run, she was also happy. It had fairly radiated from her.

"My God, it is you."

The nearly breathless voice from behind him told him he'd stayed frozen too long. He should have run. Again. It was a nice voice, though. Feminine, with a low timbre that made a man start thinking things he shouldn't.

Things he himself hadn't thought in a long time.

Definitely should have run.

She stepped in front of him then.

She was everything her voice had conjured up in his head. Kind of a little thing but definitely all female. Sandy-blond hair past her shoulders, in a loose braid. Light green eyes that made him think of spring growth. Altogether, a package that made him keep thinking of things he hadn't thought about in a very long time.

And he had no idea who she was.

"I think you've mistaken me for someone else." There, he'd managed that evenly enough. He turned to go, truly knowing now he never should have come.

"Have I?" she asked softly.

Damn, that voice. Here he'd thought he'd successfully put sexual longings into cold storage, and in less than ten spoken words she had him wanting more than anything to hear it under very different circumstances, preferably in bed.

He swore silently. Aloud he said gruffly, "Yes."

And again turned to go.

"Kane."

That voice. Saying his name. The name he'd kept because it fit, as if they'd known his soul even then. But she was now holding something out to him, her phone, with a photo on the screen.

A photo of him.

He froze all over again. This was crazy. Impossible. How could this woman he didn't know possibly have...whatever this was. Because now that he looked more closely at it he realized it wasn't exactly a photo. It looked more like one of those pictures that had had a filter applied, making it look just a bit less lifelike.

"Sean took an old picture of you and had it aged up," she said quietly. His gut knotted fiercely as she said his brother's name. "We knew it was pretty accurate when the volunteer at the museum in Seattle recognized you."

Casey. He remembered her instantly. She'd been so nice, good to him really, letting him use her pass to get into the sound lab, where he'd been able to do something he hadn't had the time or equipment to do in what felt like forever. Play music. It wasn't his guitar from home, but it was something, and had gotten him through a few rough days.

All the meaning behind those thoughts crashed into him. Sean had done that? And somehow connected him to Seattle? This made no sense at all.

Instinctively he backed away from her. This wasn't, couldn't be happening.

She spoke quickly. "Sage was so relieved to know you were alive. Every time they got closer to finding you she was terrified the next step would be finding out you were dead."

He was staring at her now. "No." It was all he could get out. He wasn't even sure what he was denying.

"Yes. I've never seen her so relieved as she was when they got home from Seattle."

"She went to—" He stopped himself. But then couldn't. "They?"

"She and Scott."

"Scott..." Realization hit. "Scott Parrish?"

"Yes." She smiled so beautifully it took most of the anxiety out of the realization that he'd just as much as admitted he was who she thought he was. "He was gone, in the service, but he came back home a few months ago."

"They're...together?"

"Very. Oh, let me take you to them. There's so much you need to know!"

"No." This time he said it fiercely. And this time he really did back away.

"It's all right," she said, much more quietly now. "I realize...you don't even know who I am, do you? I'm sorry. I'm Lark, Lark Leclair. I was in Sean's class at Creekbend High. And I'm friends with all your family."

Acid erupted inside him. "They're not my family," he bit out.

She tilted her head, looking at him not as if he'd surprised her, but as if she suddenly understood. "Then why," she said softly, "have they never, ever given up trying to find you and bring you home?"

AT FIRST, WHEN he turned and ran, she tried to follow him. But the crowd was too dense, and she too short to see over it. By the time she found something to stand on to look down the way he'd gone, he was nowhere in sight.

He was here. Kane Highwater was here, in Oklahoma City. It wasn't difficult to guess he'd come to watch Sage. They'd always been so close. But if he'd come to see his sister, why had he taken off like that at the very idea of doing just that? Lark didn't think it was her, since he didn't know her. Was it the rest of his family? His brothers? Was that who he didn't want to see? Why?

Since she couldn't find him, she had to get back to the Highwater crew. If there was any chance of finding Kane here, she knew they would. Shane and Sean might not be in police uniform today, but she'd bet they could still organize a search in a hurry. For that matter she'd bet veterans Scott and Asher could do a darn good job of hunting him down.

She didn't like that phrase that popped into her mind. Hunting him down. Not relative to this man. She was still having trouble catching her breath after the shock of seeing him. It was the total unexpectedness of him being here, that's all. Nothing to do with the fact that in the split second before she'd realized it was him she'd almost gaped at him because he was so...beautiful.

She couldn't let him get away. And she did not mean that in the way of a woman who'd spotted a man she wanted. She most certainly did not. She ran, for once her diminutive five feet two a help, because she was able to dodge through smaller spaces. But when, a little breathless from the run, she got back to where they had all been gathered only Slater Highwater, the Last Stand saloonkeeper, and Joey were still there. As she slowed she saw Slater leaning over to whisper something in Joey's ear that made the assistant librarian blush, but give him a look that made Lark feel a sort of wistful longing. And the brand-new engagement ring on Joey's finger glinted in the light.

But there was no time for that now. And as soon as Slater spotted her he straightened and smiled. "We're the least use around horses, so we waited for you while the others went to help Sage with Poke. He's a little peeved after all the photographs they wanted."

"We need everyone," she gasped out.

Joey reached out and put a hand on her arm. "Lark, what is it?"

She didn't have the wind back yet for a long explanation, so she cut to the chase. "Kane's here."

The two froze. Stared at her. She gulped in more air, steadied herself and spoke rapidly before they asked. "Yes, I'm sure. He ran. Come on, we have to move, we need everyone to search, or he'll be gone."

Slater and Joey started to move at a run, back toward where she guessed the entrance to the barn was, where Sage would have taken Poke after their performance.

Between breaths—she really needed to run more often—she tried to get the story out. "He looks just like the aged-up picture. We spoke."

"You talked to him? He said it was him?" Slater sounded beyond tense, and she couldn't blame him.

"He denied it at first. But I saw him react to Sean's name, and Sage's—" she had to pause for a deeper breath "—and when I said something about Sage and Scott going to

Seattle...he was startled and asked if it was Scott Parrish."

"Damn," Slater muttered.

"It is him," Joey said, visible excitement rising just as they dodged a group in the doorway to get out of the arena building.

As she would have expected, the two cops were the quickest to realize something was up. Shane, in fact, had gone on alert the minute he'd spotted them, perhaps from the way they were hurrying. A split second later he was striding toward them.

"What is it?" he snapped the instant he was close enough.

"Kane," Slater said. "He's here. Lark talked to him." Lark heard Sage gasp. She'd been in a stall grooming her victorious horse, but dropped the brush as if from fingers suddenly numb. "But he ran. We need to search. *Now.*"

Shane zeroed in on her and for the first time in her life Lark felt the sheer intensity of the man. But he didn't question her conclusion, which warmed her enough to be able to answer his question about what Kane had been wearing.

"Green long-sleeved T-shirt. Blue jeans, ripped at the...left knee. Black running shoes. His hair's a little long, but still dark."

Shane looked at Joey. Lark knew she had been a classmate of Kane's in high school.

"He might trust me," Joey said in understanding. "Or he might lump me in with all of you from back then, and his reasons for running."

"Lark," Sean said, decisively. "Go with the stranger, less

reason for him to take off. And she can deal, you know that."

Shane nodded, and suddenly started snapping out orders rapid-fire. "Joey, take the other end of the arena; Elena, take this end." He looked at Scott and Asher. "Can you two do what you used to do?"

The two former military men never hesitated.

"I'll take overwatch," Scott said, looking toward the upper grandstand, and Lark guessed that was something he'd done as a sniper.

Asher nodded. "I'll do a ground sweep. Group text for comms?" he suggested.

Scott nodded, as did Shane before going on, gesturing to his right. "Sean, Slater, take the perimeter out on Cooper Boulevard on that side. Lily and I will take the other side. Jessie, check the barn areas. Lark, you're with us, to show us where you saw him, then come back and help Jessie search here."

She nodded, thinking it was a measure of the respect he held that no one questioned him. Until he got to his little sister.

"Sage, you need to see to Poke—"

"I am not staying out of this!"

"What you're not doing is abandoning the horse who just won you the Non-Pro title here," Shane retorted.

She opened her mouth, looking like she was about to yell, but stopped when Scott slipped his arm around her and said quietly, "We have to know exactly where you are. You're our best weapon, Sage. When we find him, he may run from any of us, but there's no way in hell he'll run from you.

You're why he's here, you have to know that."

In the midst of the tension Lark had to smother a smile. Scott Parrish in a few words had accomplished what not many could; calm the storm that was Sage Highwater.

"He's right. If you find him, try and get him back here to Sage. Now!" Shane snapped, and they all scattered.

Lark led them back the way she'd come, again thinking she needed to run more, because when Lily asked it was all she could do to keep running and relate the conversation she'd had with Kane.

"How did he look?" Shane's fiancée asked, and Lark knew she didn't mean the description she'd already given. Lily was a human-interest reporter, and she'd begun to build a name for herself with her in-depth profiles. One she'd done on Scott a few months ago had practically turned his entire life around, and helped make it possible for him—and Sage—to come home to Last Stand.

"Too thin. Nervous. Wary." She stopped, glanced at Shane.

"Go ahead," he said, but his jaw was tight.

She took in a deep breath and said, "He reminded me of the kids I used to pull out of abusive situations. How they didn't trust anything or anyone."

Then Lark saw something few people from Last Stand ever had; their intrepid, cool, collected chief of police winced. Lily moved, grabbed his hand, squeezed it. As if her touch had anchored him he recovered. For a split second she allowed herself that same longing she'd felt when Slater had whispered to Joey, but she shoved it aside. This was too important. She knew how much this meant to all the Highwaters, and now all the ones they loved.

And they meant a great deal to her.

Chapter Four

JUST LEAVE. GET the hell out of here.

Kane couldn't remember the last time he'd spent so much time talking to himself. Lecturing himself. As if coming back this close to home could turn the clock back, as if he could undo what he'd done.

He couldn't. Nothing could. And there was no point in trying to see Sage up close, and sure as hell no point in trying to talk to her. She wouldn't—

Sage was so relieved to know you were alive. Every time they got closer to finding you she was terrified the next step would be finding out you were dead.

Lark Leclair's words played back in his head. He remembered her now, as that pretty, two-years-older blonde who'd been in Sean's year, and the subject of much juvenile male admiration from his own classmates. It was hard enough to think they'd been looking for him all this time, but Sage was…relieved? Had been afraid she'd find out he was dead?

He'd thought she would have been wishing him dead for thirteen years. Yes, they'd been close, as kids. But Sage…Sage had utterly and completely adored her father. She could also hold on to a mad better than most. The idea of her giving a damn about the person responsible for her father's death just didn't compute. Unless she wanted to find him to make him pay for what he'd done. That at least made sense.

He knew all of this was true. And yet, when he tried to make himself head back to the bus stop, or at least out to vanish amid the city streets, he couldn't seem to make his feet cooperate. Instead here he was, outside a barn behind the arena, ready to go in looking for the girl who'd been such a big part of his childhood.

And exactly what are you going to do if they're all there, gathered around her to congratulate her, as you know damned well they will be?

That would do it. He'd run. Again. He was certain of that. The mere sight of Shane, Slater and Sean would do it.

Shane, Slater, Sean and Sage. The S Highwaters. The real ones.

He'd just have to hope he could get clear before they caught him.

He walked as quietly as he could toward the large opening in the end of the barn. He was so tangled up even the sight of the big, sliding barn doors, like the ones on the main barn at the Highwater ranch, got to him. They felt so familiar, yet so strange at the same time. And the feel of the inside of the barn, the scent of the fresh hay, the straw, the leather, the unmistakable blend that meant horses to him…it nearly overwhelmed him.

He was only a few steps inside when he spotted her. The blonde again, standing outside a stall. Lark. With that voice.

He stopped, just looking for a moment. She might be a petite package, but she was perfectly put together. That dark gold hair, almost the color of Sage's show-winning horse. He wondered if she would be offended by the comparison. He doubted it, if she was close enough to Sage to come here to cheer her on.

She had her phone in her hand, was staring down at the screen. She hadn't seemed the sort to be so absorbed in a device that she was unaware of anyone around her, but what did he know?

Be grateful, because that includes you at the moment.

She tapped out something on the phone, then slipped it into her back pocket. The move drew his gaze to a lovely backside in snug blue jeans. No cowboy boots, though. Way too much heel. He wondered if being small bothered her. Not that she was really small; she was over five feet, five two if he had to guess.

He told himself he was focusing on her so he didn't have to wonder if Sage was in that stall she was standing outside. But somehow he couldn't quite convince himself that was the only reason. Because there were parts of him, parts long unheard from, that were responding with unexpected fierceness to the sight of her again. He'd thought it a fluke before, but now it had him rattled.

Then she stepped over to the entrance to the stall, leaning in as if she were talking to whoever was inside. He stood, frozen. Tried to convince himself he could move now. Could run. He'd head to the bus stop where he'd gotten off, and take the first damn bus to anywhere. Then, when he was safely out of reach, he'd figure out what to do next. Where to go. Maybe back to Alaska. That had been almost far enough, and he'd barely been inside the state.

They're not my family.

Then why have they never, ever given up trying to find you and bring you home?

It couldn't be true. They couldn't have been looking for him all this time, all these years.

Unless they want your ass in prison for killing their father.

And once more he wondered if that wouldn't be the best solution all around.

An unexpected memory came back to him, sharply, vividly. Overhearing Steven Highwater, talking to his oldest son after Kane had gotten into some scrape or other.

We can't pen Kane up, Shane. He's got the wildest spirit of all of you, and it would kill him. All we can do is help him channel it.

That had been the first time he'd been utterly certain of being understood, and it had meant the world to him. He'd resolved in that moment to try harder, to actually try to do what the man had always—usually in exasperation—asked of him.

To think twice before he plunged ahead. He'd been only so-so at that.

To keep a leash on his quick temper. He'd done better at that, but it had been a long, long haul.

To remember we love you.

Steven Highwater's words echoed in his head, hammering at him. They had loved him. And he'd paid them back for it in the worst possible way.

A faint chime yanked him out of the memory and he watched as Lark pulled her phone back out. Tapped twice, as if she were only acknowledging something. Put it back in that lucky pocket.

And started toward him.

He froze. Except…she wasn't looking at him. He could dodge out of sight and…and what? Why was he even still here? He'd seen Sage, he'd seen that glorious performance, seen she was so happy it fairly radiated from her. That was all he needed. He could go on now, and have her fixed in his mind as happy.

She was too close now—Lark. If he moved too quickly it would only draw her attention. He turned slightly, so that he was mostly facing a wall with a couple of announcement flyers posted. Pretended he was reading. She kept coming.

She was humming. It was pretty. Sounded vaguely familiar. And she still hadn't seen or noticed him.

The tune she was humming shifted into something else, something he recognized all too well. Something—

Her swift turnaround startled him. "Sage is waiting for you," she said, grabbing his arm before he could back away.

He shook his head, tried to pull free. "Don't."

"You'll break her heart. Again."

"She can't want this."

"To quote your sister, she long ago quit letting other people decide what she wants."

It was so…so Sage that it immobilized him for a moment.

And then she looked past him and said, very softly, "You can try to run again, but I wouldn't recommend it."

He spun around. And stared at the two men striding toward them. Blinked when he realized it was Shane and Slater. Together. Shoulder to shoulder. The two who had ever and always butted heads, now looking like an inseparable unit.

Against you, even they'll work together.

Belatedly he saw the two women flanking them, a redhead he didn't know to Shane's right, and a woman with a crayon-red streak in her brown hair—Joey Douglas, he realized with a jolt—to Slater's left.

He spun back around, his heart hammering in his chest. Saw four people coming at him from that direction. Some part of his brain registered one of them was Sean, and one of the women was Sage's lifetime best friend, Jessie McBride. The other woman seemed vaguely familiar, but the other man was a complete stranger.

Then a fifth person, another man he hadn't seen behind these four, peeled off and went into the stall they were passing, the one Lark had been outside.

Scott Parrish. He may not have seen him in thirteen years, but he was certain. He'd spent an hour with the guy sitting outside the principal's office at Creekbend High School. But he'd already noticed him before that day, watching Sage with a quiet sort of longing that had assured Kane he'd never hurt her. So he'd told him to go ahead and talk to her.

You saying I've got her brother's permission?

I'm saying she won't take your head off. Not that she couldn't, mind you.

And as he saw Scott go into that stall, his focus not with the others but on whoever was in that stall, the truth of what Lark had told him hit home.

Sage is waiting for you.

And the rest of the Highwaters, along with apparently a squad of friends, were all here. He was where he had never, ever wanted to be. Where he had spent thirteen long, lonely years trying not to be. Where he had sworn he would never be. And yet here he was.

Trapped.

Chapter Five

LARK HATED WHAT she saw in his eyes. It reminded her too much of all the times she hadn't been able to do as much as she felt she should. All the times she had been, horrifically, too late to stop what would likely be permanent damage of one kind or another.

It was what had, in the end, driven her from the job she had felt compelled to do, but couldn't emotionally afford.

You're too soft, Leclair. You let every case get to you, so deep you're bleeding inside all the time. Get over that, or get out.

She'd known the truth in her boss's words even then. And she'd tried, but she hadn't been able to get over it. Hadn't been able to harden her heart. Every terrified child still ripped at her. And so she'd taken his and Doc McBride's advice and gotten out. But in this moment it was as if she was right back there, and she hated the feeling. And telling herself that this was no frightened child but a twenty-nine-year-old man didn't seem to be helping much. Because she could see he was feeling just as trapped as if he were that child.

She reached for something to say, anything, any words that would soothe, help, but her brain seemed to have shut down the moment she'd looked into his eyes. Those eyes so unlike his brothers'—and his sister's—varying shades of blue. There was just something about them, about him, that had rattled her usual calm, her ability to think clearly.

So she went with her gut. "Won't it be good to get this over with?" she said, barely above a whisper.

He made a low, harsh sound. He didn't trust her; she could see—and understand—that. But she suspected he didn't trust anyone, and that broke her heart.

The troops, as she'd called them in her head from the moment Shane had started giving orders, were closing in. Kane's eyes, those hazel eyes that were looking more gold than green just now, were darting around, and she sensed he was desperately looking for an escape, for a way for this not to happen. She didn't know why he felt as he did, but she had no doubts that he would bolt at the first opportunity. She'd seen it too often to miss the signs.

"They've worried about you for thirteen years, Kane," she said, just as softly as before. "Put an end to that at least."

Something flashed in his eyes then. "It was you. Your phone. You were telling them where I was."

Somehow she knew denying that would be a mistake just now. "Yes." He looked surprised that she'd admitted it. "Because I know how desperate they've been to find you. How desperate they've always been." She studied him for a second, trying to gauge, then went with the biggest gun. "Especially Sage. She was a tough, strong girl, but that triple loss—her father, you, and then Scott leaving—nearly broke her."

Lark knew the moment after she said it that she'd broken him. Saw the surrender in his expression, the slight slumping of his body. She remembered how lean and wiry he'd always been and, oddly, remembered how his brothers had always teased him about being short of the six-foot mark when they were all there or over. But that had changed; if he was less than that now, it was only by a hair.

But most of all she saw the change in his gaze, in the hazel eyes themselves. They'd gone flat, almost dazed. It was a look she'd seen before, in children who had given up. And she hated it just as much as she ever had.

She'd thought when he realized they'd been looking for him all this time that it would have changed his attitude, but it hadn't. In fact, he'd looked worse. Which made no sense to her. Just as his response—to run—when she'd told him they'd wanted to bring him home made no sense. Unless the nastier gossips were right about what happened that day, and she refused to accept that.

And then the troops were here, and he wouldn't even look at them.

SHE'D BEEN RIGHT about one thing, that Lark Leclair. It would be good to have this over. In the tiny part of him that hadn't completely shut down he could feel a twinge of relief that it was, finally, after thirteen years, over. Sure, he'd have crap to go through, but he'd plead guilty and avoid a trial.

Go directly to jail...

The phrase from the penalty card on that stupid old board game they'd played when he was a kid slid through his mind. And he had no get out of jail free card. He doubted they issued them when you'd killed a chief of police.

"Kane."

He'd never heard anything like the way that had sounded. He didn't look up. He couldn't look up, couldn't look into Sage's face, her eyes the color of the Hill Country in spring when it was carpeted with bluebonnets. He felt himself sway, then felt a warm, steadying touch on his arm. Lark.

He'd only just met her; she shouldn't be able to do that. Steady him like that. Oddly, since he couldn't focus on what was really happening, he found himself wondering why she was here. Supporting Sage? She'd said she was friends with all of them. Was she a particular friend with one of them? Girlfriend?

And what the hell does it matter to you?

Still, since he couldn't look at them—it was like his brain was convinced he would die on the spot if he did—he looked at her. And over and above the beauty he saw the concern in her light green eyes. The caring. It was the strangest feeling he'd had in a long time. Who was this woman? How did she do that?

And then he heard light, running footsteps. Knew what was coming. Closed his eyes.

"She loves you so much." Lark whispered it as her fingers tightened on his arm. Not in a harsh or threatening way, but with that same reassurance he'd felt when she'd first touched him.

And then Sage was there, and he was engulfed in a fierce, consuming hug. He couldn't move. Felt as stunned as he had that time a mule at the Grand Canyon had head-butted him dead center in the chest so hard it had knocked the wind right out of him. And he was having almost as much trouble catching his breath as he had then.

A moment later he realized she was crying. Tough, stalwart Sage was crying. And not just quietly weeping, she was sobbing, as he'd never heard from her. He could feel the shivers going through her as she clung to him. But then she felt as if she were going to slip, fall, and he moved instinctively to catch her. Still, it was a jerky sort of motion as he lifted his arms to steady her. Much as Lark Leclair had done for him, for whatever impossible reason.

"It's all right," Lark said softly. "You're home now. Safe." His eyes snapped open, and despite the woman in his arms it was her he looked at. Safe? Hardly. Home? He saw her eyes move, toward the others who now surrounded him. Knew she was saying that they were home, not a place.

Maybe she didn't know. Maybe she didn't know what he'd done. To Sage, to all of them. Maybe that's why she seemed so determined to help. If she knew, she wouldn't have been so kind, so gentle. Not to him. Not to the man who had destroyed life as they'd known it for these people she clearly cared about.

And then Sage moved, as if she'd gotten her feet back under her at last. She reached up, although it wasn't as much of a reach she'd grown at least two inches since he'd last seen her at fourteen and was now maybe three inches less than his own five eleven—and a half—and put her hands on his shoulders. Then she leaned back to look at him, and as much as he wanted to he couldn't not look back. And the sight of those bluebonnet eyes wet with tears stabbed through to a part of him he'd thought he'd successfully numbed forever.

"I don't care where or why or what," she said fervently. "Just don't run."

His jaw tightened involuntarily, because that had been exactly what he wanted to do.

"Don't," came a warning from his right—deep, male, and spoken with the confidence of a man who could carry out what the warning implied. He looked. Scott Parrish. And in the man's eyes he saw the truth of what Lark had told him. He and Sage were very, very together. "If you hurt her again…"

The ferocity in the man's voice verified what he'd guessed. And he felt a slight easing of a tension he'd never really realized—or admitted—he'd been carrying around for thirteen years. Sage would be all right. She *was* all right. This man would see to that. That was all he'd needed. The reason he'd come here, against what small amount of better judgment he had.

He let go of her. Took a step back, ready to fight his way out of here, or get taken out in the process. But his back came up against something solid. Big and solid.

"Don't even think about it, little brother."

He had no words for the feeling that engulfed him then, because even though logic told him it was Shane, his gut was screaming because he'd sounded exactly like his father. With that same deep resonance, and that same commanding undertone that had almost anyone who wasn't crazy or stupid drunk doing as he said.

Which makes you crazy—or stupid—since you were the one who flouted him the most.

But even now he found himself obeying without thought as Shane and the others edged him into the stall Sage had come out of. He stared at the horse in one corner, the same powerful, athletic dun she'd ridden to that amazing victory. The horse's head came up, and he whickered softly.

Belatedly, those last two words Shane had said hit him. Hard. He didn't look at the eldest Highwater. He kept his gaze on the youngest, Sage. And his words came out through gritted teeth.

"I'm not your brother. I never was."

Chapter Six

LARK KNEW THE Highwaters had wondered. The Highwater family genes, at least their father's, were so strong that every one of the men looked like him, with his dark hair and over-six-foot height. Even Sage had the look, the hair, vivid blue eyes, and she towered over Lark herself.

Kane had the dark hair, but while hardly short he didn't come close to Shane's six two, and was a fraction shorter than both Slater and Sean's six feet. And where they were muscled, powerful, Kane had a leaner build, with that quick, agile sort of grace that made her think he could dart as fast as a hummingbird if he wanted to. Or had to.

But above all else it was the eyes. In this dimmer light they looked as green as his shirt, yet still flecked with an amber gold that she imagined would practically spark in sunlight.

Lark was staring at him so intently she saw the faint shiver that went through him. Reacting on instinct and training she moved, to stand next to him again. And again put a hand on his arm in support. His gaze shot to her face, and she decided that in some ways, those eyes were even more striking than the varying Highwater blues. She quickly discarded the thought both as inappropriate and unimportant at this moment. What mattered was the wrenching pain in them. Whatever the reason he'd left thirteen years ago, she knew for certain they had not been easy years.

A little to her surprise he didn't pull away from her, didn't even try. Perhaps because she was the only one here who wasn't one of them, the ones he clearly saw as aligned against him. And again, the reason why didn't matter at the moment.

She realized something else then, that Jessie and Asher had moved to the stall door, and were subtly guiding anyone walking through the barn or looking to congratulate the winner away from them all, as if on sentry duty. The Highwaters weren't just good people, they had good friends.

"Get it done," she said to Kane softly. "Then it will be over. No longer hanging over you."

She saw something shift in his gaze, knew that her words had hit home. And then Shane spoke again, in that same manner his father had, what she'd heard Sage's Scott call his command presence. "Like hell you're not," he said in answer to Kane's declaration that he wasn't his brother. "I was there the day you were born, brother. I was only six, but I remember sitting in that hospital, waiting, until they brought you out for us to see. You were a squalling, squirmy little thing, but even at six I knew you were ours."

"I'm not." Kane looked as if he suddenly felt ill. Queasy. "I'm not one of you. I've known that for as long as I can remember."

"That's crazy. Who told you that?" Sage demanded, her

voice still thick although her tears had stopped since Scott had put his arm around her.

He didn't look at her. "No one had to. I had a mirror."

Sean, the middle Highwater, spoke then, and what he said was so typical of him Lark had to smother a smile that would seem tactless in light of the tension snapping between them all. "I know what you're thinking, but I've researched the latest on the genetics, bro. Eye color isn't quite as straightforward as they once thought. It's not solely gene dominance."

She saw Kane's eyes, those different eyes, flick toward Sean, could almost sense him registering the icy-blue color. But then he looked away again.

"Remember Roxie's litter of pups when you were nine?" Slater this time. Lark gave the brother next to Shane a curious look. She knew from her own conversations with him as well as his rather fearsome reputation that he was brilliant, but where he was going with this she couldn't imagine. But his next words made it clear. "That one brown one stood out, when every other one of the six was black and white just like her. It happens."

Lark could see by Kane's expression that he remembered exactly what Slater was talking about. But he didn't look any less unsettled. She tightened her grip on his arm, knowing sometimes people in distress just needed the touch, the contact. It could anchor them in rough times, and she was guessing that for all he'd probably been through since he'd vanished that long ago day, this was probably the roughest moment he'd faced.

Kane looked down at her hand, then, slowly, up to her face. She tried to put everything she could of steadying reassurance into her gaze. She guessed he'd be embarrassed, as any adult male would be, at how much the look in his eyes reminded her of the children she'd had to pull out of awful situations. And that was the only thing that made her want to help, need to help, she told herself. Well, that and that she liked and admired all the Highwaters.

Even this Highwater, who had put them through thirteen years of worry and hell.

She heard him take a quick, shallow breath, then another. She thought if she moved her hand down to his wrist she'd probably feel his pulse hammering at a far too rapid rate. But he still didn't pull away, didn't even try to free his arm from her gentle grasp.

"They're right," she said. "There are so many explanations."

He let out a low, harsh sound that was half sour laugh, half groan, and he shook his head. Then he drew himself up—and she realized how weighed down he'd been, because suddenly the height difference between him and his brothers didn't seem much at all—and turned to face them. Shane, specifically. Then, in a flat, emotionless voice, he spoke.

"He admitted it." He didn't say who, but Lark knew he didn't have to. There could only be one answer.

Shane's gaze narrowed. "Explain," he said, and there was no doubt it was an order.

"I asked him. You know he always said he'd never lie to us. He might not answer, but if he did it would be true."

I think Dad was manic about never lying to us because our mother did so often.

The words she'd once heard Shane say to Sage, who had been only two when that mother had died, echoed in Lark's mind. Those words had made her want to immediately go and hug both her parents.

"Spell it out," Slater snapped, pounding home to Lark even more how fraught this was; Slater was usually a bit removed from emotional turmoil, more of an observer, he'd always said. But he was clearly a heart-first participant in this.

Kane's glance shot to the second-oldest Highwater. "You want it spelled out, smart guy?" he snapped, as if Slater's words had lit the tinder to a fire that had been built long ago. "Okay. I asked him if he was my father. He dodged, said he was in the ways that counted."

The male Highwaters went very still. If Kane wasn't lying, then their suspicions may have just been elevated into the realm of probability.

But it was Sage who reacted, fervently. "That's not a dodge, that's the truth," she exclaimed. "Just like he always promised."

At Sage's raised voice the horse in the corner, her beloved Poke, abandoned the hay he'd been munching and turned his head to look at the woman who had demanded and gotten his best. As if he were some sort of oversized guard dog, he moved a couple of steps toward her, and then stopped, staring at Kane as if he sensed this was the threat to her.

"Not enough of it," Kane said flatly. "So I asked him who my real father was. My biological father." He shifted his gaze back to Shane, the man who was clearly now the patriarch of the Highwater clan, even at thirty-five. Whatever he saw in Shane's face seemed to stall his words.

"And he said?" Lark prompted gently.

He didn't look at her. She could almost feel the effort it was for him to meet Shane's gaze. Then, his jaw set, he finally answered.

"He said he didn't know."

Chapter Seven

H E'D FINALLY DONE it. He'd repeated the words that had started it all, thirteen years ago. Or rather, the words that had ended it all.

They were all staring at him. Maybe they thought he was lying. Or maybe they were just getting ready to ask him the really big question. The one he'd dreaded for thirteen years.

It didn't come. Instead, the man at the door with Sage's friend Jessie, spoke. "If we're going to make it back to Last Stand before dawn, we need to roll."

There was something in the way he spoke, in the way he held himself, that reminded Kane of Scott. He wasn't sure why, or what it was, because he didn't even know the man's name.

The thought made him shift his gaze to Scott, still standing with his arm around Sage, and watching Kane as if for any unexpected moves. He remembered with sudden vividness that day they'd both ended up in the waiting room outside the principal's office. He'd known who the younger boy was—everybody in town knew who Scott Parrish was, and how much trouble he was for his already unfortunate family.

I'm the one who doesn't fit.

Scott's words from that day echoed in his mind now, the words that had made him realize that here was another person who felt as he did. The outsider, the one who didn't fit. Even Sean, whose brain worked in such an offbeat way, had at least looked like a Highwater.

He remembered the way Scott had sounded, talking about Sage with a quiet longing that had made Kane ache inside even though he'd been barely old enough to understand what it meant. It was why he'd told him that day to go ahead and talk to her, that Sage was the best at understanding people like them. The odd ones out.

And not long after, he himself was literally out. Gone, running for his life after the day he'd never, not one night in thirteen years, been able to put out of his dreams.

Kane only knew how stunned he was feeling when he realized several moments had passed before he registered what the man at the door had actually said.

Back to Last Stand.

Four words he never, ever allowed to fully form in his mind.

But they were leaving now, tonight? At nearly ten o'clock? They were in that big a hurry to get back…home? And what were they going to do about him? Just leave? Let him go?

"I'll drive," Sage was saying. "I'm so wound up I couldn't sleep anyway." She glanced at Scott. "And I'm more used to towing the trailer."

He didn't argue with her. So he knew what he was dealing with. "I'll shotgun until you get tired," was all he said.

"We'll prop you both up from the back seat," Jessie said, and the unknown man smiled. And he had the same look in his eyes watching her as Scott did when he looked at Sage.

"And we'll keep you two going." Slater, his arm around Joey, gestured at Shane and the redhead. Joey put a hand on Slater's arm, and Kane saw the glitter of a diamond on her left ring finger.

"You mean drive us all crazy with that quotation trivia thing you do," Sean said with a grimace that somehow wasn't harsh at all and made the woman beside him smile. She looked Hispanic, beyond elegant, and still reminded him of someone he couldn't place.

"I find it quite edifying," Joey said primly. And all the Highwaters laughed. They were clearly happy at the idea of heading home. And Kane suddenly realized they were all talking as if he weren't here. And he wondered if maybe he edged out of here, they wouldn't even notice. He took a small step backward.

"So the only question is," Shane said, and mid-sentence his gaze shot back to Kane, "where to put you." Kane froze. Stared. "Seven people crammed into my SUV for nearly eight hours would be a little rough."

"More room in the truck," Scott said.

"Or he could ride back in the trailer with Poke," Jessie put in, not looking at him as she reached out to pat the horse's neck. And Kane didn't think he was imagining the edge in her voice. Jessie had never been anything less than a completely loyal friend to Sage, so he guessed it was understandable she wasn't very fond of him.

And then, belatedly, he realized they were now all talking as if it were a given he was going with them.

To Last Stand.

No. No way in hell.

It was practically a shout in his mind, and Mr. Lindsay's quiet words about going back and fixing what he'd left behind had no chance against it.

"Don't be silly," said the woman who had stood beside him through all this. "He can ride with me. I'd enjoy not doing 450 miles solo." They all turned to look at her, Shane in particular studying her intently. "It'll be fine, Chief," she said quietly after a moment. The two looked at each other for a long, silent moment, and he had the oddest feeling Lark was silently asking Shane for something.

Shane was worried about her, Kane realized. Or rather, him. What he might do to her, alone in a car at night? He recoiled at the very idea, but he also supposed it made sense, given everything. To them, anyway. For all they knew, he'd murdered more than their father.

And again belatedly—which warned him of how deeply shaken he was, no matter how he tried to pretend he wasn't—what she'd called Shane registered. Chief. And his gaze shot back to the tallest of the group, the man who wasn't just imposing physically but in demeanor, as if command was somehow innate in him.

Like it had been in Steven Highwater.

He'd literally stepped into his father's shoes, Kane thought, feeling almost numb now.

There was yet another Chief Highwater in Last Stand.

Lark sensed the change in the man beside her. Was fairly certain he'd had about all he could take. It wasn't really her place—this was a family situation—but she had a lot of experience in defusing tense family situations. And the Highwaters weren't the sort to tell her to butt out. Except maybe this one.

But he's not a Highwater, not like they are.

She had a sudden understanding of how completely alone he must feel, having once been a part of this unique group, only to see it totally changed now that they'd all found the partners who would ever stand with them. And to know that he'd never really belonged—in his view anyway—in the first place.

She'd handled more than one case where such a discovery had destroyed a family. Had destroyed someone's self-image, and in a couple of tragic cases, destroyed the person themself. And while he was no helpless child, he'd been living with this, alone until now, for thirteen years. And she simply couldn't not try to help.

She stepped around him, then turned until she stood facing him. He looked a bit glassy-eyed, as if he'd retreated somewhere deep inside his mind. She knew that look painfully well.

"I promise I'm a good driver," she said, as if that were the only concern.

He blinked, and she knew she'd been right. The snap as he came back to the present was almost audible. "I...what?"

"I'm not even that tired, since I only drove up yesterday. You can sleep, if you want."

He was shaking his head now, slowly, as if in pain. As she thought he might well be. "I'm not going back there."

As if to underline it, he took a step backward. He came up against Jessie's Asher, who held his ground. He never even wobbled, prosthetic leg clearly not nearly the factor his experience as a Green Beret was.

"You're not running again," Shane said quietly, but in that tone Lark knew no one in Last Stand would ever discount. Kane's head turned sharply toward his brother.

Half brother? Does it really matter to them? I don't think so. Not this family.

"Going to arrest me now...Chief?" Kane said, his voice low and harsh.

Lark saw the last word register, but Shane only said flatly, "Is that what it's going to take?"

Kane just stared at Shane, long enough that Sean said to the man who was both brother and boss, only half-jokingly, "Just don't ask me to cuff my own brother."

Kane's gaze shifted quickly, and she saw the surprise in his yes. "You're...a cop?"

"A detective," Sean said.

"With the best clearance rate in the state," Elena added proudly.

Kane looked thoughtful which, in the midst of all this, Lark found rather amazing. "That makes sense," he said, almost to himself. "You always had that puzzle-brain."

"So," Shane said, his voice entirely different now, gentle, soft, "you didn't completely forget about us."

And again Kane's gaze shot back to the eldest. It wasn't really a stare-down; she could see Shane's expression had softened to match his voice. He had good instincts. He'd apparently sensed this was the moment to ease up, that Kane was on the verge of decision. And after a long moment when the only sound in the stall was the rustle of Poke's feet in the straw, she saw Kane swallow. Hard.

"I remember every day, dream it every night. I never forgot anything. Not one thing." He swallowed again, and his voice cracked slightly as he added in a near-whisper, "No matter how hard I tried."

Chapter Eight

KANE WASN'T AT all sure how it had happened. He'd just looked at all of them, surrounding him, and knew they would all back Shane up. They wouldn't let him run. He had the feeling they would physically stop him if they had to. And he had no doubts that they could. Their father had taught them all how to fight. Facing that, riding alone with the woman beside him seemed the best alternative.

Even if she had been the one to bring it all crashing down on him by recognizing him.

Give me a chance, Shane. I've been here before.

He doubted he'd been meant to hear her whispered words, but he had. Not that it made any difference, since he had no idea what she'd meant.

That didn't matter either, because here he was, sitting in the passenger seat of a sporty little SUV, with the petite blonde at the wheel. The car, he realized as he looked at her and she glanced his way, was the same color as her eyes, a light, springtime green. He wondered if the man in her life had picked it out for that reason. She wasn't wearing a ring, but he couldn't imagine some guy hadn't snatched her up. She wasn't just beautiful, with tempting curves, she had that kind of quiet goodness, kindness, gentleness that made you realize you weren't any of those things. Not that he needed any reminders that he wasn't.

She had the kind of caring that made a person feel guilty for going through the world with blinders on.

She was the kind of woman you built a life on.

Where the hell did all that come from?

He answered his own question. *Your own wishful thinking, idiot. You're not destined for that kind of life. You made sure of that thirteen years ago.*

So why was he here? Why hadn't he bailed out of this car at one of those stoplights before they hit the highway?

Because Shane's car's in front of you and Sage's truck is behind you. They've got you penned up like a calf to be branded.

He shifted restlessly in the seat. His thumb was tapping out a steady rhythm on the armrest.

"Is that really what you want to do? Run again?"

Her soft, low voice sent a shiver down his spine. He shook it off. What he should be worried about is how she'd apparently read him so well.

"Yes," he answered bluntly.

"Were you going to, without even speaking to anyone? Even after you've come so far?"

He gave her a sideways look. Damn, she was just as lovely in profile. "What makes you think it was far?"

"You weren't still in Seattle?"

"No." He was still trying to process that Sage—and Scott—had gone so far, looking for him. "How did they even know that?"

"One of Sean's bulletins turned up that your truck had been towed in California."

He turned to stare at her then. "One of what did what and how did that get them to Seattle?"

She laughed. "Settle in, we've got a long drive to talk."

"I don't want to talk, I want to know how—"

"Okay, then I'll talk." She said it so lightly it was hardly an interruption. "You want the digest version?"

"Just talk." He said it past a tightened jaw. Which had nothing to do with the fact that he liked to hear that low, lovely voice.

"Let's see…the basis is what I told you before. They never, ever stopped looking for you. Sean and Shane put out monthly APBs, weekly after they had your truck description and license plate."

"How—"

"I'm getting there. They followed up on any possible leads. And," she added with a glance at him before she turned back to her driving, "piled up a big list of people and agencies they owe favors to."

He blinked. "Favors?" That didn't sound like a criminal investigation, where helping would be part of the job.

"Anyone who tried to help, whether it came to anything or not."

"They kept a list?"

"I've seen it. It's long. Anyway, they knew you'd gone to Albuquerque—"

He drew back sharply. "How did they know that?"

"One of those favors. Sean said you worked at a gas station for a few days, about a year...after."

It seemed like forever ago, not twelve years. But at the same time he remembered begging the guy at the station to take him on. He'd spotted the mess from a ruptured water pipe when he stopped to use the bathroom after his last ride—a kind of creepy guy he'd been glad to get shed of—had too reluctantly let him out of his fancy sedan. It wasn't the first time he'd had somebody who'd picked him up hit on him.

You're just too darned pretty, bro.

Sage's teasing words, uttered whenever she wanted to really jab him, had played back in his mind every time.

But Joe Jeffries, who had owned the station, hadn't been one of those. He'd looked at him with sympathy in his eyes, and at that moment Kane had been hungry enough not to spurn it. When he'd offered him a hundred bucks—cash—to clean up the mess, he'd grabbed at it. It had been more complicated than he'd expected, and he'd ended up replacing some flooring and drywall, but he'd done that kind of thing before at the ranch, so did a creditable job. Joe had offered him a part-time job after inspecting what he'd done, but that would have involved paperwork he had no way of dealing with yet. Joe seemed to understand, and he'd doubled the payment since it had been more than a simple cleanup.

"Kane?"

He came back to the present with a start. "I...then what?"

"Then in the last year or so, things started to happen."

He gave a short shake of his head, trying to focus.

"Things?"

"More specifically, Joey. She remembered something, from when you two were in school together."

His brow furrowed. He'd always liked his chemistry lab partner, and not just because she'd probably gotten him through English and history class. He'd talked to her over the Bunsen burners, as they tried not to blow anything up. Or she tried; he wasn't sure he wouldn't have enjoyed it. But he couldn't remember anything he'd said that would have put them on his trail.

"And that," Lark said, "sent her and Slater to the Grand Canyon."

Geography class. When he'd told Joey he wanted to see the canyon they were starting to study. The memory was so vivid he didn't know how he could have forgotten.

I want to look up at the sky from the bottom. See if it feels like I feel…like I'm at the bottom and can only see a slice of what's there.

He hadn't even known about the list, then. Or that the place was on it.

"Wait…her and Slater? Slater went?"

"I believe that's the trip where they finally faced the fact they were meant for each other. If for no other reason than she's the only one who can keep up with him. And match him quotation for quotation."

He remembered them joking about it, back at the stop. "So…he still does that?"

"Has a quote for every occasion? Yes." Again she gave him a quick, sideways look as she drove. "I believe they talked to a gentleman named Zeb."

His breath caught. "Ol' Zeb? He's still there?"

"Along with a mule named...I want to say Casper?"

"Jasper," he said instantly. "They're both still there, still okay? When was this?"

She smiled at him. "Yes, they were. This was last summer."

He let out a long, relieved breath. Zeb had been good to him. Kind. It had been Zeb who had talked to him about the short fuse on his temper, admitting he'd once had the same problem and it had cost him everything until he learned to control it. The old man had been so laidback Kane had found that hard to believe, but he'd sworn it was true. And that Kane could—and needed to—do the same.

Easy. Just count to ten, right? He'd said it sourly, because it was so much easier said than done.

Finding the right thing to count is the tricky part. I just count ten Jaspers being stubborn in my head, and that's enough to scare the mad right out of me.

And in the middle of that serious discussion Kane had burst out laughing, the first real laugh since the day he'd left Last Stand. Just the thought of ten of the big, stubborn critters would indeed be enough to scare about anything out of a guy. And the next time he felt that leash stretching out, headed toward snapping, he'd pictured Jasper digging in his heels and refusing to give in. To his amazement it had worked. And had from then on, for the most part. At least, he felt more in control of it than he ever had. And he would forever be grateful to Zeb for that.

Zeb was old enough that he'd worried about him when he'd left. Then again, he'd also been half convinced the wiry old hand would still be wrangling mules at ninety. And he'd keep Jasper, his favorite for the very traits he complained about, going as long as possible, before retiring him to his own little acreage outside the park.

He was very thankful to know both of them were okay.

"He was the one who sent them to the campground, which is where they got the description and plate on your truck, which was how they found out it was towed. They said he remembered you quite fondly," Lark said, her voice going soft in that way that tickled his spine again.

"I'm surprised he remembered me at all," he said, almost reflexively.

"You underestimate yourself. You're quite memorable."

"I'll bet, in Last Stand." He let out a harsh, compressed breath. "Then what? How did they get from Arizona to Seattle?"

"They got the description and license for your truck from the campground at the Grand Canyon. And Shane and Sean kept sending out those APBs. I believe it was the sheriff's office in the county where it broke down that found the towing record and called." She gave him another look. "We tease Shane that him being an internet sex symbol helped all that along."

He drew back sharply. "A what?"

She laughed, and that made his stomach knot. How did just the sound of this woman cause a physical reaction? "That's a long, embarrassing story I'll leave to him to tell you. But anyway, they found your map and the Seattle brochure in the truck. And so Sage and Scott went off to search."

He was feeling almost numb now. "Scott...and Sage."

"I'll leave their story to them. And Sean and Elena's, and Joey and Slater's to them. Anyway, in Seattle they found that volunteer who recognized that aged-up photo of you." She gave him a sideways glance. "As I said, you're quite memorable. In a lot of hearts, Kane Highwater."

"Travis."

"What?"

"I'm Kane Travis. Not Highwater."

He'd said it rather fiercely, yet she reacted as if he'd merely said it was dark out at night. Did nothing rattle this woman? And why? What had she been through to give her this inordinate calm? "Your middle name, isn't it?"

"Last now."

"But you kept Kane."

"Fits."

She was silent for a moment before saying, "I think you have it spelled wrong, for the Cain you're thinking of."

And there it was. She'd understood perfectly. Had known he meant humanity's first murderer, the biblical Cain. Which told him they knew. Cain might have killed his brother, but it was the same principle. They knew he'd killed Steven Highwater.

That's why they were determined he not escape them. But then why hadn't Shane just arrested him on the spot? Why had he trusted him to be alone with this woman who was obviously a close friend?

Why on earth had *she* trusted him?

Chapter Nine

LARK GLANCED IN the rearview mirror for the set of headlights that never wavered. They were further back than most people would be, but Lark figured that was because of the horse trailer, and that it would take Sage longer to stop if she had to. No matter what the emotional turmoil, Sage Highwater would never, ever risk a horse's welfare.

Up ahead were the now familiar set of taillights of Shane's big SUV. She'd gotten to know both Shane and Sean fairly well in her years at CPS, and she knew how hard it had to be for them to let this happen this way. To let him out of their sight again, when they'd only just found him. She wasn't unaware of the level of trust they were investing in her.

And she could only imagine the conversations going on in those vehicles, with six Highwaters—or as good as—in one and four people in the other. All knowing the person they'd been missing and searching for, for more than a dozen years, was in this car with someone who was, to him, a stranger. But somehow they had managed to understand that sometimes, in fraught emotional situations, it was easier to deal with a stranger.

Her passenger had been quiet for a long time. Lark wanted to ask him where he'd gone after Seattle, but something held her back. He'd had a tremendous amount dropped on him in a short time, and when you added in that he was heading back to Last Stand for the first time in over thirteen years, she was sure he needed time to think.

He was picking at something on his jeans. When he rolled down his window, she glanced over.

"Hay," he said without looking at her as he let a couple of small bits of the stuff fly away. Then he let out a compressed breath. "I used to have to pick the stuff off my clothes all the time. The hayloft was my thinking spot."

He rolled the window back up and lapsed into silence once more for several miles. When he finally did speak again, what he said surprised her.

"Who are you, Lark Leclair?"

Given the circumstances, she was a bit surprised he remembered even her first name, let alone her last.

"A friend," she answered.

"That was obvious. What wasn't was why they trusted me to ride alone with you." She sensed rather than saw him turn to face her. "Why *you* trusted me."

"I have a little experience in judging risk."

She thought she heard his breath catch. "Don't tell me you're a cop, too? Is that why you called him…chief?"

"No. I called him that to let him know I knew he was worried, and why, and to tell him that I was looking at this from his side. Which, in a way, used to be my side too."

"So you used to be a cop?"

"No. I worked for Child Protective Services. For just over five years, although it felt like a lifetime."

There was a moment of silence before he said, "They're the ones who pull kids out of abusive situations, right?"

"Among other things, yes." She thought then of one occasion when things had turned out well. "Shall I tell you about the time your brother Sean saved the life of one of my kids?"

That got his attention; she could feel it. "Sean?"

"Yes. She was a little girl I'd been trying to get away from an abusive mother. I knew it was getting progressively worse. The X-rays on that poor child..." She stifled a shiver; it still had the power to get to her, even knowing how it had turned out. "Anyway, the mother finally snapped. Beat her bloody and unconscious. She thought the girl was dead, so she dumped the body where she thought no one would ever find it. And she wouldn't say where."

She heard him mutter a curse under his breath.

"Exactly," she agreed. "Anyway, I was in the police station, trying to think of anywhere she might take her, when Sean came in. It wasn't really his job, but I was so upset he, being Sean, wanted to help. Shane immediately gave him the okay. So he went over my entire case file, in detail, then asked me questions for what seemed like forever. Taking notes. Then he spread it all out on the table and just...stared at it."

"Patterns," Kane whispered.

Just what Sean had said that night. He truly hadn't forgotten. "To this day I don't know how he did it, but he came up with three possibilities of where the mother might have dumped...her burden, as she called her own child. We found her, half-buried, at the second one." She almost felt his shudder, registered what that signaled in the way of a lack of complete emotional numbness, before adding, "Still alive."

She saw him straighten out of the corner of her eye. He let out an audible breath. "Wow."

"Yes. She obviously had things to deal with, but she's with a wonderful family now, and thriving. And that is why I would walk over hot coals for Sean Highwater."

"And I'm the hot coals?"

"Right now I'd say you're more like a time bomb where they don't know when it's set to go off."

He let out a sharp, very short laugh. Sour, not amused. Then he was quiet for a long moment before he asked, "Do you always get so...personally invested?"

"I did, yes. It's why I had to leave the job. I just couldn't take walking into situations where I knew what was coming and couldn't do anything about it in time."

"That's what you meant, about judging risk?"

"Yes." She gave him a glance, just enough to see he was studying her intently. "And you are not that kind of a risk."

He let out a harsh breath. "Tell that to Steven Highwater."

Her own breath caught. She was used to having to assess in a hurry, a skill she'd honed in those years. And she'd rarely been wrong. Right now those instincts were telling her that

Kane blamed himself for that death. Did that mean he'd actually done it with full intent, as some—who hadn't been there—claimed? That he'd seen that pickup truck coming and pushed Chief Highwater into its path?

I asked him who my real father was. He said he didn't know.

Had that been enough to trigger him to murder? She couldn't believe it. What she could see was him reacting out of what had to be horribly fierce emotion—finding out the man you'd thought of as your father your entire life wasn't— and trying to push the knowledge away by pushing the man away.

She tried to draw on all the times she'd dealt with similar circumstances with CPS. But this was different. Kane wasn't a child anymore, and the Highwaters were friends, close friends. That changed things.

Then again, Kane clearly didn't think of himself as one of them, and if her assumptions were accurate, hadn't for years. Possibly from the moment the man he'd thought was his father had uttered that admission. So perhaps she needed to think of him not in connection with her friends, but as if he were one of those who'd found out a truth that had shattered their view of the world and themselves. True, he wasn't a kid like those she'd dealt with...but he had been when it had happened, when he'd had his life as he'd known it destroyed. And she'd bet everything she had that that kid still lived inside this man.

The road wasn't busy. The only vehicles close were Shane and Sage, so she risked a look at him. She wished she'd turned on the interior light, so she could see better. She relied so much on reading reactions in people, and his face was barely discernable in the faint light from the dash instruments. But she could still see how nearly perfect that face was, and thought again about the girls even in her own class at Creekbend, who would normally be far above noticing a boy two years younger than they, doing a breathless, wide-eyed stare at this one.

And it was that boy she spoke to now. "The whole thing sucks." He gave her a look as if the bluntness had surprised him. Which told her she'd chosen the right tack. She looked back at the dark, empty road before them. And added, "For you, your life must have looked like that road up ahead. Dark, empty. Worse even, because you had no idea where it would lead."

"You don't know the half of it," he muttered.

"No. I don't. So tell me." He gave a low snort. And didn't answer. She tried again. "Too big, huh? Okay, then just tell me...why the Grand Canyon?"

She sensed rather than saw him shrug. That was a male Highwater habit he'd apparently not gotten rid of. "Always wanted to see it."

"So Joey said."

He shifted in the seat. "I can't believe she remembered that."

"She said she asked you once, where you fit in the family. And you said you didn't. But that was before...that day."

She heard another long breath. "I always knew I didn't fit. I just never knew why. Until that day."

"So one little detail of your life wipes out all the rest? Makes sixteen years of having a family that loved you worthless?"

She heard the sharp movement in the darkness. "*Little* detail?" he snapped, anger echoing in his voice. "You think finding out your life was a lie is little? That not knowing who your father really is is a little detail?"

She hadn't planned on this, not now, but she had to counter that anger or he'd shut down completely. She could sense it just as she'd always been able to.

And so she said quietly, "It was for me."

Chapter Ten

KANE STARED AT the woman driving them through the darkness. He'd been close to developing a good mad, on the verge of calling up old Jasper, when he realized she was working him as she had probably worked kids in the situations she encountered. And clearly she'd been good at it, because stupid him, she'd gotten him to say things he never said, not out loud. But now...

"You're saying...what are you saying?"

She gave a slight, careless shrug, as if this mattered less than nothing. "I don't know who either of my biological parents are. Never have. I'm adopted."

"You say that like..."

"Like it doesn't matter? That's because it doesn't. Not to me. Marnie and Lawrence Leclair are my parents in every way that really matters. And they are the very best thing that ever happened to me."

"Lucky you."

If she noted the rather bitter edge that had crept into his voice she didn't react. She only went on in that same, light tone. "Yes. Lucky me. The only concern I ever had was not having a family medical history, but that's minor. Especially when stacked against how much they love me and I them, how they've taken care of me my entire life, how they would do anything for me and me for them."

Before that day, he'd felt the same way. He might have felt there was something off in his family situation, but he knew he was the problem, not them. And whenever there was a threat from outside, he'd always stood shoulder to shoulder with the Highwaters, ready to fend it off.

Of course, that was when he'd thought himself one of them.

Their little caravan continued through the starry night. The summer night, he thought as he saw the clock tick over past midnight; it was now Saturday, and the first day of the new season. They'd been counting down the days in Alaska, until the sun never set and the salmon started to run upstream. The people became energized, knowing they had to cram in as much as they could before the long, long winter of endless night set in again.

In the same moment he saw the gleam of water and realized they were at the bridge over the Red River, and up ahead was the sign marking the border.

The thought that all of this was happening in the same moment hit him hard. New day. New weekend. New season. New state.

Except not a new state, but the state where he'd been born and raised, what raising there had been.

"I swore I'd never come here again," he muttered.

"How often?"

He blinked. Looked away from the big sign with the still

instantly familiar Lone Star flag waving in welcome, with the usual admonition to Drive Friendly. "What?"

"How often did you swear it?"

His brow furrowed. "Every time I thought of here."

"And how often was that?"

"Too damned often."

She was quiet for a moment before saying, "I gather you tried not to?"

"For all the good it did."

What the hell was wrong with him? Why was he sitting here talking to her about what he never talked about to anyone? He wasn't used to this. Carrying on a conversation wasn't something that happened to him all that often. Carrying on a conversation about things with a decidedly personal bent never happened. He saw to that. He had pat answers for anyone who asked where he was from or why he was wherever he was at the moment. Answers that both gave away nothing and shut down the questioning, in most cases. Yet he couldn't seem to formulate one for this. Because of her?

It must be. It had to be her connection to the people who had once been his family. The only family he'd ever known.

And none of it had been real.

"I wonder why that didn't work, even when you were so far away?" she said, sounding as if she were just musing about an interesting question.

"Maybe I just hate the place too much."

"If you really hated Texas so much, I'd think you

wouldn't have to work so hard at not thinking about it."

He opened his mouth to retort sharply, then shut it again as he realized he'd be betraying that he'd so often thought exactly that. And he wasn't sure how he felt about the fact that she seemed able to read him so damned well.

"So," she said with a cheer that had to be put on, "where were you after Seattle?"

The change of subject and tone was so abrupt it caught him off guard. And he answered. "Alaska."

"Wow. As far as you could get and still be in the country, huh?"

It was getting so that he half expected her to come up not just with thoughts he'd had before, but practically the exact wording. That didn't make it any less disconcerting, though.

"Pretty much," he muttered.

"Did it work?"

"Work?"

"Make it easier to put Texas out of your mind."

Maybe she could just read his mind. Maybe that was it. "For a while."

"Why there?"

Still rattled, he answered without thinking. "Northern Lights were on the list."

"The list?"

Damn.

This had to stop. He was talking too much, and to a virtual stranger. No matter her friendship with the Highwaters, he didn't know her.

She sure as hell knows you, though.

And her friendship with his one-time family made this all even more dangerous. Floundering for something, anything else to say, he blurted out, "It really never bothers you, not knowing who your parents were?"

"I know who my parents *are*," she answered pointedly. "But no. I know the adoption agency told my parents my biological mother wasn't an addict, so there would be no effects on me from that kind of thing. And that she hadn't been raped. She was young, scared, and knew she couldn't take care of me. And so she did the best thing she could do for me, and I thank her for that every day."

"And you don't ever wonder? About her, or your father?"

She hesitated. And when she went on he could tell from her voice that she was reluctantly being honest. Another time, he might appreciate that. Right now, now that he was actually, physically back in Texas, he didn't appreciate anything.

"I won't deny that occasionally I do wonder. I don't know anything about him, so it's easier to not think of him. But her…being human, I mostly wonder if she ever thinks about me. But it doesn't bother me. Not in the way it apparently does you."

"So I'm the one with the problem, is that it?"

He saw her glance at him in the dim light of the car interior. "Well, that was an interesting jump. Since I never even hinted that. Been thinking it yourself?"

He was glad about the dim light, because judging from the heat he was feeling he was probably flushing. But she was right—again—he *had* thought it. Had wondered why he couldn't do that simple thing, not think about the man who'd sired him, whoever and wherever he was.

"Do you ever wonder...if he even knew?" he asked.

"Your father?"

"Ah. Now that's the question, isn't it? Did he know and run, or is he going about his life totally unaware? Interesting conundrum."

He stared at her. How could she be so...detached from it? For a moment silence spun out between them. Then, quietly, in that way that made him think she was wise far beyond her years, she spoke again.

"I always knew the truth, Kane. My parents never kept it a secret. I didn't find out when I was practically an adult, which had to be beyond shocking. It must have made you feel like you'd been living a lie your whole life."

That was exactly how it had felt. And it had made him suddenly, fiercely angry. Angry enough to—

He veered away from even the thought.

"What made you the angriest when you found out?" she asked, again as if she'd read him perfectly. He told himself not to answer, but as had happened from the moment they'd gotten into this damned car it came out anyway.

"That he knew. He knew all along and never told me."

"Hmm."

It was so neutral it was piercing. "That's it? Hmm?"

"Just thinking of how different our interpretations are."

"What other way is there to interpret that?" he demanded sharply.

She looked at him again, and even in the near-dark he could see the intensity of her gaze. "That he knew all along and he loved you anyway."

If she'd hauled off and slugged him she couldn't have driven the breath out of him any more completely.

Chapter Eleven

LARK COULD SENSE that she'd hit home with that one. Had he truly never realized that? That Steven Highwater had loved him just as he had his blood children, even knowing? She'd never been in such a horrible position, so she couldn't even begin to understand how he must have felt. Even when she tried to imagine what it would feel like if she hadn't found out she was adopted until she was sixteen, she knew she couldn't begin to touch the full impact of it.

Silence stretched out, but she let it, because of that sense she had that she'd hit him with something new, and hard. Best to let that echo around in his head for a while. In fact, she was a little surprised he didn't bring something else up, as a distraction. But instead he sat staring out the window into the darkness for several miles. Miles that she spent trying to decide whether to let it be, or try to prod him into talking some more.

They needed all the information they could get if this reunion was going to work—although she had no idea what it working would entail, for the Highwaters at least. She suspected they wanted him home for good, but she had no idea if that would ever be possible. At this moment in time, she suspected the very idea would send him running as fast as he could manage. So better approach it as if this were...what? A visit? A reunion, but temporary?

Her mind was spinning, and in the end the only thing she was certain of was that trying to get him used to talking—her gut was telling her he very much was not—couldn't hurt.

"What was Alaska like? And if you say cold, I'll turn the heat on as high as I can get it, even if it is still seventy degrees out."

She thought she caught a trace of a smile with her peripheral vision. "I only got as far as Ketchikan. But it was beautiful. About as different from...here as you could get."

Was that an opinion on Alaska, or Texas? Did he really hate his home that much? Or was it just what had happened here? She scrambled to keep it going, to not let him shut down.

"Did you see those Northern Lights? Are they as amazing as the videos I've seen?"

"More, in person. Because then your brain knows for sure it's real, that it's not some special effects added to a video."

"I didn't think of that, but it makes sense."

Silence descended again, and she wondered if he'd somehow taken that wrong, if he thought she'd meant...she didn't know what. Maybe that she was surprised he'd made sense. But if he was that touchy, she was probably going to make him mad eventually, without even trying.

Then he said abruptly, "I need some sleep. If you want

me to drive later, wake me up."

She was a little surprised at the offer, nearly veered off into wondering if he had an actual driver's license and how and where he'd gotten it if he did, but managed to say levelly enough, "Probably a good idea. It'll likely be a bit chaotic once we get back to the ranch."

At the word ranch he winced as if she'd struck him. Had he not realized that's where they were headed? Or had it just not registered until she said it? Maybe he hadn't been able to wrap his mind around anything more than going back to Last Stand.

"It will be all right," she said softly.

"Right." He sounded like he'd looked in that instant.

"You'll work it out. You've all waited so long…"

"I should never have come." His voice was the harshest thing she'd ever heard. "I knew it, knew it all along, but I did it anyway."

"Because it was time."

"No. Because I was fu—freaking stupid."

She hated that he thought that, but was amazed that he bothered to clean up his language for her. *He hasn't lost everything you taught him, Steven Highwater.* And it was that realization that made her say, casually, "If it's too horrible for you, you can come home with me. I have a foldout couch in my den."

His head snapped around. "Are you insane?"

"Not the last time I was checked," she said lightly.

"You don't know who or what I am."

"I know that a man I respected more than anyone other

than my own father raised you for sixteen years. That's a better start than many, many kids get."

"And look what happened to that man," he said, still in that harsh tone.

"We'll get to that. Eventually. But it will keep. Right now why don't you try for that sleep you need? There's a pillow and a blanket in back. That seat reclines, or you can stretch out on the back seat if you want."

He gave her a sideways look. "What if I wanted you to stop so I could get out to get back there?"

"Or run? I don't think so," she said, giving him a wide smile. "Although I have to admit, the image of Sage chasing you down on her horse is amusing. And if you think she wouldn't, you're mistaken."

"She's done it before."

Was that the slightest, barely noticeable trace of humor in his voice? Oh, she hoped so. "When was that?"

"When I hid her favorite toy horse. She was ten."

"Oh, my gosh."

Her shocked tone wasn't faked; she could imagine the feisty Sage's reaction. Even then she'd been known as what her mother had called a "tough cookie." Lark had always figured she'd had to be, not only being the only girl with four brothers, but Highwater brothers to boot.

"Yeah, well, I was only twelve. I didn't get the power of a ticked-off female yet."

With no mother to show you. Knowing their mother was not a subject any Highwater wanted to talk about, she simply asked, "Did she catch you?"

"You have to ask? This is Sage we're talking about."

Yes, it was. And he was talking. Almost normally, almost like anyone talking about a childhood memory. She felt her own tension as she tried to keep it going, tried not to say anything that would make him go silent again. She tried to keep her voice light, as if this were indeed a perfectly normal conversation.

"So how did you make it up to her?"

There was a moment of silence, and she was afraid she'd blown it. But then, so quietly she had to concentrate to hear it, he said, "I wrote her a song about the horse. How he just wanted to see a little of the world before he settled down on the ranch."

Her breath caught; she hadn't expected that kind, that personal of an admission. "Perfect," she whispered. "Do you remember it?"

"Mostly."

"Sing it for me?" He went very still. She kept her tone as casual as she could. "It'll help keep me awake." *And I've always heard about your voice, I've just never heard it.*

He didn't respond, and her gut was telling her she'd pushed about as hard as she could. But she didn't want to give him the out of saying "never mind" either. Let him decide. So she stayed silent. And after a long, quiet moment spun out, it paid off.

His voice came out of the shadows, a living, vivid thing that seemed to wrap around her heart. The words were simple, exactly what a twelve-year-old—a talented twelve-year-old—would have come up with, but that voice made it so much more, gave an adult spin to the words she doubted even he could have guessed would have such import years later. He sang it softly, almost distantly, as if he were lost in the memories it stirred up.

I'm just a poor ranch horse
Destined to spend my day
Messing with cattle
Earning my hay.

But before that destiny hits
Before I spend my life
In endless days of work
Free of trouble and strife.

Let me run, just a little bit.
Let me run, just a while.
I'll come home, I'll be good,
Just let me run a while.

Lark had never quite felt like this before. All the things she would have said, that they'd far understated the beauty of his voice, that the tune was lovely, that for the situation the lyrics couldn't have been any more perfect to calm down his angry sister, she couldn't say. Because she knew instinctively that he would shut down. And it took her a moment to think of something to say. Her gut feelings had worked so far, so she went with them again.

"Well, great," she said wryly. "Now you've got me feeling sorry for the horse."

She didn't think she was wrong in sensing him relax a little. "It worked with Sage."

"Did he come home?"

He let out a very small laugh, an almost sheepish one, and she felt like a prospector who'd seen the glint of gold. "Yeah. I muddied him up a bit so it looked like he'd been traveling, and put him back on her shelf while she was asleep the next night."

"Oh, nice touch. I like a man who thinks of the details." *Well, that was a stupid thing to say...*

Again silence spun out in the car. Then, unexpectedly, he asked, "What do you do now?"

She took it as a good sign that he was asking, even if it was just to break the silence. And he seemed to have forgotten his intention to sleep.

"I work for the private adoption agency my parents used."

"Why?" He sounded startled.

"So I can specialize in placing the kind of kids I couldn't help before."

He was quiet again for a moment before asking, "Do you tell them you're adopted?"

"If I think it will help. It's not a secret, something I try to hide."

Another silence. Then, "You live in…"

He couldn't even say the name, she realized. There truly was a lot of repair work to be done if he and the Highwaters were going to heal the breach.

"Yes. My parents moved to Austin a few years ago, for

my dad's job, but I love Last Stand, and the agency's there, so I stayed." She grimaced. "Not real thrilled with my apartment right now, but that's another story."

"What's wrong with your apartment?"

"Not the apartment itself, my neighbors. On both sides. They seem to be on a noise campaign to make sure I never get a full night's sleep."

"Oh."

The silence was longer this time. She supposed she should be glad he didn't just say "Move." Expert as he obviously was on the art of moving on. Physically, anyway.

The question was, would he ever be able to move on from the past?

Chapter Twelve

KANE LOOKED AT the clock on the dash, realized it was now twelve hours since he'd first looked into that arena and seen his sister putting that dun horse through his paces. Twelve hours, and here he was halfway back to… Damn, he couldn't even say it in his head, now that he was so close.

He was having trouble processing all this—he knew that. It just seemed strange to him that with everything that had happened since he'd gotten off the bus that had dropped him near the showground, the person he was most fixated on was sitting a bare two feet away.

He told himself it was because she was the only one besides Jessie and her man who wasn't really part of what had once been his family. He hadn't missed the engagement ring on Shane's woman's finger—he didn't even know her name—and he'd seen Joey's earlier. He'd bet Sean and his elegant lady were headed that way, and he'd put money on Sage and Scott, too, if he had it to throw around.

So all the Highwaters were matched and set. Obviously happy.

And then he tumbled back into their lives.

They've worried about you for thirteen years…

Worried about him? Or been hunting him down?

Especially Sage. She was a tough, strong girl, but that triple loss—her father, you, and then Scott leaving—nearly broke her.

His little sister had always been the best at understanding, the best at caring, even if she did hide it half the time under that tough façade. That had always been just self-defense, born of being the only girl.

If any of them could ever forgive him, he'd always known it would be Sage.

"Joey says you two were lab partners, in chemistry."

The abrupt statement rattled him out of his reverie. "I...yes."

"She also says she wouldn't have made it through the class without you."

Memories of those days, huddled over stained books, bottles and test tubes, and the Bunsen burner that only worked half the time, came flooding back again. How she had always been so understanding. And so many times, she'd given him a different way of looking at things, a way that made sense to him. "And I wouldn't have made it through English and history without her."

It was a moment before she spoke again. "Sean said you once told him over a puzzle that just because a piece fits in a place doesn't mean it belongs there."

A chill swept him, and the warmer memories fled. "That's exactly how I felt." He hated the way his voice sounded, and swore under his breath. "Why the hell were they even talking about me at all?"

"I told you. They never, ever stopped looking, wondering…or caring."

He bit back a protest, a denial. He saw her, in the dim glow from the vehicle's dash lights, turn her head to glance at him again.

"Maybe," she said softly, "the reason you could never forget Texas is we never forgot about you."

A sour, sharp, short laugh escaped him. "Seriously?"

"Maybe when Texas popped into your mind for no reason, it was someone here thinking about you."

He stared at her then. Her gaze was back on the road, so he couldn't really see her expression, and it was too dark in here to really see her eyes anyway. "That's…crazy."

"Whimsical I'll grant you. But is it any more fanciful than muddying up a toy horse to make it look like he'd been out running for a while?"

He looked away then, staring out into the night. "That's different," he finally said, a little lamely. "I was a kid." When she didn't respond he couldn't help asking, "How could someone who did what you did for a living, who saw what you saw, think that way?"

She glanced at him again, and he saw that her expression was completely sincere. "I left that job so I could stay that way."

He didn't know what to say to that. He didn't know what to think about it. He'd never spent so much time and effort trying to figure out a woman he'd met less than a day ago. But then, his life hadn't leant itself to getting to know anyone well, because that took time. And he never spent much in any one place.

This was driving him crazy. Not for the first time he wished there was an off switch for the brain, so he could just take a break from thinking about all this.

Why isn't there, Dad?

Because, son, who would turn it back on again?

The memory hit hard, vividly, and his gut knotted so tightly it was a moment before he could catch a breath.

Son.

He'd called him that, often. Even as he'd known it wasn't true.

...he knew all along and he loved you anyway.

He couldn't do this. He couldn't deal. He needed to be back on his lonesome road, only dealing with the people he had to...to survive.

He heard a musical notification, a sweet little riff, realized it was coming from the dash area and apparently a relay from her phone. A glance at the screen—he wasn't used to any car built in the last fifteen years, other than the occasional ride while hitchhiking—told him it was an incoming text. And his gut knotted all over again when he saw Sage's name.

"That's our signal. Time for a gas stop," Lark said.

Gas stop. Of course, towing the trailer Sage would be getting lousy mileage.

Lark changed lanes, as if she were readying to take the next off-ramp. Were they all going to stop? Maybe he could slip away. Maybe he could—

Right. Slip away from two cops, a couple of other obviously tough guys, and the little sister who'd always been able to practically read his mind. Not to mention the woman beside him, who seemed to be darn near as good at that as Sage was.

Just keep your mouth shut. You can't say anything stupid if you don't say anything at all.

They did all stop, at a truck stop on the outskirts of Fort Worth. It was a fairly large setup, with a market, washing stalls, and a kids' playground in addition to several rows of gas pumps. And busy, which explained why they were routing themselves around the city instead of through it, he guessed; Friday night traffic, even at this hour.

Oddly, it seemed the two non-family guys, Scott and Jessie's Asher, were in charge of keeping him on a short leash. Maybe the Highwaters were afraid they'd kill him if they got him alone.

And despite his determination not to speak, when he finished in the multi-stall restroom complete with showers and was washing his hands, he looked at Scott and said, "You and Sage."

"Completely," he said.

Kane nodded. "Good." It was all he could think of to say. But he noticed the man's eyes were green. A darker green than Lark's, which were the color of a spring meadow.

"Very," Scott agreed. As they stepped back outside he looked northward into the darkness, then gave the man beside him another glance. "Don't even think about it," Scott said.

"He means it," came Asher's cheerful voice from behind them; he'd been waiting outside. "He was a sniper, and a damned good one."

Well, that was just his luck. He supposed Scott had taken the military as the out from his life in Last Stand. Kane could understand that. Might have done it himself, when he was old enough, except he hadn't dared risk his identity standing up to a background check.

"And he was a Green Beret," Scott said, nodding at Asher, who seemed to be hanging back. Probably in case he took off running and Scott couldn't take him down.

He nearly laughed at the absurdity of him trying to escape these two.

"I get it. I'm doomed."

Hell, I've spent most of my life that way.

"No," Scott said quietly. "You're going home."

Kane winced as if the guy had punched him. "Same thing," he muttered.

Scott stopped. But he did it in front of Kane so he couldn't keep going. "Look, I get what it's like, growing up feeling like the odd one out. The problem child, the useless one in my case."

Kane did know. He'd heard the story for years, how Scott hadn't been a donor match for his deathly ill brother, but his younger brother had been. It was probably why he'd been able to talk to him that day in the principal's office.

"Your point?" he asked, his voice cooler than he'd actually meant it to be. He'd liked the guy, then.

"Just saying it doesn't have to stay that way. It didn't for me. Not saying it wasn't harder than hell, it was. But I took my life back. I own it now, and what anybody else thinks doesn't matter anymore."

"Congratulations." It came out in that same cool tone, and he made himself add, more sincerely, "I mean that. I know where you were."

"Yeah. A bad place. So if I can stomach coming back to Last Stand, you can too."

Kane followed him back to where everyone was parked, thinking with every step of the biggest, insurmountable difference between those returns.

Nobody suspected Scott of murder.

Chapter Thirteen

STANDING NEXT TO the gas pumps, Lark gave Shane a last look. He nodded at her, acknowledging their talk and confirming the decision they'd made. When she'd told them she sensed if they pressured him he would run, they'd trusted her.

She was aware of how hard it was for all of them, having just found him after all these years, and again felt a warmth at their faith in her. But that was for later; now she only nodded in turn and walked back to her car, arriving just as the other trio of men arrived. Scott and Asher retreated, leaving Kane there, although she had the feeling neither of them liked the idea.

None of the Highwaters had actually spoken to Kane at this stop. On her recommendation they had kept their distance, and sent the other two men with him when he headed for the restrooms. She knew he noticed by the way he looked warily back over his shoulder at his family.

Or rather, the people he hadn't thought of as his family in thirteen years.

"Want me to drive so you can sleep?" he asked now, very politely.

"I'm not sure."

"Another five hours is a long stretch." So he remembered the drive from Fort Worth to Last Stand? One more thing he hadn't succeeded in wiping from his memory. When she didn't answer he drew back slightly. "I've got a license. I won't crash."

She thought again about asking him where he'd gotten it and how, but decided this was not the time. "Maybe I'm a little afraid I'll wake up in Alaska."

He gave her a startled look, then a rueful smile. "Not unless you're really tired. Alaska's nearly three thousand miles; that's three days pushing hard sixteen hours a day. So shall I drive?"

"I…yes. That would be a nice break for me for a couple of hours." She wondered if she would regret it.

When they were back in her SUV, she studied him as he adjusted the seat for his much longer legs. She knew Alaska was a long way away, but she didn't have the distance—or the driving time—in her head. He obviously did. And it struck her why. "You thought about driving here?"

"No. No car. Thought about hitching again, but there are places on the way where potential rides are few and far between."

"I would think hitchhiking would have been dangerous for someone who looks like you did then. Or now, for that matter."

His head snapped around. "What?"

"Beautiful, I mean."

His jaw dropped. He was gaping at her. Did the man

never look in a mirror? Then, slowly, he seemed to recover. And looked away. She thought the moment had passed, but then he muttered under his breath, "Look who's talking."

He started the engine before she could react. Which was probably just as well, given that she knew her cheeks must be red because she could feel the heat. They were back on the interstate and headed south before he spoke again.

"It happened, a couple of times. In the beginning."

She'd been so flustered at the implied compliment—which made little sense, she'd been complimented on her looks before—that it took her a moment to realize he was referring to what she'd said about hitching being dangerous for him. He was incredible now, but she also remembered what the sixteen-year-old Kane had looked like, and it was quite believable that he'd be a temptation some couldn't resist.

And the heat retreated rapidly, as it always had when she'd been confronted with a kid who'd been through the worst hell. But maybe he didn't mean that.

"Somebody who gave you a ride hit on you?" she asked lightly.

"Lady did, once. I almost took her up on it. But she changed her mind."

And of course you abided by her wishes. Because no matter what you think, you're a Highwater. "And...the other time?"

"He wasn't so polite about it."

Her throat tightened. "What happened?"

"Knife to my throat." She swore under her breath. He gave her a startled glance. "That was pretty vehement."

"Predators like that were the other reason I quit." She didn't want to ask, afraid of the answer, but she asked anyway. "Did he...hurt you?"

His jaw tightened. She could see it in the faint glow from the dash lights. "If you mean did he succeed in raping me, no. I fought him off, thanks to...what Shane taught me."

The fracture in his voice before he could get out his brother's name almost broke her heart. "Dare I hope you hurt him in the process?"

He gave her another startled glance. "Bloodthirsty?"

"In certain situations, absolutely. Did you?"

"I might have...left him bleeding a little." Another sideways look. "And I kept the knife. Came in handy later."

"Good."

When she looked at him again his gaze was fastened on the road. But he was smiling a little. And that warmed her far more than it probably should have.

He was a smooth driver. But then, from what they'd learned he'd at some point driven at least from the Grand Canyon to near Yosemite. Probably more, since he'd had the truck they'd later found towed when he was working at the national park in Arizona. She should ask him about that. If he'd been on some sort of mission to visit national parks.

Northern Lights were on the list.

What he'd said when he'd seemed a bit disconcerted ran through her mind again. What list? Joey had said they'd talked occasionally in the lab about places they'd like to go or see, which is how she'd known about the Grand Canyon, and later Seattle. Maybe he'd been making a list all along, and what had happened that day thirteen years ago had just sent him on the journey earlier than he'd planned.

Something else occurred to her. Had he ever gotten his high school diploma? Had he stuck somewhere long enough to get a GED at least? Or did he not care? One of the kids she'd pulled out of a horrible situation once hadn't cared, hadn't thought it would make one bit of difference to her miserable life. Once she was in the system at fifteen she'd had no choice and had to go back to school, but she hadn't been happy about it. And even though her role was officially over at that point, the girl had come to Lark.

She'd known Shari was smart; she'd just never been motivated, had been swamped by the load she'd been carrying. So Lark had laid out a list of options, of things she might like to do in her life, and pointed out the paltry number of them she'd be able to do without that diploma. The key had been telling her that if she got that diploma she could conceivably get out of the system earlier, be declared emancipated. That had been like lighting a fire, and only two years later Shari had returned to show her the GED certificate. And thank her.

She let out a long breath as the memory came back to her. There had been some good moments, even some triumphant ones in that work. There just hadn't been enough, for her at least, to outweigh the bad.

"What were you doing in Alaska? I mean, working, or what?"

"Worked in a...store."

Her brows rose. "That came out oddly."

"I'm not sure what you'd call it. It's a combination hardware, sporting goods, fishing, clothing store with a snack bar."

She laughed. "Sounds like a true one-stop shop place."

"Pretty much."

"Did you enjoy it?"

"Yeah. Mr. Lindsay is a good guy. He took me on when—" He stopped abruptly.

"When what?"

"When I have zip in the way of references. At least long term."

She kept her tone one of simple curiosity. "What's the longest you were ever someplace?"

He hesitated, but finally said, "Yosemite. I worked at a rafting outfit, who did the Tuolumne River. I'd learned a bit about it on the Colorado when I was there." Another half shrug. "I was there for a couple of years."

"Because you were stuck because your truck broke down?"

"Partly, yeah."

"What was the other part?"

"It was beautiful," he said simply.

"What was the least beautiful place you went?"

She was keeping the questions ordinary, and it seemed to be working. "No question," he said dryly. "L.A. But that was because of the people, not the place."

"What was the strangest?"

He seemed to think a minute. "Death Valley, I guess. Or maybe Mono Lake."

"The most impressive?"

He gave her another sideways glance, but answered easily enough after a moment's thought. "I'd say the combination of Mount Saint Helens and Mount Rainier."

"Because the one could go like the other?"

That got her a smile. "Exactly."

"Scary thought," she said. He seemed almost bemused that she'd followed his thoughts. "How'd you get to Alaska?"

"Hitched."

"Through Canada? How—"

"On a fishing boat."

"Oh. Was it like those shows on TV?"

He laughed. "Not really. Far less dramatic. But then we didn't hit any storms, and I got off at the first stop."

"Catch any fish?"

"Enough to take time for that first stop."

"And you decided to stay there?"

"It was kind of decided for me." Another one of those sideways looks, but this one was wary. "Mostly because my first night there was that rare combination in Ketchikan, a clear winter night. And I saw the Northern Lights."

"Which is why you went?" He nodded. "And should I not ask what the other reason was?"

"I got in a bit of a fight with one of the long-time crew guys on the boat. I figured that canceled my return trip."

"Over what?" she asked, truly curious.

He let out a long, annoyed-sounding breath and gestured at the windshield, as if to indicate everything outside. "This," he said flatly.

"Texas?" He nodded. "Then I hope you upheld our reputation," she said very primly. The short, sharp sound he made could have been either disgust or laughter. She couldn't tell in the dim light.

"It was the old Alaska stole the biggest state title thing. I don't know why it set me off. Shouldn't have. It doesn't matter to me anymore."

"And yet now you're back," she said quietly.

"Against my heart, my gut, and my better judgment."

"Then I guess it's up to Texas to prove you wrong."

She only hoped they could.

Chapter Fourteen

Ms. Lark LeClair was as smart as he'd thought she was. He was almost certain she'd planned it when she said she needed a stop just before they hit Temple. His first clue was when she'd taken the keys with her.

As if she thought I was going to steal her car. Maybe she does. That's far from the worst thing she probably thinks I've done.

Not that he needed a car if he was going to run.

When she'd come back she'd said—not asked, just said—she'd take the wheel when they started out again.

"Don't trust me?" he'd asked.

"We're getting close enough I don't trust you not to run," she admitted. Which only proved again how smart she was. Because now that they were headed west out of Austin, with the sky behind them beginning to lighten as dawn approached, the moment they passed the first mileage sign with the name, that name on it, he reacted as if someone had tried to brand it on him.

Last Stand, 60 miles.

Sixty miles. He'd sworn never to set foot in Texas again, but that he'd die before he'd go back to Last Stand. And yet here he was, sixty miles away.

"You were right," he said, his voice strangely hoarse.

"It happens," she agreed lightly. Then, with a glance at him and a world of compassion in her voice, she said, "Getting that white-knuckle feeling?"

As it happened, his knuckles were no doubt white, although he couldn't see them in the darkened vehicle. But he could feel his fingernails digging into his palm as his hands clenched into fists. He consciously relaxed his fingers but his palms still stung, and he wondered if he'd actually drawn blood.

"I never should have done this." His voice still had that strange sound, maybe because his throat was so tight he could barely get enough air. "It was a really bad decision."

"There's a kids' picture book about a magical pony named Murphy who helps people. One day he makes a bad decision for the best reason, and then it takes all his magic to make things right."

He blinked. Stared at her. There had been something in her voice, some undertone he couldn't name. But it was something he shied away from. Not knowing what else to say, he said, "There is?"

"Yes." He saw her mouth quirk. "I wrote it. Because sometimes, for some of my kids, I felt like it would take magic to make things right."

He didn't want to dwell on the apparent fact that she was thinking of him as one of "her kids"—she couldn't be much older than he was, after all—so he focused on something else. "You wrote a book?"

She laughed. "Hard to believe, huh? I'll tell you the whole story, what inspired it someday, maybe. But it was for the little ones, mostly. They ended up using it at CPS. Reading it, or looking at the story in pictures if they were too young. It seemed to calm them down. And get them used to the idea that someone might actually want to help them. Then they started giving a copy to them and that really helped. Something about having a possession of their own, or being given a gift."

She was making him feel...something. Amazed at her, yes, but also uncomfortable. He'd been so wrapped up in his own twisted life for so long he didn't tend to think about the misery other kids had gone through, and much younger than he had. The only thing he could think to say was an inane "That's nice," so instead he said nothing. She went on anyway, that same light note in her voice, so unlike his own harsh croak.

"In fact, I was kind of plotting a new one when I ran into you."

"You were?" Hmm. That came out better.

"Yep. When I was trying to find the restrooms at the arena, I was thinking I'd need a trail of breadcrumbs to find my way back. Then I started thinking a story like that might be a good way to teach kids to pay attention to where they were, to maybe leave a trail of some kind so they could find their way back."

"Assuming they want to go back." The harsh note was there again.

"There is that," she agreed. "But that was my job, to find

out if they should go back. Or not."

On the last two words her voice had been the one to take on a low, rough tone. And he could sense the pain she still felt. "And if you found reason a child should not go back to whatever situation it was?"

"I fought tooth and nail to see that it didn't happen." She said it so fiercely that it made her next words, and the change in her voice to one of utter sadness, wrench at him in a way he'd never felt before. "And sometimes it did anyway. Sometimes they sent that child back."

"And were you right about what would happen? Like with that little girl?"

"Too often. But then, just once is too often."

He couldn't think of anything, no words that would ease the pain in her voice. He wasn't even sure why he wanted to do that, ease her pain. She was the one who'd gotten him into this mess, after all. Well, after he'd made the colossal mistake of giving in to the urge to go to the Derby in the first place.

"Sing something else for me," she said abruptly.

"What?" he asked, startled.

"'The Yellow Rose of Texas,' maybe. I'll bet you can smoke that one. Or maybe 'Deep in the Heart of Texas,' since the stars are really out tonight."

"If you're trying to make me happy to be back here, it's not working," he said sourly.

"Right now I'm trying to make me happy."

He thought again of the horrible sadness in her voice. Thought again of the little girl Sean had helped her find barely in time to save her life. Thought of...so many damned things. And didn't he know better than most that sometimes music, the right music at the right moment, could help? Hadn't he spent countless nights aching for his old guitar, and ending up singing softly without it because it was the only thing that seemed to ease the building pressure?

"I can't...sing those." Not after years of trying not to even think about Texas. Singing those anthems would be beyond painful.

"Then sing me...Sage's song. The bluebonnet song."

God, that would be worse. How does she even know about that song?

Idiot, as close as she obviously is to...everyone, of course she's heard about it. Sage used to brag about it all the time. But...he couldn't. He just couldn't. The pressure was already building—soon it would be unbearable. "I—"

"Please."

The tiny plea was like a knife twisted in his gut. *Deal. Deal with it now, or wait until you're in damned Last Stand, where it will hurt even more. You're going to be back there in less than an hour, face to face with it all, so you'd damned well better buck up now.*

Buck up and get it done.

Just like the man he'd thought was his father for sixteen years used to say.

And because he didn't know how to say no without betraying what a mess he was, or because he truly didn't want to say no, not to her, not when she asked like that, in that voice, he swallowed hard and started the song he'd written for his little sister all those years ago.

It included all the things Sage loved about her home. The open spaces, the hills, the river, the horses, her family. He had his eyes closed, remembering the day he'd first sung it for her, her twelfth birthday. Remembering the look of awe and love on her face.

He started quietly, barely above a whisper, but when he hit the last verse he let it out because he had to, because the pressure was too much.

And that's what I think
Every time I see a bird on the wing
As blue as the wide Texas skies
And the bluebonnet hills that in spring
Turn as blue as my sister's eyes.

His voice broke on the last note, and that was what seemed to linger in the air. He was so tangled up right now he didn't care.

"My God," she breathed. "Why aren't you…famous? On the radio every time I turn it on? Have your own streaming channel?" She gave him a startled look. "You don't, do you?"

He let out a harsh laugh. "No." But he couldn't deny her words warmed him.

"Why not?"

"I don't want to be famous." *Any more than I already am, in that town we're headed for. Make that infamous, no doubt.*

"But your voice is incredible. So is the music. And you obviously have a way with words."

"I hid out a lot in libraries, when I didn't have anyplace else to go." He slammed his jaw closed, thinking that was the most pitiful thing he'd ever said. "Still do," he ended rather lamely.

"That's a good place," was all she said.

"They were warm, at least. Or cool, depending."

That wasn't much better, idiot.

"So you read a lot?"

"Yeah. They left me alone when I was reading."

"What did you read?"

"Sometimes about where I was going next. Sometimes about where I'd just been. And sometimes about places that don't really exist."

"Sometimes those are the places I wish did exist the most," she said quietly.

He stared at her in the darkness. How many times had he finished some book or story set in a fictional place and thought exactly the same thing? That he'd be happier there, that it would be easier to survive.

She unnerved him, with how she understood. He lapsed into silence. And at some point he had dozed off, because he jolted awake when a gentle hand touched his arm.

"Kane. We're home."

Home.

He sat frozen, unable to move, afraid to even look around. It was full light now. He'd actually slept through Last Stand, to…wherever this was? Because it wasn't the ranch. It was a large building with a paved lot and covered parking.

"Where?" He sounded as confused as he felt.

"My place." He blinked. Looked around, but there was no sign of other cars, not Shane's SUV or Sage's truck with the horse trailer.

"Your place?"

"We all thought it might be easier if you got some sleep here, and then…we'll deal."

He stared at her. "You want me at your place?"

"I want you not to run," she said frankly.

He didn't want to run, not from her. Which was crazy. But then, all of this was crazy. Full on.

"What about…them?" He didn't explain who he meant, knew he didn't have to. "They agreed to this?" Why would they do that? They finally had the guy who had caused their father's death within reach and they were leaving him…with her?

"They've waited thirteen years. It won't kill them to wait until this afternoon. Come on, wandering man."

She got out of the car. And after a long moment of fighting the feeling of numb shock that had engulfed him at realizing he was actually back in Last Stand, he got out and followed her.

Chapter Fifteen

HE WAS AS skittish as any scared kid she'd ever dealt with. But for Lark, it was impossible to think of Kane Highwater—or Travis, as he insisted—as a kid. He was only two years younger than her, after all. And in tough roads walked, he was much, much older. It wasn't ordinary sadness that put that shadow in his eyes.

Those hazel eyes that didn't match the rest of the Highwaters'.

She watched him as he stared into the mug of coffee she'd poured him. He certainly did right by those worn jeans, and that equally worn T-shirt was just snug enough to tell her there was likely a healthy six-pack of abs beneath it.

Of course, there was also the simple fact that he was nothing less than beautiful, in a way that almost left her breathless. And definitely had her reminding herself that she needed to stay detached, to help everyone through this situation that would be awkward at best, or turn into disaster at the worst. Kane might need a representative, but the Highwaters were her dear friends.

And the situation was hardly the same anyway. Kane didn't need saving, not from the family who had never, ever quit looking for him, worrying about him…or loving him. He just needed to know that. To believe it. She could help with that. She had before. It would just be a little more tangled, because of her connection to everyone involved.

"Awake yet?" she asked.

"I think waking up requires going to sleep," he muttered.

It had been rough for her, too, although after the long drive she had, finally, a bit before noon, slept for a couple of hours. Once she'd managed, by trying to further plot out her idea for a new book, to put him and his presence in the next room out of her mind long enough to relax. When she'd awakened it was late afternoon, and she knew sleeping any longer would mess her up for tonight, so she'd given up and gotten up.

"It's hard in a strange place, I know," she said. *So what's my excuse?*

"It's hard," he said flatly, "in this town."

"I know that, too."

He at least looked at her then. "But you…love it."

"I do. I visit my folks in Austin often, and it only reinforces that I don't like big cities. I'm happy here." She gave a wry smile. "Well, except for my neighbors."

To her surprise, she thought she saw him flush slightly. "Is the woman next door always so…energetic?"

Lark nearly blushed herself; she'd heard the familiar noises, not unusual at any time of day on the weekends, but had hoped he was asleep. "Yes, afraid so. And often. Especially on the weekends."

"Nice," he muttered again, back to staring into his coffee.

"Might be, if it was ever the same man more than once."

"Maybe she likes it that way."

"Maybe. Does make me wonder what she's running from, though." His gaze shot back to her face. She shrugged. "Occupational hazard, from an occupation I can't seem to leave totally behind."

Something in that wary gaze shifted, softened. "I'm guessing you've seen a lot of things you can't leave behind."

"Yes."

"Quitting didn't help?"

"It helped in that I'm not piling up any more." She drew in a deep breath. "Have a muffin?"

His gaze darted away again. "Not hungry." Then, after a moment when he almost visibly remembered his manners, he added, "Thank you."

"Let me rephrase then. Have something to eat to stall heading out to the ranch?" He went very still. And after a long, taut moment she said softly, "If you wanted to run, you should have done it by now."

"I didn't want you getting the blame for letting me escape."

"Thank you. I think."

She thought about it for a moment, then went over and picked up her phone, which had been on the charger all night. She opened up the text she'd gotten while he was in the shower. She had been busy baking the muffins, trying to distract herself. And they'd almost gotten burned when, after the water had stopped running and she'd heard footsteps in the hall, she hadn't been able to stop herself from glancing that way. And with only a towel wrapped around his lean waist, Kane was an amazingly beautiful sight. Almost exactly as she'd imagined. Lean, strong, perfectly proportioned.

What she hadn't imagined were the scars. Even from here she'd seen them. A thin, curving one that seemed to wrap around his left side, a jagged, thick one just above the towel on his right side, and a nearly matching one on the inside of his left arm. And when he'd turned—thankfully without noticing her—to step back into the den, she saw yet another on the back of his right shoulder.

She'd guessed his life since that day had not been easy, but foolishly she hadn't really thought it might have been dangerous. She remembered what he'd told her about the predator with the knife, and wondered if one of those scars was a souvenir from him.

Shoving aside the thoughts she slid her phone across the counter to him. He stared at her for a moment before he looked down.

She knew what he was seeing.

Sage: Is he still there?

Me: Yes.

Sage: Thank God. Bring him out ASAP, please. I can't wait any longer.

"It's time to put an end to her torment, don't you think?"

His gaze flashed back to her face, just in time for her to see what she'd suspected all along. Sage was the key. She was his Achilles' heel, the way in, the one thing he hadn't been able to write off.

And after a moment he sighed, but nodded.

And so it begins.

A LITTLE TO his own surprise, he turned down her second offer of an early dinner before they left. Partly because he didn't want her to go to any more trouble, and partly because now that he'd decided he had to face this, he didn't want to put it off.

He stuffed his dirty jeans and shirt into his backpack, having put on his last clean clothes. They happened to be the least worn, too, which he'd likely be glad of later. Bad enough he was going to have to face them, without looking like the vagabond he was in the process.

He closed up the couch, folded the blanket and stacked it and the pillow on one end. He heard a thump through the wall from next door. Was she at it again? After a moment when no more sounds came, he decided not. And felt a bit relieved for reasons he didn't want to analyze but couldn't seem not to.

It was strange. A couple of times he'd been an inadvertent witness to sex, once at a restaurant he'd been working at when he'd walked in on the manager and her boyfriend in the back room, and once when the trucker who'd given him the ride into Seattle had been busy in the sleeper compartment with a woman he'd found…somewhere. Neither had bothered him particularly, he'd just shrugged it off and left them to it.

So why the hell had just hearing the activity next door, through a damned wall, gotten him so hot and bothered? Had being back in Last Stand screwed up his brain that much?

Or was it the fact that the first woman to wake up that part of him in a very, very long time was just feet away? Whichever it was, it had set off a chain of imagining that careened from wondering what—if anything—she wore to bed, to what she looked like asleep, with that silky golden hair spread on a pillow, to thinking about how soft and warm she would be, how silken and smooth her skin would be, what those soft, full breasts would feel like rounding into his hands, how—

Damn, just remembering his imaginings was making him hard all over again. And when he heard her in the doorway he froze, knowing he didn't dare turn around until he had himself back under control.

"I bagged up a couple of muffins. You can eat on the way."

Well, that was a distraction. He looked at her, over his shoulder, since his cock was a bit slow to calm down. He'd been too on edge out in the kitchen, but now the idea of fresh baked goods was very tempting. Then he inwardly grimaced at the word he'd used, wondering what the hell was wrong with him. He grabbed at the first words that popped into his head.

"You really baked muffins?" Stupid, you know she did, you smelled them baking.

She looked oddly embarrassed. "I needed to do...something."

"I would have thought being up all day and driving all night would have been enough."

"I'm...a little nervous."

She didn't look at him when she said it. As if he were the one making her nervous. The first thing that shot through his mind was that she was feeling the same thing he'd been, after her neighbor's vigorous activities this morning. Then reality slammed into him.

She's probably anxious to be rid of me. The guy who killed a man, and destroyed her friends' lives.

He was silent until they were back in her small SUV and she'd handed him the bag. He caught the same lovely aroma he'd smelled in the apartment earlier, and to his surprise this time his stomach woke up.

"Thanks," he said. "For the shower, too."

"You're welcome." Her brow furrowed. "I should have asked if you wanted to do laundry. But you can do it at the ranch."

Laundry? He didn't tell her for him laundry usually consisted of washing things in a sink, with warm water if he was lucky. Then trying to find a place for stuff to dry, which was always—

At the ranch.

It suddenly hit him that she expected he'd be staying there. Long enough to do laundry, anyway. And suddenly her little foldout couch—even with the sound effects through the wall—seemed like a haven.

Right. And you can go through that crazy hot and bothered thing again, every time you think of her just down the hall.

And for far from the first time in his life he had to decide between different kinds of dangerous.

Chapter Sixteen

LARK DROVE SLOWLY through town. Kane was staring out the window, but she wasn't sure if he was seeing anything or if he'd mentally shut down with the shock of being back here. Because she was certain when he'd come to the Derby he'd had no intention of coming here. He probably would have quietly slipped away if she hadn't run into him and recognized him. Maybe be on his way back to Alaska by now.

Something occurred to her then. "Are you going to miss a flight back?"

"No."

There was an Alaska-style chill in the two-letter word that kept her from pushing. But she was still curious. Had he intended to stay all along? Or was it simply that he couldn't afford the round trip? That seemed to her more likely, both because of the state of his worn clothes and his steady antipathy toward the place he'd been born.

But not to Steven Highwater.

Something struck her then—a distinct possibility, a reason for his wandering. Had he been looking for his biological father?

She couldn't think of a way to ask without risking the small rapport she thought she'd built with him. So instead she talked about what they were passing, about what was new or changed, while in her mind grateful they did not have to drive past Valencia's restaurant, where the accident had happened. The only things she saw him really react to were the big, stone library building, and the statue of Asa Fuhrmann out front.

"Joey's working there now?" he asked.

"Yes. She's the assistant librarian. Emma Corbyn is the librarian."

"She always did have her nose in a book." He looked back toward the building. "What happened to him?" he asked, nodding at the statue's base, where a sizeable chunk was missing, and a new plaque of explanation had been installed.

"It happened on Minna Herdmann's birthday celebration last year. This year was uneventful, thankfully."

He blinked. "She's still alive?"

Lark did the math quickly; the town matriarch would have been ninetyish when Kane had gone. "She is," she said, cheerfully. "A hundred and three now, and feisty as can be." Then, more seriously, she went on. "Anyway, a truck ran a red light and hit a tour bus. The bus ended up in the wine tasting room. The truck rolled and ended up there."

He looked back at the statue. "Whoa."

She knew she had his attention now so, quietly, she kept going. "The truck caught fire. Two people died. It would have been three, if not for Shane. He risked his own life to pull the survivor out."

It was a moment before he said, in a tight little whisper, "That sounds like him."

"Yes."

Then, more strongly and now with an edge, he added, "Just like his old man, huh?"

"In the most admirable way, yes."

The edge became bitter then. "Mr. Heart-of-Last-Stand, who never left for fear the place would cave in without him."

She wasn't sure what drove her to ask at that moment, but it was an instinct that had paid off before so she went with it. "What list of places are you working through?"

His head snapped around so sharply, and his expression was so shocked, it took her a moment to realize. When she did, her eyes widened in shock of her own. In understanding.

"It's his," she whispered. "It's…a bucket list?"

He looked away, and she could sense the tension even without seeing how tight his jaw was, and how his hands had curled into fists. But she knew she was right. He hadn't been looking for his biological dad at all. He'd been going every place Steven Highwater had never gone.

She wanted to ask more questions, wanted to understand why, if he felt as he seemed to about the Highwaters, he would have done that. It was hugely significant, and she desperately wanted to know. But with that same sense that had driven her to ask at that moment she knew if she pushed she would get nowhere. Except perhaps to make him even more guarded, maybe even enough to make that escape.

And so she backed off, talking only of general things until they were at the Highwater ranch. She turned onto the drive and slowed as they approached the big gate with the centered lone star. She saw Kane staring at the small pillar with the keypad. He watched as she keyed in the code Sage had texted her and the gate began to slide open.

"Sean's been busy," he muttered.

She smiled at him. She could sense his unease, and she could hardly blame him. He hadn't been here, to this place where he'd grown up, for more than a dozen years, and this automated gate hadn't been here then.

"Yes," she agreed. "They all have. The house is the same, although they updated the kitchen a while ago. In time for the surprise party they threw Shane when he became the youngest ever chief."

It wasn't until they were driving through the gate that he asked, "When did that happen?"

"About three years ago now." She glanced at him. "Where were you then?"

His brow furrowed. "I..." It stabbed at her that he had to think to figure it out. What a life he must lead. Or perhaps it was her, always and forever here in Last Stand, who was missing out. He'd certainly seen more of the world than she ever had. "Lake Tahoe," he finally said.

"Oh, I've heard that's beautiful," she said.

"It is." He was back to staring down the long, curved drive that wound through the grove of trees. "The water's so clear you can see bottom, even way offshore."

"Sounds like one of those pictures of a boat where you can't tell if it's floating or flying."

His gaze shot to her face. One corner of his mouth curved upward. "It's exactly like that."

"How long were you there?"

"Not as long as I would have liked, but it was winter, and I didn't have—" He broke off suddenly, looked away, down at his hands. His right was clenched, she saw.

She could guess what he'd stopped himself from saying, that at the time he hadn't had the clothes necessary for a winter in the Sierra Mountains. Obviously he must have acquired warmer clothes since, if he'd gone to Alaska. What had he done with them?

Left them in Alaska, idiot. Because he's planning on going back as soon as he can. As far as he can get from Texas.

She slowed as they neared the edge of the grove of pecan and oak trees. Caught herself holding her breath as she waited for him to look up. When he did, he went pale. She brought the car to a halt. He simply stared toward the big, sprawling ranch house, and opposite it the large arena, with the main barn beyond that. She couldn't even begin to imagine what it must feel like to be back here, to see it much as he must remember it, since little on the outside had changed.

And suddenly she felt an odd, potent shift somewhere deep in her heart, and she knew in that moment that if he asked her to turn around, she would do it. It would damage her relationship with people she cared greatly about, but she would deal. She could not, would not force this.

And she would just have to explain to the Highwaters why they should not, either. And hope they trusted her enough to listen.

"Do you want to keep going?" she asked softly.

"I didn't think I had a choice." His voice was flat. Not angry, not even bitter, just flat.

"We'll turn around and leave right now, if that's what you truly want."

His head snapped around. "You'd...do that?"

"I would."

He stared at her. "Why?"

"If there's anything I learned in those five hellish years, it's that some things are better not rushed, or pushed. Human emotions happen in their own time, and require processing."

A fierceness came into his voice then. "I'm not one of your cases."

"But the kid you were when you were last here could have been."

"I am not," he said in that same fierce tone, "one of those kids."

"No. I think you're a man who's physically moved on, but has never really dealt with what that kid lived through."

"They send you to shrink school for that job of yours?"

"Yes." He looked startled. "I found some of it useful, in a controlled setting, but I too often had to make snap decisions based on instinct and gut feelings for it to be much help."

"Snap decisions?"

"Like whether that parent was truly capable of beating their child severely enough to require hospitalization. Or worse."

His voice was low and harsh when he asked, "And the other way around?"

She knew perfectly well what he meant. "I won't deny it happened that a kid would strike a parent. But I never had a case where that wasn't self-preservation." Even as she said it she found herself trying to think of ways what had happened that day in front of Valencia's had been self-preservation for him.

He made a low sound she couldn't name, except that it was full of pain. But before she could ask again what he wanted to do, the front door of the ranch house opened and two people stepped out. And in that moment she saw in his changeable eyes the urge to run.

Sage. And Shane. His little sister and his biggest brother. The two who likely struck the most panic in him.

"It would make a much bigger statement to run now than to not have shown up at all," she said.

"If I was going to run I should have bailed out of the car back in Oklahoma."

"True." She reached out then, laid a gentle hand on his arm. Felt the rock-hard, tensed muscle beneath her fingers. "I'm glad you didn't," she said softly. "And I think, eventually, you will be too."

He didn't look convinced. At all.

But he didn't tell her to turn around.

Chapter Seventeen

KANE WAS USED to urgent signals from his gut. Most of the time it was hunger, and when it got fierce he knew the signal was about to be sent to the brain that he was dizzy or light-headed. Or sometimes it was that that last batch of scraps he'd scrounged from wherever was a little far past the expiry date, and he was going to pay for it messily.

And sometimes it had been a warning. Those times when that gut knotted up, when it screamed at him that the guy driving that innocent-looking delivery van had an ulterior motive for that ride he was offering. Or was going to expect a payment Kane had no interest in giving.

But it had been a while since he'd felt the two together, nausea and tension, as strongly as this.

Since the day, hiding out in the small library in the distinctively named Truth or Consequences, New Mexico, he'd seen that six-week-old news piece headline. *Police Chief Killed In Traffic Incident.*

That was when he'd learned what had really happened. What his short-fused temper, which had made him push away the man who had just shattered his world, had caused. He was dead. And in that moment Kane had wanted nothing more than to walk in front of a truck himself.

He'd seen that headline—ironically on a day he'd actually been thinking of going home—and it had been the lid coming down on the coffin that Steven Highwater's admittance that he was not his father had thrown him in. Darkness had descended anew and had never lifted again, not really.

That was the moment when he'd first faced the impossible convergence of hatred and grief for the man he'd loved as his father his entire life, until he'd found out he'd lied to him his entire life.

Traffic Incident. Incident. Not accident.

That was when he'd known they'd realized from the get.

"You'll get through it," Lark said, jolting him out of the morass of memory. And only then did he realize that, when she'd put her hand on his arm, when it had been so…when it had somehow eased the nausea a bit, he'd twisted around to grab her hand. "I'll just drop you off and—"

"No!" Panic jolted the protest out of him, and he didn't even care if it made him sound like a coward. "Don't leave."

"This is a reunion that should be private," she began.

"Please. Stay. I can't… Please stay."

To his immense relief she gave in. "All right. Unless they want me to leave," she warned.

Then I'm going with you.

He gave his head a sharp shake as she began to ease the car forward.

It looked the same. Oh, the barn had been painted recently, and the arena fence repaired, and there was a spot on the upper level roof of the house that had been redone. Was that still Sage's domain, the upstairs? He couldn't see the individual wings from here. One for each of them, the senior Highwater had always said, because he wanted his family under one roof. Here on the land that had been in the family since the revolution.

Mine's probably a junk room now. Or maybe a shooting range.

Crazily he wondered what they'd done with their father's rooms, the master suite that sat somewhat isolated from the rest, beyond the den where they most often had gathered.

You belonged there then. Or thought you did. And so did they. Now they know better.

She parked the car near the house, but didn't turn the engine off. He looked at her.

"Last chance to run," she said softly.

He stared at her for a long, silent moment, vaguely aware of how his breathing had gone fast and shallow. Then he took in a deep breath, swallowed, and closed his eyes for a moment.

"They lost a good one when you quit," he said roughly.

"Considering the source, that's one of the best compliments I've ever gotten."

His eyes snapped open and he looked at her, at the concern and support in those light green eyes. But then the two Highwaters were there and it was time, as the man he'd thought was his father used to say, to fish or cut bait. His brain wanted to skitter back to that time when he'd asked what that meant, and had gotten both an answer and praise for wanting to know. Just as they all did from the man who loved the history of language just as he loved the history of Texas.

He'd been one of them then. Now, he didn't know who—or what—he was.

He got out of Lark's vehicle. Took in another deep breath. It felt crushing, overwhelming to be back here, at the only real home he'd ever had or known.

Should have run, should have run, should have run...

A trumpeting neigh came from over near the barn, and his head snapped around. He saw the dun horse Sage had ridden to victory just—God, could it truly have only been last night?

He caught a movement out of the corner of his eye, a slight shift of blond hair, as if Lark had tilted her head. Or nodded toward the horse. She was looking at Sage, whose brow furrowed, then cleared.

And then Sage turned those bluebonnet-blue eyes on him. "Come on. I'll introduce you officially."

He felt a slight easing of the pressure in his chest. He could do that. He could meet a horse. That sounded easy compared to everything else that was about to happen. He glanced at Lark, hoping she saw in his expression that he knew what she'd done, made the silent suggestion that this might be an easier start. And that he was thankful.

The horse trotted over to the fence the moment he saw them coming. Or saw Sage coming, more likely. He stretched his golden-brown—that shade so close to Lark's hair—head out for a pat from her, then looked at Kane curiously.

"This fifty-thousand-dollars-richer-today boy is Highwater's Hot Poco," Sage said, nothing short of pure love echoing in her voice.

He hadn't heard the impressive total of her prizes last night. He tried to think of something to say. All he could come up with was, "That should keep him in hay and sweet feed for a while." Then, his sluggish brain caught up a little. "Poco? Poco Bueno bloodline?"

She nodded. "He just turned four. We got him as a yearling."

"And turned him into a champion in three years," he said softly, reaching out tentatively, old instincts and knowledge taking over as he patted the strong neck, leaving the more familiar nose pats to his clearly beloved owner.

He was aware that Shane was standing a couple of feet behind Sage. *Got her back, huh? Like you always did. For all of us. Even me.* But he didn't—couldn't—look at him. Until he spoke.

"Come on into the house."

Suddenly all the tension was back and he went rigid. "Was that an order, Chief?"

"A request."

"Really?"

Shane let out an audible breath. Kane felt a touch, Lark's hand at the small of his back. It seared him in ways that made him remember things that had never happened. But it also took the edge off of his tension. As it always seemed to.

Shane gave a slow shake of his head. "I'm only responsible for what I say. Not what you think I meant."

Shane-isms. He'd almost forgotten. Even when he'd last seen him, at twenty-two, he'd been full of them, just as his father had been.

"I figured you'd hit me with 'Life is tough, but it's tougher when you're stupid,'" he said, the pressure easing a little more.

The corners of Shane's mouth twitched. "Doesn't fit. You're not stupid. I do have one for you, though."

"'Never approach a bull from the front, a horse from the back, or a fool from any direction?'" he suggested rather tightly.

"No." Something came into Shane's voice, something that was so quiet and gentle Kane almost couldn't believe it was coming from this man. "If you're on the highway to hell, turn the hell around."

Chapter Eighteen

"Your fiancé," Lark whispered to Lily, "is amazing."

She meant it, too. She'd always admired the man, but had been throat-tighteningly moved at both his words and tone when he'd so cogently and exactly defined Kane's situation and at the same time offered him haven.

"He is," Lily Jones agreed, with the smile of a woman utterly, totally in love.

Lark had watched Kane step through that front door, back into the house he'd grown up in. Sean and his Elena were in the kitchen, Slater and Joey were seated at the table in the dining area, and Sage was pacing while her Scott, arms folded as he eyed their approach warily, leaned against the kitchen bar.

She could see the tension in every line of Kane's lean body, could see it in the way his eyes scanned, darted, and—when he spotted the portrait on the living room wall of Steven Highwater—widened.

He almost broke and ran then. She could feel it as certainly as she'd ever felt anything. And she spoke quickly, quietly, but urgently to Lily.

"Please don't take this wrong, but I think…it would be

easier on him, and maybe everyone, if just for now it was only his siblings."

Even as she said it, Elena looked over and made eye contact. With one dark, elegant brow raised in question, she nodded toward the back of the house.

"Obviously Elena agrees," Lily said, nodding back at the other woman, who whispered something to Sean, then walked over and did the same to Joey. "And I think you're right. I'll try to round up Scott, too, although knowing him he won't be eager to leave Sage just now."

"Only for a little while," Lark said.

Lily went over to Scott and began to talk softly. It was clear the man was reluctant, but after a moment and a glance at Sage, he nodded. Lark looked back at Kane just as he, apparently realizing what was happening, looked from the departing quartet to her. And at the look on his face she couldn't stop herself from walking over to him.

"Don't," he said, hoarsely. "Don't go."

When he'd said it in the car, he'd sounded almost scared. When he said it now, it sounded pleading.

"This is between you and—"

"I'd like to have somebody here who doesn't hate me. Somebody on my side."

Lark didn't know which stabbed at her more, that he truly believed they hated him, or that he believed she was on his side. She was, but she hadn't expected him to accept it yet.

"They don't," she assured him, but she could see he didn't believe it.

She didn't know what to do. She looked over her shoulder at the gathered Highwaters. Slater, Sean and Sage were looking at Shane. All of them were strong, self-possessed, and confident, but there was no missing who they looked to as the head of the family.

And now the absent piece was back. Were they looking to Shane for guidance? No, she thought suddenly. They were looking to him to start what they had already planned. They'd probably stayed awake rather than sleep after the long drive, discussing what had happened. And she had the feeling that it had probably taken all of them to keep Sage even partially grounded.

"You're the one we called when we walked in on a situation like this," Shane said. "We trusted you then, and we trust you now."

Her breath caught; that kind of trust coming from this man was an honor. And technically he was right; troubled and torn-apart families had been her bailiwick. Still she hesitated, because this was so different—they were her friends.

"Stay, Lark," Sean said quietly. "You have more direct experience than any of us with the personal side of…wounded families."

Slater stood up from the table. "The whole is more than the sum of its parts," he said. "We were, once. Help us be again."

And finally she looked at Sage. Sage who said nothing, but the battered, wounded part of her heart that bore Kane's name shone in her eyes. And in that moment she felt Kane take her hand, squeeze tight.

"Please," he whispered again. "Don't make me do this without you."

It seemed an odd way to put it, some wandering bit of her mind thought. Don't make me do this alone. She'd heard that before, but this was more specific. Personal.

Because we've spent time together now, and he knows I'll be on his side if he needs it. That's all it is.

"All right," she finally said.

The Highwaters were all looking at her, silently waiting. And she realized that they truly had handed this over to her.

"We'll still love you no matter what," Sage said to Lark quietly, the first thing she'd said since they'd come into the house.

Lark gave the youngest Highwater a smile. "And because you understood that's what I was worried about, I'll start this. But in the end, it's up to you five."

Kane had gone still again. And when she looked at him, she saw the concern in his eyes, along with his own worry, nerves, and the myriad things that must be hammering at him right now. And again, going with instinct, she took his elbow and guided him toward the big table near the kitchen. Sean had told her once about the big family meetings they had there, and she doubted they'd ever had one bigger than this. As big, perhaps, as when their father had been killed, but not bigger.

Kane was clearly reluctant—she was sure he'd rather have stayed on his feet, able to run—but he went.

And she tried to think of where and how to start.

This wasn't the old table. A sudden image of the old arrangement flashed into Kane's mind. Steven Highwater at the head, Shane at the other end, Slater and Sean down one side and he and Sage on the other. Usually laughing, and teasing each other until the boss—for he'd been that above all—made them settle down.

There were eight chairs now, two on each side. They all had someone now. That should make him feel better, shouldn't it? Did it? He didn't know. The only thing he was sure about was that he'd been heading for this for thirteen years, even when he'd thought he'd been running away from it.

And now it was time to face it. He didn't dare hope they could put it behind them, but maybe, just maybe, he could. He wasn't even sure where that hope had come from, but if he had to hang a name on it, it would be Lark.

It went against every instinct he'd developed since he'd last been in this house, but he sat down. Sage immediately took the chair beside him, as if she, too, had remembered the old arrangement. He didn't look at her, couldn't look at her, so stared down at his hands resting on the tabletop. They wanted to curl into fists, but he forced himself not to do it.

I'll start this.

Lark had said that, but she wasn't sitting down. He wondered why, why she was still on her feet behind him. Was it a sort of symbolic "I've got your back" statement? Or did she just not want to get any deeper into this than she already was? He couldn't blame her for that. She'd already done so much.

Or maybe she just didn't know where to start.

Not that day, please don't start with that day…

"I'd like to give you a list," she said, "and see if it rings any bells."

Surprised, Kane half-turned his head, although he couldn't see her. In varying degrees they looked puzzled, except for Shane, who simply waited with that steady calm.

"The Grand Canyon. Zion National Park. The Great Salt Lake." Shane drew back slightly but said nothing, and she went on. "Death Valley. Lake Tahoe." Now Slater straightened, staring at her. "Mount Shasta. Crater Lake." Sean had glanced at his older brothers, but now realization was dawning in his eyes. "Mount Rainier and Saint Helens. The Space Needle. Northern Lights in Alaska."

Kane closed his eyes for a moment, now that he knew where she was going. Why this, he didn't know, but at least it wasn't what he'd been afraid of.

He risked a glance at his little sister. Sage was frowning, and looked around at her brothers. "I don't get it."

"You wouldn't," Slater said softly.

"You were too young," Sean said. "He wouldn't have talked about it with you."

"Then tell me." She was sounding anxious now, and that was not Sage Highwater's typical state. At least, not the Sage he'd known.

"It's Dad's bucket list," Shane said quietly, and her eyes widened.

"And where Kane has been in the last thirteen years," Lark added softly.

Sage's still wide-eyed gaze shot back to the brother she'd been closest to. It was one of the hardest things he'd ever done, but he met it. "You did Dad's bucket list for him?"

It was a moment before he could speak, and when he did even, he could hear the harshness of his voice. "I did. And don't think I don't know I'm the last person who should have done it."

"Or perhaps the first," Slater said, and the quiet understanding in his voice made Kane's breath stop.

He looked up at the man who had always been cemented in his mind as the most brilliant guy he would ever know. He swallowed, hard. And when he spoke, he felt as if the words had been ripped through that wall he'd put between himself and...everything. "It was the only thing I could think of to do—"

He stopped abruptly, feeling an inch from losing it. He clenched his jaw, hard enough that he felt it up to his eyes. Focused on the tightness, to keep everything else out.

"You can deal with all that later," Lark said briskly, "but right now let's flip the coin."

Kane blinked, distracted. "What?"

"They know now what you've been doing." She looked at Shane. "Time for your side of that. I gave him the chronology of your search, so maybe focus on the why."

"Why?" It burst from Sage. "Because he's our brother."

"But I'm not." A little to his own surprise there was no anger, just acceptance. A sad sort of it, but acceptance. He knew it because he didn't have to consciously relax his fingers anymore.

"Like hell you're not," Shane said, almost icily. "Just because our mother was a drunken fool doesn't make you any less ours."

"And it isn't your fault that we weren't enough to keep her sober," Sean said.

Kane's head came up sharply, in the same instant the other three Highwater heads snapped around to stare at the middle sibling.

"You thought that…too?" Slater asked, and Kane thought this was the first time he'd ever seen him disconcerted.

"I thought I was the only one," Sage said in a tiny voice, as if she had honestly believed the toddler she'd been when her mother had finally drunk herself to death could have somehow stopped it.

"Apparently we all did," Shane said ruefully, and Kane realized this was something new to them, something they'd all thought but never admitted, even to each other. He wasn't the only change happening at this table.

"None of you are responsible for the decisions your mother made," Lark said firmly. "Her illness, her failings, they were hers and hers alone. Not yours."

Shane, looking so much like his father, focused on Kane. "Did you feel that way, too?"

Slowly, Kane nodded.

"It wasn't your fault," Sean said firmly. "Just like it wasn't my fault she…strayed."

"Whoa." That from Shane.

"What?" Sage yelped.

"I used to think that, that I hadn't been…enough, when I wondered if what we suspected was true." He gave them a smile. "Until Elena convinced me I had an overblown sense of my own influence at age two."

Chuckles came from around the table, a welcome bit of relief. Kane barely registered it; he was too busy processing what their words were betraying.

"I'll trade you," Sage said wryly. "Feeling like you're the make-up baby is no fun, either."

Kane shifted his stunned gaze going from one sibling to the other. "Wait…you all…you knew? That I wasn't his? All along? And you never said anything?"

"We didn't *know* anything," Shane said. "Either way, it didn't matter a damn to me. Or to him." Shane didn't specify, but they all knew who he meant.

"I thought it, but didn't know it," Slater said. "Didn't care."

"Once I did the math, I suspected," Sean said. "But they're right. Made no difference."

"I was too young to realize any of that," Sage said rather sharply. "All I knew for sure was I missed you and my heart was twice broken." Kane recoiled at that, but Sage rather mutinously didn't back off. "And so why would we say anything when we weren't sure and it didn't matter to any of us anyway?"

"It mattered to me," Kane muttered. "I hated it."

"Only one person to blame in any of this," Shane said

firmly. "And she's long gone."

"And this," Slater said, his tone very dry, "is why virginity was so prized in the old days before DNA. You always knew who the mother was."

For a moment the others looked at him in shock. But then Sage let out a small chuckle. The rest followed and the impossible happened. Kane Highwater—for at this table that's who he was, at least in this moment—laughed along with his family.

Chapter Nineteen

KANE WANTED TO hug Lark for this. He never would have expected for this to happen at all, let alone barely an hour after he'd set foot back on the Highwater ranch. But she had done it, had somehow known what to say, and so here he was, with the people he'd once had as family, and not only weren't they threatening to arrest him, they weren't even angry, yelling, shouting, or shooting visual daggers at him. Instead they were laughing.

And he was breathing again, almost easily. He knew better than to have any faith it would last, but for now, he'd take it gratefully. And remember it. Not that it would offset all the bad, but at least it was something, some small crumb of comfort.

He looked across the table at the men he'd grown up with. It hurt to think of them as his half brothers, when for more than half his life they'd been simply his brothers.

They'd changed so much, and yet stayed the same. Shane had grown into the solid, powerful man Kane had always known he would, but he was still steady and unwaveringly fair—and full of Shane-isms. Slater was as smart as ever, but instead of teaching in some ivory tower he was here, running the historic Last Stand Saloon and from what Lark had said, loving it. Sean was probably the most changed of the brothers, still with that intricate brain but now having gained a calm confidence totally unlike his younger, rather geeky self.

But of them all, it was Sage who had changed most. The wiry, quick, determined and gutsy fourteen-year-old he'd left behind had blossomed, become a beautiful woman. The blue eyes that he'd never forgotten, that had often haunted him, were just as bluebonnet blue, but they were rimmed now with thick, dark lashes that matched the long, silky fall of her hair. Yet he would bet—no, he knew, based on her performance in Oklahoma City—she was still as determined and gutsy as ever.

As if she had felt him studying her she looked at him. And suddenly something in those eyes changed, shifted. Softened. "I never got to thank you," she said quietly.

He blinked, startled. What had he ever done except cause her pain? "For what?" he asked, not sure he wanted the answer.

"Scott told me it was you who told him to go ahead and talk to me, back in high school."

"Oh. Yeah."

"He said you told him I was the best of all of us at putting myself in other's shoes."

"You were."

"So I'm trying to put myself in yours."

That quickly his chest was tight again. Because there was no way even the empathetic Sage could forgive him for that long-ago day. He was almost relieved at the sound of light, running footsteps on the porch. A moment later the front door banged open.

"Marcos," Sean warned, but his obvious amusement sabotaged his effort at a stern tone.

"Oops," the boy who'd come in said as he turned to close the door more quietly. But then he was running again, toward them. Kane stared at him, wondering. He looked maybe ten or twelve, with bright dark eyes and dark hair. He reminded Kane of someone, but he couldn't think who at the moment.

"Sean, Sean!" he yelped as he skidded to a halt beside Sean's chair. "I saw a coyote and a roadrunner! It was so cool and—" The child's enthusiastic account broke off abruptly as he spotted Kane. "Who's that?" he asked warily.

Sean slipped an arm around the boy's shoulders and gave him a loving squeeze. "My brother," he said firmly.

The boy's forehead furrowed. He glanced around the table at Shane and Slater. "But they—" He broke off again, and his gaze shot back to Kane. "Oh! He's your brother who was gone? You finally found him?"

"Lark did," Sean said, nodding at the woman beside Kane.

The boy looked at her. Smiled with obvious familiarity; clearly she was known to the boy, and in a good way. "That's great. They've been looking forever and ever."

"I know," Lark said, smiling at the child.

And finally, the boy looked at him, giving him a tentative smile. "I'm glad you're okay and you came home. Now they won't be sad about you anymore."

There had been such simple certainty in the boy's voice, and such sincerity that Kane couldn't have spoken if he'd had to. Sean squeezed the boy's shoulders again and said quietly, "Your mom's in the den with Joey and Lily. I'm sure she missed you, since you've been out riding the hills all day."

The boy grinned, nodded, and darted toward the back of the house where the others had gone. Kane watched him go. Elena. That's who he looked like. Her son? His breath caught. *Their* son, hers and Sean's? Lark hadn't said anything about that, on that long drive. Surely she would have mentioned it. And Sean could only have been about twenty, so—

"He's come such a long way since you and Elena have been together," Lark said to Sean, as from behind him she squeezed Kane's shoulder, as if to let him know she understood where his mind had gone. "You're good for him. Helping him break out, just as you did. His father would be pleased."

So no, Kane thought as Sean shrugged, but with a pleased smile. "I hope so. He's good for me, too." He glanced at Kane. "He's almost as big a nerd as I was."

The memories came back in a rush, of Sean glued to a game console, the times he'd gone down the rabbit hole as they'd called it, when that complex and differently wired brain of his led him from thought to tumbling thought and momentarily closed off the rest of the world to him.

He remembered the time they'd been at the coast, on the beach, and they thought they'd lost him. But he'd only been distracted by finding a bottle with a strange label, which had sent that brain careening down possibilities. When they'd finally gone back and found him, he'd pointed out that he hadn't been lost, he'd been in the exact same place all that time.

Kane had agreed his brother had had a point. And Sean had thrown an arm around his shoulders like he had Marcos, and said triumphantly, "See?"

And suddenly it was all too much. He felt himself going chilly. Shutting down, Zeb had called it. It happened sometimes when it all swept over him, what he'd lost, what he'd done. And it had never been stronger than it was now, here in this house again.

He pushed back his chair, intending to get up, but couldn't quite find the strength to stand at that moment.

"Has anybody gotten more than a couple of hours' sleep since yesterday?" Lark asked.

"Not so's you'd notice," Shane said, his tone wry.

"I think you should all rectify that, or the crash could be ugly."

Sean glanced at his watch. "It's barely sunset. I don't know if my brain will accept that it's time to go to bed."

"Mine will," Slater said, then added with a wiggle of his eyebrows, "Joey will help."

That drew Kane's attention. He looked at his older brother, memories of those long-ago days in the lab at Creekbend High School, and his sweet, caring lab partner running through his mind. "You and Joey?"

"Absolutely. I adore that woman."

Slowly, Kane nodded. "I can see that happening. She was always so darn smart, just like you."

"Food first," Sage announced, standing up suddenly. And when Kane looked at her he couldn't read her rather intent expression.

"I think," Lark whispered to him, "she doesn't want you out of her sight yet."

How the hell did she always know?

"Food sounds like an excellent idea," Shane agreed. "Especially since it's that huge batch of lasagna you made when you wouldn't sleep when we got home."

"Couldn't sleep. Big difference."

Sage walked over to the oven, turned it on and set the temperature. Then she went to the refrigerator, taking out a huge oblong dish covered in foil.

"You won fifty grand," Slater told her, his tone teasing. "You could order in food for all of us for months."

"Hah," Sage said, but she was smiling as she gave her brother a mock glare. "That money's going for more entry fees, I'll have you know."

"You earned it, you spend it," Shane said easily.

Sage shifted her gaze back to Kane. He felt pressure to say something, but had no idea what. Finally he said simply, "It was a great ride. You did earn it."

"He's a great horse," she said. "He's the one who earned it."

"So he's dining on sweet feed and carrots tonight?" he asked, remembering the old traditional treat for a horse who'd done well.

She gave him a grin then that knotted up his gut. "Yes. Want to come help me reward him?"

He hesitated, but Lark squeezed his shoulder in reassurance yet again. "Go," she whispered. "Sage deserves this."

Yes, his little sister did. She was what had drawn him back here, after all. It would be stupid, now that he'd done it, not to at least spend some time with her.

At least, until the fantasy ended and they were face-to-face with the reality of that day thirteen years ago.

Chapter Twenty

LARK HAD NEVER seen the Highwater men look so exhausted. They might not want to admit to it, but the shadows around their eyes and the way they rubbed at stubbled jaws—except for Slater, whose neatly trimmed beard also got a rub—betrayed it. And the way, when the oven dinged that it had reached the temperature their sister had set, it took them a moment to react. Sean was closest, so he went over and put the big glass dish in the oven and shut it, none too gently.

"Dad's bucket list," Shane said, his voice touched with wonder.

"I never would have expected that," Sean said as he came back.

"Yeah," Slater said, staring at the door Kane and Sage had left through.

The three of them shifted their gazes back to her. "Assessment?" Shane asked.

She drew in a breath. "He's not a kid, not one of my cases."

"But you know the history, just as you did when you were with CPS," Sean said.

"Yes. And if that's the assessment you want I'd say, if he were that kid, that he's wary, distrustful, very tired, and...haunted." All three Highwater men pulled back a little at that. "Did you think that he'd be any less haunted by that day than you are?" she asked quietly.

Slater shook his head. "I thought maybe more."

She nodded. "Because even though your father's death was an accident, even if it never would have happened if he hadn't put that foot wrong, he still blames himself."

Shane let out an audible breath. "Thank you, Lark. We wouldn't be here, even to this point, without your help."

"I just got lucky and recognized him."

"You're the one who talked him down when he was ready to run," Shane pointed out.

"And it's more than that," Sean said firmly. "You get people, understand people."

"Not just kids," Slater added, "that's just where you probably learned to be brilliant at it."

She couldn't deny all the praise pleased her. But something in Shane's steady gaze made her stay silent, waiting.

"Clearly Kane trusts you," he said.

"As much as he trusts anyone at this point, perhaps," she said.

"Yes. Which is more than any of us."

"Which I don't get," Sean put in. "He's our brother, why doesn't he trust us?"

"He asked me to stay when we got here because he wanted someone here who didn't...hate him."

The astonished looks she got nearly made her smile;

clearly that idea was utterly foreign to them.

"Did he...actually say that?" Slater asked, looking horrified.

"He did. In so many words."

"Damn," Shane muttered. "We've got a lot of convincing to do."

"Another piece of advice?" Lark suggested.

"Anything," Sean said, his tone heartfelt.

"Don't rush it. Tell him, but then let him process. This is an amazing occasion for all of you, but for him it's simply overwhelming."

"You've already done so much that I hate to ask," Shane said. "And I know you have a job, but...will you hang around here for a while when you can? Help...not us, help him?"

"I work on an on-call basis, so I have free time," she assured him. She hesitated, then went on. "But I...this is so personal to you all—"

"And we trust you just as he does," Slater said.

"If you really think I could help."

"I think," Shane said, "you may be the only one who can."

"HE'S BEAUTIFUL," KANE said quietly.

"And strong and gutsy and smart," Sage said as Poke head-butted her hand insistently, the one that held the last bit of carrot.

"And bossy?" he suggested.

Sage laughed. And again that odd sensation flooded him, that happiness he was so unused to. It had always made him happy to hear Sage laugh, from the first time she'd done it when he'd made faces at her when she was two.

"He is that, too. Aren't you, Poke?" She gave him the last bite and patted his nose as he crunched happily.

Kane leaned his forearms on the top rail of the fence. When he'd left here, that rail had been about even with his shoulders. Now it was noticeably lower. He hadn't made the Highwater six-feet-or-better club, but he was close. But then, he wouldn't really be a member anyway.

He turned his head to look at the person who made him regret that the most. "You should be proud. You fulfilled your biggest dream."

She gave the horse's nose a final stroke and turned to face him. "That dream hasn't been my biggest for a long time."

"But you always said—"

"My biggest dream," she said, cutting him off, but with a gentle voice, "changed thirteen years ago." He winced, but she just kept going. "Ever since then it's been for you to come home."

"Sage," he began, but stopped when she held up a hand.

"We never, ever stopped looking, stopped hoping. I can't tell you how many hours went into that search, how many bulletins Sean put out, how many calls he made. And Shane, straight-arrow-by-the-book-don't-ever-trade-on-the-name-or-the-rank Shane, pulled any string he could grab trying to find you."

He didn't know what to say. He couldn't even deal with what she was saying, not when there was only one reason he could think of for the two cops in the family to be looking so hard. Nor would he put it past her big brothers to protect their little sister from the ugly truth by not telling her why they were hunting him so hard. Maybe they'd decided on that long drive to give her a day or two of thinking all would be well before they dropped the hammer.

That thought sliced deep, and he suddenly felt utterly exhausted. He dropped his head down to rest on his forearms.

"Come on," Sage said. "We'll eat, get some sleep...and work it all out tomorrow."

Tomorrow. She said it as if it were a given he would still be here, when where he would be the next day hadn't been a given for him in...thirteen years.

When he wanted to run from here more than he'd ever wanted to escape anywhere.

It would make a much bigger statement to run now than to not have shown up at all.

Lark's words echoed in his head, and they held the ring of truth. If he ran now, it would say that he was a coward and afraid to face what was coming. But he could handle that—he'd thought it often enough himself.

What he wasn't sure he could handle was what it would do to Sage if he vanished again. He didn't know why, but she obviously still cared, and he'd already hurt her so much...

He'd been right when he'd told Lark if he was going to

run, it should have been back in Oklahoma.

His breath jammed up in his throat all over again as he remembered how she had reached out then, how her hand, so gently, had touched his arm.

I'm glad you didn't. And I think, eventually, you will be too.

He doubted that. Couldn't see any way that could happen.

Forest for the trees, son, forest for the trees.

How many times had old Zeb said it, about not seeing the big picture? He'd always told Kane he was talking about Jasper the mule, that the animal could only see and react to what was right in front of him, what was happening now. But from the timing of the remarks, Kane had guessed the old man had meant it for him as well. And he'd always wondered what the hell the old man had expected him to see. The truth was pretty damned simple. And ugly. Very, very ugly. Because by then he'd known. Known what he'd truly done.

"Coming? I promise, I make a wicked-good lasagna."

He couldn't deny the thought of food, real food, was tempting. Beyond tempting. So when she headed back toward the house, he followed. Wasn't like he could just take off on foot here. They'd be on him like a horsefly in summer.

"You're really cooking now?"

She gave him a sour look. "We all cook. I made sure of that. Damned if I was going to let them shove that chore onto me just because I'm the girl."

He chose his words carefully. "Anybody can cook. Not everybody's got your knack with horses." And it was true. It had been obvious from the time she was old enough to even sit on a horse—which had been at about age three, if he remembered right—they had responded to her. The only other one in the family who came close was Shane, and that was because most creatures, animal and human, realized it would not do to cross him.

She had stopped dead when he'd spoken. And then, unexpectedly, she threw her arms around him in a fierce hug. And she didn't explain, just released him and started walking toward the house again, going on as if it hadn't happened. Which was just as well, because he was getting that overwhelmed feeling again.

"So we all cook," she said. "We divvied it up, and we all learned how to fix five different things, and we each do a week. That leaves two days for leftovers or takeout, without feeling like we're having the same thing every day."

"And who put that clever plan together?" he asked, already knowing the answer.

"You have to ask?" she said archly. Then she smiled, so widely it fairly screamed happiness. "Of course the menu's gotten bigger with Lily, Joey and especially Elena. The food that woman can fix! She makes enchiladas that will knock your boots off, in the very best way. I'll ask her to make them for you ASAP."

And there it was again, that assumption that he would be here. That he would be staying, not just in Last Stand, but here, on the ranch.

That he was tired enough of running to stay.

That he wanted it over with, even if it meant giving up the freedom he'd always felt was stolen anyway.

That he loved her enough to stay because it would hurt her all over again if he didn't.

All the while his gut was screaming at him to leave while he could.

And right now he wasn't sure which would win.

Chapter Twenty-One

Lark watched him as he looked around the main room of his wing of the ranch house, clearly shocked.

"Does it seem different?" she asked.

She already knew the true answer; the Highwaters hadn't done much of anything here, in Kane's wing, except keep it clean. She suspected Sage spent some time in here, when she got to missing her youngest brother. And because it was a sign of their hope, because nothing had changed, down to his beloved guitar on the rack beside the rather elaborate sound system.

"No."

"You looked surprised. What did you expect?"

He gave her a look that was nothing less than incredulous. "I expected it to be gutted. Burned down. Bulldozed. Something."

He meant it. Down to the bone, he meant it. And this was why she'd come back here with him, alone, although she knew it was difficult for his family to let him out of their sight again.

It took some effort to ask simply and without inflection, "Why?"

"Because they hate me. They must hate me."

"Keeping this wing of the house exactly as you left it doesn't seem like hatred to me. More like...hopeful." She went for a quick switch. "Why did you do the bucket list?"

She saw his eyes widen, saw him take in a quick breath. His mouth tightened, as if fighting to hold back words. But they came out anyway. "So I could live with myself."

It was her turn to be surprised; she hadn't expected him to admit that. Had he still been that kid he'd been then, she wouldn't have expected him to have even realized it. Clearly Kane Highwater—and she still thought of him that way, never mind his insistence the name was no longer his—had done a lot of growing and thinking and learning since that long-ago day.

Again she worked for that matter-of-fact tone, sensing that any pushing or prodding would be a mistake. "Which infers that you know the truth. That the reason you expected them to hate you is because you hate yourself."

"I expect them to hate me because I killed their father!"

He'd snapped it out with a no-guardrails kind anger she had seen before. It burst from him as if under pressure, and she guessed it was a kind of pressure she couldn't even begin to imagine. But then it was gone, and she knew that somewhere along the line he'd learned to reel it in. She chose her next words carefully.

"If it had been, say, Shane showing Poke in Oklahoma City, would you have come?"

His brow furrowed, whether in thought about what she'd asked or that she'd asked it at all she didn't know. The answer came quickly enough that she suspected it was the latter. "No."

"So it was Sage who drew you."

"I...she...I knew what it meant to her, to accomplish that dream. I couldn't not come."

"So you could cut off your brothers, but you couldn't cut off Sage." He frowned, as if he didn't like the way she'd put that. *Tough, Texas boy. Because you still are one, no matter how hard, fast, or far you run.* "Doesn't seem quite fair, does it? Why them, but not her?"

He looked away again. She wondered if his solution to things that were hard to think about was to avoid thinking about them at all. She wouldn't really blame him if it was. He had more to avoid than most. But she'd made the point she'd wanted to make, and her gut was telling her she couldn't push much harder right now. So again she changed tack.

"I've told your family to go slow, but I hope you realize how hard that is for them right now." His gaze darted back to her face, and for a moment she thought he was going to protest that they weren't his family at all.

But instead he surprised her. He looked away again, but said, "Thank you." His voice was low, and rough.

"If you really want to thank me, promise you won't take off during the night."

He grimaced. "Would you believe me if I did promise?"

"Yes," she said simply.

His gaze shot back to her face once more. "Just like that?"

"Yes," she repeated. "If you had really cut yourself off from them, you wouldn't have come at all. And you certainly wouldn't have spent your life completing that bucket list."

"I didn't complete it."

Interesting, she thought, that that was what he seized upon. "What's left?"

"Hawaii. I knew I'd never be able to afford that. L.A. was bad enough." When she didn't speak, he grimaced and shrugged. "At least it wasn't New York City. I couldn't afford that, either, but I might have tried."

She smiled at that, not even sure why. "I'm glad you didn't." Then she gestured around the spacious suite of rooms. "You've got the knowledge that they kept this wing for you, for all these years. Will you think about that and at least try to get some real sleep, now that you have privacy, and a lock on the door?"

His mouth quirked. "Sean's been able to pick the toughest locks since he was fourteen."

That took her aback, but after a moment she found herself smiling again. "Well, that's a handy talent for a detective."

He smiled, but it was a fleeting thing. As his smiles always seemed to be. "I...thank you for staying. It made it...easier."

"I'll settle for that," she said. "It won't be easy for a while, but you can get there."

"I doubt it." He gave her a sideways glance then. "Unless you're around to referee."

She knew then that she'd made the right choice. "As it

happens, I will be in and out for a while." He blinked. "Shane asked me. For your sake." She gave him an embarrassed smile. "He seems to think I can help."

He was staring at her now. "And you said yes?"

"Presumptuous, huh?"

He slowly shook his head. "A relief. Among other things."

And with the look that had then come into those changeable eyes of his lingering in her mind, she left him to get that much-needed sleep.

And she heard the click of the lock as she went.

※

KANE DIDN'T KNOW how long he'd been standing there after she'd gone. He only knew the place felt empty now. How could she have taken root in his mind so quickly? Sure, he'd been alone with her on that hours-long drive, trapped in the car with nothing to do but talk or feign sleep. Or sit in pointed silence, which she didn't deserve. She'd done nothing more than recognize him. From that damned photo Sean had come up with.

I can't tell you how many hours went into that search, how many bulletins Sean put out, how many calls he made.

He wasn't surprised at that. Sean with a puzzle to solve would never quit until he did.

And Shane, straight-arrow-by-the-book-don't-ever-trade-on-the-name-or-the-rank Shane, pulled any string he could grab trying to find you.

He was surprised at that. Beyond surprised. Because Shane was as close to a replica of his father as there could be. Honorable, honest, kind, fair—all those noble adjectives, they all had always applied to Shane. He was the walking definition of like father, like son.

Which probably explains you, too.

He began to pace around the living room of this wing that had once been his private domain. Maybe it really was genetic. Their father had been who he was, and his father, whoever the hell he was, had…not been. Maybe it was that unknown sperm contributor who had sealed his fate. Maybe it was whoever that man was that his mother had turned to, probably in a drunken haze, for whatever reasons had driven her.

And they had all thought it was their fault, somehow. That any of them had believed that, that the men he'd always thought invincibly confident all had the same weak spot—each without any of the others apparently knowing—had astonished him.

And then there was Sage. *Feeling like you're the make-up baby is no fun.*

He'd never really thought about that aspect, for her. He should have. But no, he'd been too wrapped up in his own private misery. Selfish bastard, just as his mother had been a selfish bi—

He abruptly realized where he was in the room, standing next to the rack that held that beloved old guitar. Realized he'd actually reached out for it, and recoiled as if it had morphed into a rattler.

He couldn't get away and into the bedroom where it was out of sight fast enough. That room hadn't changed either. His chest tightened when he spotted the framed image on the wall over the dresser, the caricature of Sage he'd done when she was ten, a still-little girl dwarfed by her cowboy hat and the horse that stood docilely behind her, his chin resting contentedly on her shoulder.

He remembered how his little sister had demanded he do one of himself so she could have it in her room. That had been awkward, trying to draw himself, but she'd said she wanted it with his guitar, so he'd made the guitar huge and pretty much hidden himself behind it. He figured she'd probably burned it by now.

But then, a lot of the things he'd figured had happened here since that day apparently hadn't.

He poked around a little more. Found some clothes in the closet and drawers, which surprised him; he would have thought they'd tossed his crap long ago. The jeans were too short now, which put an expression on his face that was half smile, half grimace. He slammed that drawer shut and opened the next.

The T-shirts were snug but wearable. He just had to decide if all this was still his. Deciding no one else would want any of it, he pulled out something to wear tomorrow. Something different than the three-day rotation that he felt as if he'd been wearing his entire life.

Tomorrow.

He'd thought it like it was nothing. Like it was a matter of course.

He slammed the second drawer shut. Tried to make himself think clinically, unemotionally.

Play it like you got lucky and ended up in a hotel somewhere for the night. Take advantage while you've got it, because you won't be here long.

He sat down on the edge of the bed. Worked up to lying down. Laughed sourly at himself when he automatically kicked off his worn sneakers before he swung his feet up. Made a mental note to check for socks. Those he could definitely use; he didn't have a pair that didn't have a hole somewhere.

He'd thought he'd go out like a light the moment his head hit a pillow. Instead it was as if a switch had been thrown, and his brain snapped back into high gear. In between his glances at the windows at the slowly fading long summer light, his mind was caroming around from the mistake he'd made going to Oklahoma City, the bigger mistake he'd made coming here, and the worst mistake of agreeing to stay under this roof even for one night. His brain was fairly buzzing, until he wanted to scream at it to stop.

This was crazy. He hadn't slept in nearly two days—how could he not be already unconscious?

He tried again. Had no idea how long he lay there before he leapt up, furious with himself. It was full dark now, so he snapped on the bedside lamp. Started pacing, slamming his fist into his palm. Walked back to the nightstand to look at his watch, that cheap thing he'd picked up in a discount store in Oregon that had amazingly kept going for three years now. Nearly midnight.

Out of morbid curiosity, he walked into the bathroom, flipping on the light as he went in. He'd forgotten how nice it was, how spacious. He crossed over to the sink and looked at his reflection in the mirror. His eyes—those non-Highwater eyes—looked as bad as he'd figured they would, so bloodshot they were almost scary. With his hair tangled and his jaw three days unshaven, he was pretty much a mess.

For some reason, that made him think of Lark. Lovely, luscious Lark. He doubted at her worst she ever looked this disheveled.

I'd like the chance to dishevel her, though.

He spun around, giving his head a sharp shake. What the hell was wrong with him? She was a kind, sweet, generous woman who was trying to help, and here he was, lusting after her like a man who...well, who hadn't lusted after a woman in a very long time.

He was leaning against the edge of the bathroom counter, staring into space, his eyes so tired now he could barely focus on the shower right in front of him.

The shower.

It hit him that he could take a shower. A long one, not just the hasty, lukewarm things he'd been taking at the apartment above the store because he didn't want to run up Mr. Lindsay's costs any more than he had to. He knew each wing had had its own water heater, to avoid running out if everyone was getting ready at the same time. But surely the one for this wing wouldn't be turned on?

He turned back to the sink and turned the hot side on. Stuck a finger in the stream. Realized with a self-disgusted laugh that room temperature in Texas in June would be practically hot water in Alaska, relatively speaking. So he'd take that shower as it came, since he was used to it and—

The water had turned hot. The water heater was on. Startled, he shut off the flow into the sink. Wondered who had thought to turn it on, and long enough ago that it was hot now. Sage was his best guess. Or maybe Shane, taking charge in that quiet but unstoppable way of his.

He reached in and turned the faucet in the spacious shower, tiled with the whimsy he'd chosen himself all those years ago, a replica of the Lone Star flag on each wall.

Smart kid.

A very special kid.

The memory hit him like yet another punch to the gut. The day this room had been done, when he'd been twelve, and the grinning tile installer had gestured at the star he'd just finished and spoken to Steven Highwater. The man Kane still, at that point, thought was his father.

But that man had known. Had known all along Kane was not his.

...he knew all along and he loved you anyway.

Again Lark's words hammered at him. And with them came the image of her, looking at him with such kindness and concern. He'd traveled a rough road, but surely he wasn't so far gone that he would mistake that for something more. Because why on earth would a woman like that be attracted to a man whose life was as screwed up as his was?

He stripped off his clothes and stepped into the shower, wishing he could scrub hard enough to wash away the last thirteen years.

Wishing he could scrub hard enough to erase that single moment that had shattered everything.

But he couldn't. He knew that. And the knowledge hovered like the dark cloud it always was, threatening to lower and envelop him forever. He felt it, heavier than ever, nearing, ready to try again to push him over that final edge.

And then she was there again, in his mind, with those lovely light green eyes, that silken fall of blond hair, and the darkness receded. Which amazed him, because nothing had ever pushed it back so quickly before.

His hand compulsively slid down over his belly, then lower. He didn't resort to this often, but right now he thought the pressure might kill him if he didn't ease it. He told himself to flip the water over to cold, to put a chill on his body's reaction to just the image of her in his mind. But he wasn't sure the water would be cold enough.

And then it was too late. He couldn't stop. And moments later he heard his groan of her name echoing from the tile walls of the shower.

For a long time after he stood with the water pouring down into his face. He remembered the days, in the beginning, when his sixteen-year-old self had done that so he could at least pretend he wasn't crying.

He didn't cry anymore. He didn't think he had any tears left in him.

He didn't go back to bed. Instead he sat down on the couch in the living room, staring into the darkness. And finally, without really being aware of the moment he let go, he slept.

Chapter Twenty-Two

"He hasn't come out yet," Sage said as she poured Lark a cup of coffee. Then she slid the bottle of creamer over to her, saying with a wry smile, "This is Slater's brew this morning, so you might want to double up on this. He likes his coffee strong enough to peel paint."

Lark laughed, but she did double up on her creamer. "Probably from pouring it down those who have overimbibed at the saloon."

"Probably," Sage agreed, "even though Shane says all that means is you've got a wide-awake drunk."

She smiled as she said it, but she was looking toward the doorway that led to Kane's wing of the house. Lark had seen Scott pulling out as she'd arrived, no doubt on his way to his job at Lock and Load, the local shooting range, now open all weekend. Since he'd started there the place was booming, what with the extra hours open and the chance to get pointers from a genuine American hero. Lily's profile of him, published in the *Defender* newspaper, had seen to it that all of Last Stand knew exactly what Scott had done for his country.

Lark had come back as she'd promised, early this morning. She'd had a restless night, and no amount of laughing at herself—she couldn't sleep when he was down the hall, couldn't sleep when he wasn't—had seemed to solve that problem. That had better improve tonight; this was not a situation she wanted to deal with when she wasn't thinking clearly from lack of sleep.

She had something she needed to do this afternoon, something she refused to miss, but other than that she was clear. She'd talked to her boss, at the agency and Mrs. Cruz had been, as usual, kind and understanding. Lark had told her she'd keep her scheduled appointments, but to please not schedule any new ones for her for a few days. She had no idea how long it would take for things to settle here, how long it would be before they would find any sort of comfort level.

She told herself to just enjoy spending her days here on their ranch, the very kind of surroundings she'd been wishing for, but she kept wondering if Kane would take the first opportunity to light out once more. But if he was really determined to do that, she didn't think she could stop him. Even if she did want to be his babysitter, which she definitely did not, she could move in here 24/7 and not be able to do that.

Her next thought had been literally moving into his wing, which had brought on some images in her head she had no words for.

"Lark?"

She snapped back to reality. "Sorry. Just thinking." *And you don't want to know about what.*

Sage gave her a wry smile, her expression half sad, half hopeful. "Lot of that going around here today."

"Speaking of which, where is everybody else?"

The smile was better this time. "My brothers are crazy in love. Where do you think they are? Well, except Sean, since Elena had to take Marcos home."

Lark could guess, and it made her grin. But Sage's expression suddenly changed, shifted to one of dismay. "I said my brothers. But I was thinking of Shane, Slater and Sean. Not Kane. Even though he's here. He's really here."

"But he hasn't been, Sage. After he left, how long did it take you to get over looking for him, expecting him, talking about him as if he were here?"

Her friend let out a weary sigh. "A long time."

"And it will take time to get back in the habit." *And I hope more than anything that you have to, my friend. That he stays.*

That she wasn't at all sure that would happen she kept to herself.

She took another sip of the admittedly powerful brew just as she heard the door at the back of the ranch house open, close, and then footsteps. She turned and saw Sean headed toward them, looking none too happy. She saw him glance toward his sister, and saw nothing less than pure apprehension in his gaze.

And she knew before he said it what he'd come to say. And wished she could say she was surprised.

"He's gone."

Sage's own coffee mug came down hard on the granite

countertop. She stared at her brother, pain welling up in her eyes.

"How gone?" Lark asked. "Are his things still there?"

Sean had been so focused on Sage he seemed startled when she spoke. "You mean that backpack?"

"Seems that's all he has."

Sage winced, but Sean's brow furrowed. "It wasn't there. Unless he put it out of sight somewhere."

"At my place, he put it under the bed. I got the feeling he was used to doing that, so he could grab it and run if he had to."

Again Sage winced, but she moved. Turning on her heel she waved at Sean. "Let's go look. And pray Lark's right."

She watched the two go. Hoped they'd find the small, battered pack where he'd put it at her place. Because if he was really gone, it was going to shatter Sage. And do the rest of the family no good, although the Highwater boys would hide it deep. At least, until their women drew it out and eased the pain.

She let out a little sigh. The change in all the Highwaters in the last year was rather amazing. And she begrudged none of them, even if she did feel a bit wistful, and doubtful that she would ever find such happiness herself.

She looked around the warm, comfortable ranch house. This was definitely a home, and she found herself thinking that there really was something to keeping a family together under one roof. Steven Highwater had thought ahead, and arranged the house with its separate wings in such a way that all of his children could have their own, private space, in the hopes that they would stay. And they had, each for their own reasons, not the least of which was belief in and loyalty to the man who had loved them all.

Including Kane.

She sighed as she walked over to rinse out the last of her coffee, glancing into the ceramic mug half-expecting to see it partially eaten away, such was the power of the Slater Highwater brew. She looked out the window over the sink, toward the big barn. Saw the covered hay storage alongside it. They must have just had a delivery, because it was fuller than the last time she'd been here.

Hay.

They'd been just outside of Oklahoma City when he'd said it, after pulling a couple of clinging bits of hay from his jeans.

I used to have to pick the stuff off my clothes all the time. The hayloft was my thinking spot.

She set down her mug and ran for the door.

※

HE HEARD THE running footsteps from below. Light steps. Sage? No, they weren't boots. Not cowboy boots anyway. And Sage always wore those on the ranch. At least, she always had.

What the hell do you know? She was fourteen when you destroyed her world and left.

Lily? Joey? The elegant Elena? Wait, maybe the kid? No, he'd heard something about Elena having to take him home last night because her mother—the redoubtable Mrs. Valencia of Creekbend High School, and the reason Elena had seemed familiar to him from the first—wanted them home for church this morning. He remembered the nausea that had swept him when he'd realized Elena was connected to the restaurant, the restaurant it had all happened in front of.

And then he felt the slight tingle that began at the back of his neck and worked its way down between his shoulder blades, and he knew.

Lark.

And sure enough, just a moment after he heard the sound of someone climbing the ladder, the top of her lovely golden head appeared. How the hell had she known?

And in the way he'd already come to know, she disarmed him instantly with that sweet smile and a charming admission.

"See what you get for mentioning this was your thinking spot?"

The memory hit him then. He had said it, on that long drive, as he'd released the fragments of hay out the window to the night wind.

He tried for some armor. "Do you ever forget anything?" he asked dryly.

She walked over and dropped easily down into a cross-legged position beside him. "Not when it's important to me."

"Why on earth would that have been important to you?"

The smile again, and it had the same disarming effect.

"You want a list?"

He looked at her for a moment. Then said, rather tightly, "No." He didn't want to hear her list. Didn't want to know what was on it. And what wasn't.

"I like your shirt," she said. "It's a great place."

He had to look down to remember which one he'd pulled on. A T-shirt from historic Gruene Hall, the oldest continuously functioning dance hall in the state. The place he'd once dreamed of playing music one day in the future.

Before his future made a U-turn.

"It's nice to wear one that doesn't have holes in it." His mouth quirked. "And if it was Sage who turned my hot water on, I should thank her."

"Actually, it was Lily who thought of that, and Shane did it." She smiled. "They tend to work together that way."

He didn't know what to say. "I'm...glad they're happy."

"He deserves it, maybe more than anyone, after he gave up everything for his family."

He tilted his head slightly, not wanting to ask, because he didn't want to hear the answer. But she told him anyway.

"I don't suppose you know he quit school and came home after it happened. Stepped into those big Highwater boots, in more ways than one."

He closed his eyes as pain roiled up inside him anew. He hadn't known. But now that he did, he wasn't in the least surprised. "Of course he did."

"And never once has he complained."

His eyes snapped open. "He wouldn't." He desperately tried to change the painful subject. "When did he and Slater start getting along?"

"About the time Joey made Slater face why he was always at loggerheads with him. Because he didn't quit school and come home."

He shook his head in slow wonder. "Little Joella. And Slater."

"Yes." She was quiet for a moment before nodding back toward the house. "They were all afraid you had run again."

"I said I wouldn't." *But you should have, when you had the chance. Should have "gotten while the gettin' was good" as old Zeb used to say.*

"I know. And I know they could trust you. But I don't think they do, yet."

He was staring at her now. "How could you? And why would they ever?"

She held his gaze steadily. And then, in a tone so full of understanding it made his chest tighten, she said quietly, "Perhaps because we all want to."

Chapter Twenty-Three

IT TOOK LARK some time to convince him to come back to the house. She didn't blame him, understood when he stopped to give Poke a stroke on the neck and a pat on the nose. The horse seemed quite accepting. Kane clearly hadn't forgotten what he knew about horses. And had apparently learned a bit about mules. She smiled at the memory of how glad he'd been to hear Jasper and Zeb were okay. It gave her hope.

When they finally got back into the house she blessed all the timing gods, because Joey was alone in the kitchen. Her friend looked up, and the smile that lit her face when she saw Kane should have been enough to thaw all of his reservations at once.

Joey set down the coffee mug she'd gotten out and ran around the kitchen island to them. Lark felt Kane stiffen, but then Joey was there, throwing her arms around him.

"I didn't get to do this before," she said, hugging him tightly. "It's so wonderful to see you. I wish it hadn't been so long, and I thought and worried about you so often, but you're here now, and…oh, don't mind my rambling. I'm just so glad and it's bubbling out."

After a moment, he hugged her back, although Lark could see he felt awkward about it. She couldn't imagine it was because it was Joey, but the only other answer that came to her, that it had simply been a long time without such human contact, made her very sad.

When she finally let go, Kane was staring down at her. He looked as if he were searching for something to say, and finally got some words out. "You were...one of the memories I didn't mind."

To someone who didn't know, the words might seem slight of praise, but Lark knew Joey understood from the moisture that suddenly gleamed in her eyes. She also knew they never would have gotten as close as they had to finding him without Joey's help, remembering things he'd said back in those days they'd been lab partners at Creekbend High School.

She saw Kane tense up again when footsteps sounded from another direction. From Sean's wing, if she was judging right. And a moment later she knew she had been as he came into the room. He was carrying a tablet, making some taps on the screen as he went. Lark thought it was just because it was Sean and he was rarely far from a device of some sort, but then he walked up to Kane and handed it to him. His brother took it, but with lowered eyebrows.

"Seemed like you didn't quite believe how long and hard we looked for you," Sean said. "There's your proof. Every bulletin, every email sent and received, and a log of every response we ever got. Only thing that's not there is the first couple of weeks before we went wide." Sean let out a compressed breath. "Back when we were hoping you'd come home any minute."

Kane stared at the screen for a moment, then looked up at Sean, then back at the tablet.

"You'll see Detective Parker at Last Stand PD started the case. He's how we knew you headed west and got to Albuquerque. When he retired and it went cold, Shane took over, since he was on the department by then. And then he and I have been working it together since I came on." He nodded at the tablet. "Page on through."

Tentatively, in a way that made Lark wonder if he'd ever used a tablet, if perhaps he'd never been able to afford such luxuries, he swiped at the screen. Scanned the new page, then repeated the action. He went on and on, and she lost count of how many pages and reports. Then he stopped, slowly shaking his head as he looked back at Sean.

"Yeah," Sean said. "It's a freaking huge file."

Kane put the tablet down on the dining table as if it were suddenly burning his fingers. Lark tried to think of something, anything to say, but before she could come up with anything Slater arrived from his—and Joey's—wing of the house. He was also carrying something, a sheaf of papers, but he walked over and planted a kiss on the nape of Joey's neck first. Joey's smile, and the way she reached up to stroke Slater's neatly trimmed beard, warmed Lark to the core.

She heard footsteps on the stairs, and knew it had to be Sage. Wondered how Kane would react to her.

Then Slater turned and set the papers, which Lark could now see looked like a financial statement of some kind, on the table and slid them toward Kane. "We had to sell a couple hundred acres a while back, to cover some remodel and new equipment debt. The McBrides bought that chunk that made the boundary between us weird."

"Jessie's running a mustang rescue now," Sage said as she came into the room. "And that's where she keeps the new ones until they settle."

"And that," Slater gestured at the paperwork, "is the most recent statement on your share of what was left after we paid off what we had to."

Kane looked utterly blank. "My share?"

"You do own a fifth of the place," Slater said.

"I...what?"

"The ranch," Sage said, looking at him in obvious puzzlement.

"And before you say something stupid, Dad's will was updated every year."

Slater gave him a pointed look, and Lark realized he was expecting Kane to assume the will had been done before their father had found out he wasn't Kane's father. And she saw the point register in Kane's eyes.

"So," Slater continued then, "the sale was at six thousand an acre, half to the payoff, the other half divided between the five of us. Since you haven't been spending any, it's sitting at a nice 200K now."

He stared down at the paperwork, looking utterly bewildered. "Why...would you do that?"

Slater looked taken aback, a rare enough occurrence to be notable. Joey looked startled, and Sage had stopped dead in her tracks. "I think you know why," Lark said quietly, "you're just afraid to believe it."

In that moment she heard a light, cheerful, rather nimble whistle coming from the last unheard from wing of the house. All of the Highwaters looked up. The three who'd grown used to it smiled.

"Sounds just like Dad, doesn't he?" Sean said.

"Exactly," Slater agreed.

"Remind me to thank Lily for bringing that on," Sage said. She looked at Lark. "It hurt a little at first, because it sounds exactly the same, but now I wouldn't trade it for anything."

Lark smiled at her friend. Then she looked at Kane and her smile vanished.

He had gone stock still and utterly pale. He spun around, away from them. Instinctively Lark grabbed his arm. Felt the tension fairly radiating from him in the rigidity of his muscle under her fingers. He could put her on the floor easily, she knew that. He might have put ranch work behind him, but he was still strong, and clearly hadn't led a life of ease since he'd left Last Stand. But he stopped. Looked at her.

She looked at him, and in the hazel eyes, so different, she saw the truth, that he was a fraction of an inch from breaking.

"I can't take any more of this," he said, his voice so low she doubted anyone but her could hear him. "I'm sorry. You tried, but—"

"All right," she said. And then she looked at the Highwaters. She knew her expression was worried, but she hoped they still trusted her enough to go with what she was about to say. "I think a break is in order. I have something I need to do this afternoon, a follow-up sort of special occasion that won't take long. Kane," she said, looking back at him, "why don't you come with me?"

He stared at her. Said nothing. But she thought she felt a tiny bit of the tension ease out of him. She looked back at the family once more. They did not look happy. She tried to think of a way to reassure them.

"How about we bring back lunch?"

In the end, reluctantly, they agreed. And Lark wondered if she'd ever be able to properly thank them for the huge amount of trust they'd put in her.

The best way to thank them was to help them heal this breach.

And that was her goal. She practically chanted it to herself as they drove toward Last Stand. That was the goal, and she'd better focus on that. Never mind that it was so darned hard to do, because Kane—under whatever name—was incredibly distracting.

She didn't think she'd ever met someone she wanted to know every last thing about. She was as curious as the next person, but she wasn't one to pry, and if someone had secrets, she figured everyone was entitled to that. But with this man, she wanted to know it all. Not just the silly stuff like his favorite color or food—had he ever even thought of such things in what had to have been, at least at first, a struggle just to survive?—but everywhere he'd been, what he'd been doing, how he'd endured, and what he wanted to do now. She didn't want to just know what he thought about, she wanted to know *how* he thought.

She'd learned a lot in that long drive through the darkness, but she still wanted more. And she'd never felt that way about anyone in her life.

Of course, the fact that he was the most beautiful man she'd ever seen might have something to do with that.

He was restless, the tapping of his fingers on the armrest, the head on a swivel action told her that. She supposed he was fighting the instinct for flight every second he was here. She understood, but she was determined that wouldn't happen. If he took off on her, she'd never be able to face the Highwaters again. She'd never forgive herself.

And she'd always wonder if he felt the same spark when they even accidentally touched.

"We're not going far, just over past the hospital. I have a follow-up with a couple we matched with one of our long-term fosters."

"Right." Then silence.

"This hasn't changed much," she said as they drove along the narrow route into town.

"No."

"Town's not all that different, either. Some new buildings, businesses, but most of the long-timers are still here."

"Mmm."

"Population's grown a lot, though."

"Okay."

This was worse than drilling in a dry hole, as her father

would say. Finally, a little too sweetly, she asked, "Planning to take the money and run?" His head snapped around. "Ah. So you are listening."

"I'm not touching that money."

Slowing for a turn, she looked at him. "Why?"

"It's not mine. Nothing there is mine."

She was a little bit in awe. She'd put together a pretty good idea, based on what he'd said and things she'd learned in her work, what his life must have been like. And yet he was turning down all that money?

"I see you kept the Highwater integrity, however misguided in this case."

"I'm not a freaking Highwater!" It broke from him sharply.

"So you keep saying."

"What do you want from me?"

It came out in the same way, as if involuntary, although much less sharply. And when she glanced at him again she saw he'd closed his eyes. His profile was as beautiful as the rest of him, and the semi-circles of thick, dark, and impossibly long lashes only accentuated that.

She was alive and breathing, therefore had appreciated good-looking men before. But no one had ever taken her breath away—or made her overheat—the way this one did.

What I want from you would probably shock you. It shocks the heck out of me.

She smothered a gasp. This was crazy. Utterly insane. And it had to stop. The middle of this Highwater family crisis was hardly the time to indulge in such thoughts, especially about this man who was the epicenter of it all.

"I want this to work out the best way possible for everyone."

She'd swear she could feel him looking at her now. And when he spoke his voice was entirely different. And the drawl sounded like he'd never set foot outside of Texas. "Well, that was nice and practiced. Use that a lot at CPS, did you?"

"Only because it's the truth."

"I am not," he said, and she could practically feel his anger even if the carefulness of his enunciation hadn't told her he was a hair away from yelling, "one of your damned cases."

"No. You're not. You're not a kid, you're a man. More of one than most I've met." And then words she hadn't meant to say slipped out. "And none of them ever knocked me silly the way you have."

Well, now you've done it. He'll probably bail the first chance he gets just to get away from you, and you'll have to go back and explain to the Highwaters why.

Served her right for getting involved in this in the first place.

Chapter Twenty-Four

KANE STARED AT her as she drove. Her cheeks were flushed, and he wondered if she regretted saying what she'd said. Then he wondered if he was wondering about that to keep from thinking about the effect she had on him in turn.

"But with your looks, you're probably used to that," she said, her tone wry.

It was a fact, albeit one he didn't care for, that a lot of women—and some men—seemed to react to him that way. It was odd. When he looked in a mirror, something he generally avoided except for shaving, he didn't see what they saw. The composition, the structure, whatever it was that made him stand out to those people. What he saw was the guy who'd destroyed lives. And ended one.

"It happens," he said after a moment. "But it's nothing to do with me."

"The real you, you mean? The you on the inside, not the perfect exterior?"

He should have known she'd understand. But that didn't mean he wanted to discuss it. So he took the out her last words offered. "Far from perfect. I've mucked up that exterior a bit."

"The scars?"

He drew back. "How did you know about...that?"

The color in her cheeks deepened. "I glanced down the hall at my place, after your shower. I'm not used to having anyone..." Her voice trailed away.

"Oh." He remembered walking down her hall with only the bath towel wrapped around him. Was glad he hadn't known she'd seen him. Was really glad she didn't know how his shower in the middle of the night last night had gone, how he'd relieved some of the pent-up pressure with images of her in his mind.

"How'd you get them?"

"I got in a lot of fights, in the beginning."

"Easy to do when you're angry at the world."

He couldn't deny that. "Sometimes I still am." It came out sounding like a warning. Did he want her to take it?

"Sage always said you had a short fuse, as a kid."

A riot of thoughts exploded in his mind. They talked about him? When? Now, he could understand. But that had sounded like it had been before he'd made this crazy trek. She and Sage talked about him before? Why? And why about that in particular, his edgy temper?

The only reason he could think of was that Sage blamed that temper for what had happened. And maybe she was right, maybe it was true. Maybe if he'd done as he'd been told so many times back then, or if he'd found a trick like Zeb had and learned to keep it under control earlier, learned to use the power of his anger to fix whatever had sparked it, the man who'd tried to teach him that might still be alive. Maybe—

"She also said it was usually triggered by unfairness or injustice, and in defense of some person or animal."

He blinked, the wild train of thought derailed. "What?"

"She told me a story three or four years ago about how you stopped some guy from abusing a horse once, even though he was an adult and you were just a kid."

"Jerry Schmitz," he said, the memory snapping into his mind and pushing the rest aside. "He was using a whip. The horse was bleeding from it."

"She told me. She was so proud of you. Said even when the man turned on you, you stood your ground. That you—" Her breath caught, and she turned her head from the road for a split second to stare at him. "The scar on your ribs."

She really had seen him. It was all he could think. "Yeah," he muttered. The thin, curved line was his souvenir of that incident, left after Schmitz had whirled around and struck, probably before he realized the person who had grabbed his arm to stop him was a fourteen-year-old kid. That, at least, made him stop.

Or maybe it was because at the time, he—and everyone—had known him as Police Chief Steven Highwater's son.

"In fact," she said as she slowed for the stop sign before making the turn that would lead them toward town and, he guessed, her prior engagement, "that story was the inspiration for this."

She reached into the leather bag behind her seat and

pulled out what looked like a children's book and handed it to him. Then she went back to driving, making the turn.

He stared at the large picture book with the bright green cover. *Murphy, the Magic Pony*, the title read. The cover image was a whimsical drawing of a pinto pony, sitting on his butt as horses rarely did, with a leprechaun-style hat perched jauntily on his head and a too-clever expression on his face. And he couldn't help it, it made him smile; the pony looked as if he'd be winking at the reader in the next instant.

And then the author's name on the cover drew his gaze. Lark Leclair.

"This is the book you told me about?"

"Yes. But I didn't tell you what inspired it. After Sage told me that story I thought about how brave you were, to stop an adult that way, and that it was so unfair that…things went so wrong for you just a couple of years later. So in the story the child who helps the pony gets his help in return."

He had to swallow before he could get the words out. "I didn't feel brave. Just…angry."

"And rightfully so." She smiled. "I'm taking it as a birthday gift for one of the first kids to see the book, back when I was still with CPS. Joey keeps a few at the library, too, and hands them out where she thinks it might be useful in one way or another."

He ran a finger over the drawing on the cover. "It's a good image," he managed to say. And he was sitting here wanting to read a book that was obviously designed for kids about a quarter his age.

"Yes." Something in her voice made him look over in time to see her mouth twist slightly. "Unfortunately, the same artist wasn't available to do the interior illustrations. I'm not as happy with those."

He opened the cover, stopped at the title page where she'd signed it, telling Chris—the kid she was giving it to, he assumed—the future was his, to build what he wanted. *Nice thought. Too bad it's not always true.* But he hoped that, at least someday, the child would realize the import of the gift of the personalized copy.

He flipped through a few more pages, looking at the images that were bright and colorful, but lacked the clever whimsy and style of the cover. "I see what you mean. They're serviceable, but not as…alive."

"Exactly," she said, sounding oddly relieved. "Some people don't get why I'm not satisfied with it. They all think it's fine."

"Maybe you need to have been a scared kid to see it." Damn, what was it about this woman that had him saying crap like that?

"I'll bet you could do it better," she said. "I've seen the caricature of yourself you did for Sage, with the guitar. It's just full of the exact kind of life and energy I wanted for the book."

She'd seen it? So, Sage hadn't burnt it, or ripped it to shreds? He wasn't sure how that made him feel.

He also wasn't sure if he was more embarrassed that she'd seen it or pleased that she'd liked it so much. "I'm not good enough for a book."

"You could be. I could see that. In fact, it would be fitting, given that I had that idea for another story right before I saw you at the arena."

He remembered what she'd said about breadcrumbs. Hell, he remembered every word she'd said since he'd first laid eyes on her.

"I thought I'd use Murphy again, but I can't quite see how," she finished.

"Use something else. Something smaller." He had no idea what instinct had made him say that. "So between the two books, they see even a little bit helps."

She threw him a startled glance. A slow smiled dawned on her face. "Perfect. Something small and cute. A raccoon maybe."

And he had the thought that he'd do a hell of a lot more than make up some silly drawings for that smile. He had to look away, so intense was his reaction. He looked back at the book in his hands. Opened it to the first page of the story, wondering if he'd have time to read the whole thing before they got there.

But then his gaze was snagged by two short lines of text alone on the white expanse of the page opposite.

For Kane
Wherever you are, I hope you found help.

He froze, staring at the words in disbelief. He couldn't look at her, didn't dare. "Why...did you do that?"

"Because I meant it. And it seemed only fair, since your heroics inspired it."

The absurdity of that gave him back a bit of control. "I'm no hero."

"You were to that horse," she countered. "And in your sister's eyes."

Sage. It always came back to Sage, the person he'd hurt the most.

They were on the outskirts of town now, in what appeared to be a fairly new residential development. Set amid trees, they were large houses, but not pretentious, with spacious yards. Many of which boasted play equipment. So a place for families. Like the one Lark had apparently helped build here as much as the contractor had built these houses.

She pulled into the driveway of a house mid block, painted a cheerful yellow and white and shaded by a couple of big trees. She turned off the engine and put the car in Park. And then she looked at him.

"I'll just...wait here," he said, feeling awkward. Again.

"No, please. Come in with me."

"But they don't know me." *And if they did, they wouldn't want me in their house.*

"That won't matter. They're wonderful, welcoming people. They—"

She broke off as the front door burst open and a little boy raced out, yelling "Lark, Lark!" at the top of his lungs. The child—he was no good at kids' ages but guessed he was maybe six or seven—was headed for them at a dead run, the joy in his face unmistakable. And Kane found himself getting out of the car just to be able to see this completely.

The boy barreled into her, throwing his arms around her

waist and hugging her fiercely. And she hugged him back, just as fiercely.

Kane looked up as two adults came out onto the front porch of the house. And they were smiling almost as widely, even at him, as if the simple fact that he'd come with Lark was enough for them to welcome him.

"...an' I'm having a party later! Kids from school are coming. I wish you could stay."

"You," Lark said, giving the boy another hug and tousling his hair, "will be so busy having fun you won't even notice."

"Mom made me a big cake and everything."

"Lucky you!"

"I am lucky, huh, Lark? They picked me!"

"You are," she confirmed. "But so are they, to get you."

If it hadn't been for the obvious fact—judging by the decorations—that it really was the boy's birthday, he would have thought she'd set this up just to make a point.

When they were back in her car, after an hour of watching the obviously contented and much-loved boy page excitedly through the book about Murphy, Lark gave him a sideways look. He'd already learned this tended to mean she was about to slam him with something that would make all this even harder to process.

"He seems really happy," he said quickly, trying to forestall whatever she was going to hit him with.

"He is. He was my last CPS case." She seemed to hesitate, then apparently decided. "He was abandoned as a baby by his biological mother. Literally dumped on the doorstep of the church on Main Street and was in foster care until last summer."

He could almost feel a tightening in the air as she headed toward the reason she was telling him this. "Sucks," was all he said. All he could say.

"Turned out he wasn't her husband's. And when her husband found out, he sold everything out from under her and took off, leaving her and their two children homeless and penniless."

And there it was. The point stabbed deep, and he didn't doubt he'd be bleeding profusely had it been a true blade. And the worst part was, he knew it was true. And she was making him face something he had never really faced. That in fact, under the circumstances, he'd been lucky. He could have easily—had Steven Highwater been a lesser sort of man—ended up dumped somewhere, unwanted. Instead he'd accepted the boy who wasn't his, and treated him as if he was.

Until the day when, just a couple of miles from here, that boy had found out the truth and pushed out in anger. And that amazing man had died in the street.

Chapter Twenty-Five

"IF THAT WAS supposed to make me feel better, it didn't."

His voice sounded harsh, broken, and Lark wondered if she'd pushed too hard, or in the wrong way. Maybe her instincts were too rusty, maybe she didn't understand as well as she thought she did, maybe she just should have stayed out of this altogether.

But it was too late now. She'd done it. She drove toward town in silence, her mind racing, trying to think of some way to mitigate what had apparently been a misjudgment on her part. She'd thought he might need to remember the good parts of his life here, to get past what had happened since, but maybe he wasn't ready. Maybe too much had happened too fast. She hadn't given him enough time to sort out everything he'd been hit with in the last forty-eight hours.

As they neared town she decided to not make the turn up toward Main Street until Pecan, since making her usual turn on Oak would mean they went by his brother's saloon, and her next usual choice, Hickory, would take them right past the other two brothers' bailiwick, Last Stand PD.

Although she was already realizing it might have been

pointless, judging by the traffic. It was the first weekend of summer, and it had brought out residents and tourists alike. When she pulled into the first parking place she found, which happened to be being vacated by someone apparently leaving services at the Catholic church, Kane still hadn't looked up. He hadn't moved or said a word since she'd told him Christopher's story.

Really bad choice there.

She took in a deep breath before she turned in the driver's seat to look at him. "Considering this was to give you a break from all the pressure and stress, it hasn't really worked, has it?"

"I'm fine."

That was so blatantly untrue she didn't even bother to point it out. But before she could think of anything to say there was a light tap on the hood of her car. She looked up to see Marcos standing there, grinning at them.

"I'm going to go say hello," she said. "You do what you want. I'm through making things worse for today."

His head turned sharply. He looked at her for a moment before he shook his head slowly. "The truth isn't your fault."

"Then come with me. Maybe then I won't feel so guilty."

His gaze narrowed slightly, as if he suspected she was guilt-tripping him. Which she couldn't deny.

"And," she added, "so I don't have to explain to Marcos. He's still a little shy with strangers. He was quite withdrawn before Sean came long, had been ever since his father was killed overseas. He might think you didn't get out because you don't like him." At his frown she said, "And that's not a guilt trip, that's the truth."

That this worked, that he, albeit reluctantly, got out of the SUV when she did, was something noteworthy. And when Marcos had tentatively said hi to him, he'd managed a smile and a "Hi, Marcos."

He didn't want to hurt the feelings of a kid he barely knew. So as angry as he'd admitted he was—whether or not he still was—he hadn't gone down that road so far as to take a swipe at a kid.

Or was it that Marcos was a kid who'd lost his father? Was it empathy that had restrained him? Because for all his anger about the lie he saw his early life as, he'd still been a kid who'd lost his father. His father in the real, day-to-day, loving and taking care of you sense. Which to her was the only one that mattered.

When she could see him across the hood of her vehicle—she was too darn short to see over the roof—she saw his expression tighten for a moment. She glanced the direction he'd been looking and saw why. Sean was here, standing a few feet away talking to Father Nunes. The relatively new priest who had taken over after the passing of the previous one had quickly become a moving force in his parish, and in Last Stand; he had a lot more energy than the aging Father Garza.

Lark walked around the front of the car to where Kane and Marcos were.

"You should come some time," Marcos was saying to Kane. "Father Nunes is a lot different than the old priest. He's a lot more fun after, too."

"Mmm." It was all Kane said, the barest of acknowledgments. And then Sean spotted them. He went still for a moment, then started toward them. Kane tensed even further when his brother stopped next to Marcos and put a hand on the boy's shoulder almost protectively.

"Hey, buddy," Sean said.

"Hey, Sean." Marcos grinned up at Sean, a wide, untroubled expression. Then he looked back at Kane. "Mom says I can call him Dad after they get married. That my father wouldn't mind."

Lark's breath caught. Her gaze locked on Sean, and she'd swear he was blushing a little. "An announcement you'd like to make?"

"Not yet," Sean said. Then, to Marcos, "Go inside and find your mom. I think she's with Mrs. O'Brien. Who brought cookies."

The boy's grin widened and he wheeled around and took off at a rapid trot.

Sean watched him go until he was safely back inside the church building. In turn Lark watched Kane watch his brother. When Sean turned back, Kane said neutrally, "In talks with the priest to convert?"

Sean looked startled. "No. I just like him. He's a good guy. And he helped Scott, when he first came home." Sean's gaze narrowed. "When he didn't want to be here."

Lark thought—she wasn't certain of anything at the moment, after her misfire—she could read the slight change in Kane's expression. She'd told him a bit about Scott on that long drive, and had called up the profile Lily had written about him for her "Hometown Heroes" series on her phone and given it to him to read.

He really made good.

Yes, he did.

The exchange had been quiet. She'd wanted to say more, but sensed it was too early. And a moment later he'd said wryly, "I guess I'm lucky the sniper didn't take me out at the arena."

She'd had to tread carefully with that one, decided to retort in the same tone. "He only would have if Sage asked him to."

He hadn't said anything then, but she'd sensed if he had, it would have been: "I wouldn't blame her."

"You and Marcos are tight," Kane said abruptly to Sean now, and Lark wondered if maybe he'd fallen into the same memory she had.

"Yes," Sean said simply. "I love the kid." He smiled then. "Can't wait for him to call me Dad, crazy as it will feel."

Kane looked away, and Lark saw pain flicker across his face. Apparently Sean saw it too, because he said softly, "Do you think it matters a damn to me that Marcos isn't biologically mine?"

Kane's gaze shot back to his brother. "But she didn't cheat on you."

"No." Sean hesitated, then said, just as quietly, "You were the most innocent bystander, as it were. And Dad knew that."

Lark saw that hit home. And she wanted it to reverberate for a while, so she didn't say anything as Sean—reluctantly, probably still afraid Kane was going to take off—turned and went after the boy who would soon be his son. She smiled inwardly, although she'd known from the first time she'd seen Sean and Elena together they were headed that way.

"Shall we look around?" she asked Kane instead. He looked up Main Street warily. "There are enough visitors here today you can blend in. Or we can go the other way."

The moment she said it she wished she hadn't, for that way was Laurel Street and Valencia's. If there was anyplace she was certain he wouldn't want to go, that was it. He paled slightly, but said nothing. Hastily she started walking in her original direction, further into downtown. After a second's hesitation, he caught up with her. She grabbed for anything else to say, settled on something she'd wanted to say since they'd left Chris's new home.

"I'm sorry I told you about Chris. I thought it might help, but I was obviously wrong."

He refocused on her, as she'd wanted. "It made me face the truth. I killed a better man than I will ever be."

Lark's stomach knotted, and her chest tightened. Yet Kane was walking along, glancing around at the shops and businesses on Main Street, as if he'd said nothing unusual.

As if he'd been living with the idea for a long time.

She didn't know what to say to that. And for a moment or two, she couldn't bear to look at him, couldn't bear that expression on his face. And she was grateful when he didn't push her to answer. Then unsettled even more when she realized that was probably because he thought he already knew the answer.

They'd barely made it a half a block, were in fact in front of the bakery, when he said wryly, "I think you overestimated my chances of going unnoticed. Or underestimated the grapevine in this town."

She realized then that more than one person on the street was staring at them. Or rather, at him. Apparently she'd messed that up too, her prediction that he could blend in. But then she noticed that most of the ones who were really staring were female. She watched for a minute or two, registering their expressions before she responded.

"Personally," she said evenly, "I think you're underestimating the effect you have on women."

He blinked. "What?"

"None of these people are familiar to me, most of them are acting like tourists, and it's mostly woman doing the looking. You may think they know who you are, but I think they're just gaping at an amazingly good-looking man."

He stared at her for a moment, then a muscle in his jaw jumped. "You have no idea how much I hate that."

"I might. I hate being short, but I can't do anything about it any more than you can do anything about your looks."

He blinked. "But you're not short. You're..."

"If you say petite, or worse, cute, I'll be the one doing violence," she said, exaggerating the warning in her voice. She saw his lips twitch again, as if he were again fighting a smile. She wished someday he'd quit fighting it, but guessed that time was far in the future.

They were now in front of the western outfitters store,

amusingly named Yippee Ki Yay, and Kane glanced at the window display. In one corner was some hunting gear in camouflage, which he looked at for a moment, which in turn made his change of subject logical.

"Scott...he's settled back here now?"

"Yes. He and Sage are as happy as can be."

"Sean said...he didn't want to be here."

"No, he didn't. He only came back for his brother's funeral. But then he and Sage collided and the inevitable happened."

He turned to look at her. "Funeral? His brother's cancer came back?"

She grimaced. "No. His self-centered stupidity won out in the end. He drove drunk and wound up in a lake."

Kane's eyes widened. "After everything they all went through for him? And the hell they put Scott through?"

She nodded. "They did put him through hell." She studied him for a moment, telling herself not to say it. But then she realized it was far too late for her to pull back. Or maybe it was simply that the pull toward him was just too strong. And the question came out.

"Which do you think is worse? Being lied to by an utterly honest man who wanted to be your father enough to do it, or to be like Scott, thrown away by the man who really is your biological father because you're of no use to him?"

He went very still. And for once he held her gaze as he said coolly, "How about both?"

And Lark realized she should have thought of that. That from where he stood, they were both true for him.

Chapter Twenty-Six

KANE WAITED FOR her to say something else that would slice him to the bone. She definitely had the knack. And she did it with such care, such gentleness. The problem was, with her, he was certain the care and gentleness was genuine. She really did care. And no amount of telling himself the care was for the Highwaters, her close friends, seemed to stop him from hoping that wasn't all it was.

"Lark!"

The call came from behind him, and he looked over his shoulder. A little girl was running toward them, smiling widely as she dragged the woman holding tight to her hand along with her.

"Brittany!" Lark exclaimed, and bent to hug the girl. A moment later the woman he supposed was the girl's mother also enveloped Lark in a big, and obviously heartfelt hug. Another successful adoption story?

"We just saw Detective Sean, and now you!" the child exclaimed happily.

Lark glanced at him, and his jaw tightened. The last thing he wanted was to be introduced—with explanations—here on Main Street. And as if she'd read his look, as she seemed to so often do, Lark gave him a reassuring glance and said merely, "This is my friend Kane," before asking the girl about her plans for the summer.

Later, when they moved along, he let out a compressed breath and said, "Thanks, for not...explaining who I am."

"They wouldn't have known the story—they weren't here then," she said. Then, with a studying look he'd come to know presaged something rather monumental, she said, "Remember the case I told you about, where Sean found the baby left for dead?"

He nodded. She only smiled. With a jolt it hit him, and he looked up to spot the woman and child who were a block ahead now, looking up at the Asa Fuhrmann statue in front of the library. Then he looked back at Lark.

"Her?" he asked. She nodded. "Wow." Then he looked at her curiously. "Do you always stay so...close with the kids you've helped?"

"Not always. For the first year or two, yes. But Brittany is a special case because of the circumstances."

He couldn't argue that. "You're...an amazing woman, Lark." Then, afraid he'd let too much of what he was feeling into his voice, he added, "For a short person, that is."

Her gaze shot back to his face. And then she laughed, lightly, much more happily than his attempt at a joke deserved. And he thought he would crawl across an Alaska glacier to hear that wonderful sound.

When they went back to her car, to his surprise she didn't head back to the ranch, even though they had a bag full of sandwiches for that promised lunch—that she had had to buy—in the back. And he was too grateful for the reprieve to ask why. Instead she drove to a spot along Hickory Creek, where you could park and watch the water. It was lower than it could get in spring, but still not summer-dry yet. There was a log in a spot near the rushing water, and when she went over and sat on it, he followed. He wasn't even sure why.

Right. Keep telling yourself that. You just want to be with her. Even when she rips your guts out.

"May I ask you something?"

His mouth quirked wryly. "You're asking permission now?"

"About this, yes."

Uh-oh. "Go ahead," he said warily.

"When did you know...he had died?"

His gut knotted fiercely. It was a moment before he could get the words out. "Not until weeks later. In New Mexico. I saw a headline." He closed his eyes against the rising pain again. "Crazy. I'd just been thinking maybe I should go back, go...home. Then I saw that old story. How he'd died. Realized...I'd done it."

"Kane—"

His eyes snapped open again. "He named me right, didn't he? He should have spelled it like the first murderer, though."

Those delicate eyebrows lowered. "What?"

"I'll bet he never thought it would be him I'd kill, though. He—"

"He didn't name you."

He blinked. "What?"

"Sean told me, back when we were working a case together and were waiting to testify, that his father had wanted to name you Seth."

He stared at her. "Why would he...do that? Give me a name that fit with the Highwater names?"

She gave him a smile he couldn't quite interpret, then she said softly, "Probably for the same reason Scott and Sage plan on naming any kids they have with 'K' names so you wouldn't be the only one. They love you. To them, you're their brother."

He had no words for that. He couldn't even begin to process how it made him feel. And after a moment Lark went on.

"Sean said your...mother had insisted on Kane."

His gut twisted again. "So she knew what she'd birthed."

"Stop it. She wanted the biblical spelling, but he wouldn't have it. Shane remembers the argument." Her mouth twisted, and her expression was as close to distaste as he'd ever seen on her. "I never knew her, but when I heard that I knew I was glad I hadn't."

For a moment he simply couldn't breathe. His lungs had lost the capacity to take in air, and he couldn't seem to make them work. "No." It came out like a low moan, but he couldn't seem to help it. "No, no..."

She reached out toward him. "Kane—"

He threw up an arm to ward her off. He couldn't let her touch him. He didn't deserve to have her touch him. She was good and sweet and beautiful and he was dark and ugly inside, no matter what the outside looked like.

"Don't. You don't understand."

She touched him anyway. She enveloped him in a hug that was more full of warmth and caring than anything he could remember. "Tell me what I don't understand," she said gently, coaxingly. "It's choking you—let it out."

The gentleness broke the dam inside him. "You don't understand," he said again. "My name...that's what...how I...that's why I pushed him away."

"Tell me," she said in that same tone, holding him closer.

"He was taking me to lunch because I'd made the baseball team." The memories were boiling, the wall he used to hold them back weakening. "I...confronted him. I'd always known I didn't fit. My name, my eyes... But that day I made him tell me the truth. That I wasn't his."

He waited for her to give him some platitude, or some variation on what she'd said before, that Steven Highwater had loved him anyway. She didn't. She simply waited. And that made him able to go on.

"I was yelling at him. He made us move into the doorway space of Valencia's, so we wouldn't block the sidewalk." His mouth twisted. "After he'd admitted I wasn't his. Always worried about everybody else. I asked him if...my name was Kane so he'd never forget that...that betrayal. He...started to deny it, but I knew it had to be a lie. And I had to get away from him before it came out. So I...pushed him. Hard. And ran."

"Kane—"

"Don't you get it? I killed him. Maybe I even meant to

do it."

"I don't believe that."

"I dream about it, all the time, and in the dreams I meant it. In the dreams I wanted him...dead."

"Guilt and loss can torture people into believing things that aren't true. And that can cause bad—and by that I mean faulty and untrue—dreams."

He shook his head. "It's still my fault. I don't know why the hell Shane hasn't arrested me yet."

She was looking at him as if she'd just realized something. Something that stunned her a little. "I need to tell you something. And I need you to listen, even though it will be painful."

"What else is new?" he muttered.

"Just hush and hear me out. Please?"

How was he supposed to say no to that, when she was looking at him with such caring in her eyes? "You must have charmed the hell right out of those kids you dealt with," he said with a grimace.

"I'll take that as a compliment," she said. And before he could find the words to tell her that's how it was meant, she was going on. "Elena was there, at Valencia's, that day." He blinked. Of all the things she could have said, he had not expected that. "Kane, she held him. She heard his last words. And his last words were that it wasn't your fault."

He pulled back, almost violently. Stared at her.

"His last thought," she said quietly, "was to relieve you of any fault. Does that sound like a man who did not consider you truly his son?"

For a long, silent moment he could not form a single word. And when he finally did, they came out hoarse, and harsh. "He would say that. Because of the kind of man he was."

"He also told them to find you, to tell you. He knew you would blame yourself."

"Rightfully."

"There was a scrape on the outside of his left boot. They were brand-new boots. They thought it was a result of the accident, but Sean and Shane now believe his foot came down wrong and his ankle buckled, causing that scrape. If not for that, he would have stayed on his feet."

He knew she meant to alleviate his hell. But it didn't change the bottom line. If he hadn't shoved him away, it never would have happened.

Chapter Twenty-Seven

"I WAS AFRAID he wouldn't come back with you," Shane said as he put his coffee mug in the dishwasher while Lark disposed of the sandwich wrappers. "He's still so edgy I feel like he'll take off at any moment."

Lark wondered if he thought Kane would actually run off on Sage, who had taken him out for a ride over the ranch. He'd seemed willing, probably more to get away from all of them again. Or maybe he'd decided he really would take off, and didn't want to do it without saying goodbye to Sage, at least. Lark was having trouble judging his state of mind at the moment. And she knew it was because she'd become personally invested in the outcome.

Even as she thought it she knew there was more to it, much more. Because it wasn't just the Highwaters she'd known for years she cared about. It was the one who had disappeared after the tragedy that had forever changed his family.

And how you've come to feel about him. Let's not forget that...

"I get that feel, too," Sean said. "He's like a suspect ready to run. And I don't know why."

"We can't figure that out until we know why he stayed away so long," Slater pointed out logically.

Lark took a breath, then said, "He thought if he came back he'd be arrested."

Three heads snapped around. Three sets of Highwater blue eyes stared at her. "What?" Shane finally demanded.

"At the arena, he wasn't just goading you. I think he really believed you would."

"Why?" Slater asked, rather sharply.

"I think you all know. Because...in the beginning you all wondered, didn't you? If he meant what happened that day?"

"But now we know he didn't," Sean said. "Elena was there. She told us what Dad really said with his dying breath, that it wasn't Kane's fault."

"I know that." She glanced toward the door, then back at them. "But he didn't." She told them, in detail, exactly what Kane had said. She saw Sean frown at one point, although he didn't speak.

But Slater did, sounding more anxious than she had ever heard him. "He knows now? You did tell him?"

"I told him. But...he has dreams, nightmares. And in them he meant to kill him." She used the harsh words intentionally. "Even though he didn't actually know your father was dead until six weeks later."

"But that's—"

"Crazy?" she said, cutting Shane off, something she probably would never have done were this not so crucial. "No, it's what's born of a sixteen-year-old boy who's had not just his life but his entire perception of self shattered, a boy who's scared to death and has no idea who he is or where he belongs. And then he finds out something horrendous happened because of him, and so decides he must be evil and belongs nowhere."

She'd wondered occasionally what it would take to ever rattle the Highwater men. Sean was clever enough to work out anything, Slater was ever cool and insouciant, and Shane was...well, Shane. But she knew now. Because every one of them was looking a little pale. She understood, because until she'd spoken the words out loud, until she'd heard them almost hanging in the air, she hadn't realized how very wrong she'd been when she'd told herself Kane didn't need saving.

"There's one more thing you should know," she said, remembering suddenly. "When he found out your father had died, six weeks after, he was in New Mexico. And he was thinking about...coming home."

There was a sudden, collective intake of breath from them all. "Damn," Shane said, and it was the most heartfelt oath she'd ever heard.

She took in a breath of her own and went on. "But when he found out, it changed everything for him. Again. And this time when he ran, it was because he thought of himself as a fugitive."

Sean was staring at her. Then, slowly, he said, "He doesn't know about the inquiry, either. What the witnesses said."

Her brow furrowed. She had a vague memory that there had been a proceeding, shortly after the incident, but no details. She sighed. "I'm sorry, I didn't remember that. I felt awful, because I admired your dad, but...we'd all been prepping for our graduation, and then..."

Sean, who had been in her class at Creekbend, grimaced wryly. "I remember."

"I was a little too self-absorbed back then," she said apologetically.

"We all were," Sean said.

"It's the nature of the beast, at that age," Slater said. "Don't feel guilty."

That admonition was one she hadn't needed in a long time. One of the first things they'd told her at CPS was that she couldn't feel guilty when things went wrong. What they hadn't told her was how not to. Oh, they'd made counseling available, she'd even gone a few times, but in the end, it still came down to the thing she finally had had to acknowledge: she simply didn't have the required ability to separate herself from the misery she encountered.

"Believe me," Shane said rather fervently, "you're the very last person who ever needs to apologize to us. You've already done so much..."

"Amen to that," Sean said softly.

"Indeed," Slater agreed.

Lark's throat tightened, and she was grateful when Joey arrived at the front door.

"Sunday dinner's kind of a thing with us," Sean explained when Elena—and Marcos—arrived just moments later, lugging bags and boxes that, judging by the luscious aroma, was dinner.

"More in the car," Elena said with a smile, and Lark couldn't help smiling as every Highwater male dashed out the front door.

"How goes it?" Joey asked Lark as she helped sort out the things Elena and Marcos had brought in. The aroma alone had her stomach growling.

"I'm not sure. He's out riding with Sage."

"They're back," Slater said as he lugged in a couple of large aluminum trays, Shane at his heels with two more. "Sage is untacking Poke."

That caught her attention. "She rides her big prizewinner around the ranch?"

Shane grinned. "He gets offended if she doesn't."

"Truth," Sean said, setting down three large bags of delicious-smelling stuff on the counter. "She rides another horse, he sulks."

Lark laughed. "I had no idea." Then she glanced at the array of trays, boxes and bags on the counter. It looked like a full-on buffet of enchiladas, tamales, fajitas, and several other dishes. "That's a lot of food."

"There's a lot of us," Lily said as she came in from Shane's—or more likely their, now—wing of the house.

"I counted eleven for tonight," Elena said as Sage came in the front door. They all looked at her, asking without words.

She shrugged. "It went okay. Good even. But he got weird again when we got back here." She sighed. "I'm going to go clean up. And hope he comes in on his own."

Shane's jaw tightened, but he only nodded. He turned to

help with the food, and as he moved, Lark heard a slight sound from the front door. It quietly edged open, only slightly, and she knew it was Kane. She stifled the urge to immediately go to him; she wanted to see what his reaction to this gathering would be.

"It's understandable," Lily was saying briskly. "We're a lot to take even under normal circumstances."

"Normal? I think I'm insulted," Slater said with a grin.

"That," Joey said with a teasing jab at his arm, "is because it's the only time you don't get to run the conversation."

"I don't always do that," he protested.

"Do what?" Sean said, a bit too innocently. "Go off on some esoteric musing nobody but Joey can follow?"

"Says the guy whose mind goes down rabbit holes so complex they come out in another time zone?" Shane said dryly.

Lark smiled at the teasing family interaction, but at the same time wondered how it was making Kane feel. Would he want to be part of it, or would it just make him feel more of an outsider? Would he want to come in and try, or would he run?

"I could, of course," Elena said in a very formal tone that didn't quite hide the humor in her expression, "solve this entire dinner table chatter problem by bringing my mother."

Lark burst out laughing. She'd had Mrs. Valencia in high school, and remembered all too well the chilling effect the teacher everyone was afraid of but knew was the best could have on an unruly class.

The chatter went on, but Kane didn't come in. And after another minute Lark broke and went to the door. He was just standing there, the strangest expression on his face. And she realized it was a combination of exactly what she'd half-expected: longing and wariness.

"It will be all right. You won't have to say a word if you don't want to. And Elena cooked, so you'd be crazy not to eat."

He shifted his gaze to her. "Why are you doing this?"

"Because I care," she answered. "About them." Then, almost against her will, she added, "About you. More than I would have ever expected."

Something else came into his eyes then, something fiercer, hotter, something she barely got a glimpse of before he looked away. But it sparked an answering heat in her, and she knew she was well on her way down a very steep slope.

When he came in the gathered group reacted to him perfectly, as if his presence was utterly normal and he belonged as much as any of them. And he ate, she noticed. That didn't surprise her since she was sitting next to him and had heard his stomach growl the moment they'd started uncovering the various dishes of food.

He didn't speak, just ate, but Lark saw his gaze darting around the table as he followed the conversations. They went from reliving Poke and Sage's victory, to the ranch, to the big upcoming rodeo next month, often simultaneously.

"Grandma should come more often," Marcos declared finally. "Maybe she'd even laugh. It's the most fun."

Sean gave the boy a smile so full of love Lark felt her eyes sting a little. "She should."

"As long as she's not in teacher mode," Slater said with a grin.

"I'll take her over Mr. Borden," Joey said sourly. Kane's head came up sharply at the mention of the teacher of that long-ago class. "If it hadn't been for that guy," Joey went on, nodding toward Kane, "I would have flunked Chemistry I."

"He was a jerk," Kane said, the first words he'd spoken at the table.

Joey nodded. "He didn't think girls had any business taking chemistry." She smiled wryly. "Now, in my case he might have been right, but still…"

"You weren't that bad," Kane said quietly.

"With your help," she said. She grinned then. "I'll never forget the look on old Borden's face when you switched your beaker with mine right before he got to us to check our results on that balancing the reaction in…whatever that solution was. He asked how you'd screwed it up, and stared in shock that I'd gotten it right."

For the first time since he'd sat down at the table Kane smiled. "The look on his face…"

"I always felt guilty about that. That was the ding that took you from an A to a B+."

He lowered his gaze to his plate again. "It was worth it."

Joey smiled almost triumphantly, and Lark knew she'd done that with full intent. And their smiles told her that everyone at the table knew it.

Except, perhaps, for Kane himself.

Chapter Twenty-Eight

L UXURY. Kane wandered around, thinking that was the only word for it. He had this whole wing to himself—a private bedroom, full bathroom, and the main room with all the comforts of life. He'd only had a short time to live in it before everything had gone to hell, but he remembered the novelty of having a place to get away from the natural chaos of the family.

Now, it was the nicest place he'd stayed in in thirteen years. In the beginning he'd slept wherever he could, often during the day when he could get away with pretending he was just a stupid kid who'd partied too late, or sometimes in a library, where he'd always made sure he was seen reading first, so it would seem like he'd just dozed off. Then, after he'd been at the canyon for a couple of months and Zeb had sold him his old truck—for less than it was probably worth, although the gruff old man would never admit it—he'd slept in the back at the campground, which he'd paid for with odd jobs around the property.

And it hadn't been lost on him that the reason he'd been able to at least keep from starving to death was Steven

Highwater's insistence that they all be competent at some basic things. Even Sage, at fourteen, could wield a hammer or a wrench with some proficiency. So he was good at fixing things, repairing things.

Everything except your own life.

Fixing his life was an idea he'd always assumed beyond his reach. Some things were just unfixable. What he'd done that day was one of those things.

Just 'cuz you don't think you can don't mean you don't try.

Zeb's words came back to him vividly. They'd been talking about something else, but as so often with the old guy, Kane had had the feeling it was meant specifically for his situation. And there had been no way he could make Zeb understand that was impossible without confessing what he was running from. And he hadn't wanted to see the look that would come into those steady, knowing eyes if he told Zeb what he'd done.

He walked over to the desk in the corner. Remembered the hours he'd spent there, doing homework, or drawing. Avoided looking at the papers that sat to one side, the ones Slater had given him, with that astonishing statement that the hundreds of thousands of dollars were his. That was insane. He had no right to that, or one-fifth of the Highwater ranch. He reached out and turned them face down.

Without thinking much about it he pulled open the top desk drawer. Swallowed tightly when he saw his half-used sketch pad was still there. He pulled it out, set it on top of the desk. Stared at it for a moment, wondering if it would still help, as it had before when his thoughts had been so tangled. Only this, or music, had ever helped. He sat in the chair, and grabbed a pencil out of the cup just within reach.

It came out so quickly he knew it had to have been in the back of his mind since Lark had told him about her idea. In a matter of a few minutes he had a raccoon with a puzzled expression staring down at a trail of breadcrumbs. He made the mask around his eyes a bit exaggerated, paused, then began to add a hat similar to the one Murphy the pony wore, to tie the two stories together.

He wondered if she'd actually do it, this second book. He thought she would. She was the kind of woman who accomplished what she set herself to. She was also the kind of woman who recognized when to quit, to save herself. As she'd had to do with CPS.

He was glad she hadn't felt that way with him. Anyone less than her would have walked away by now, if not kicked him out of her car back in Oklahoma. But that wasn't Lark.

When he'd finished with the raccoon with the hat at a rather rakish angle, he sat and looked at it for a moment. He realized he felt a little less unsettled. He tore off the page, folded it and stuffed it in his back pocket to show to Lark when she came back tomorrow. The idea made him smile because he knew that the drawing would make her smile. And that was about the only thing he was certain of at the moment.

I care about you. More than I would have ever expected.

The words made him ache. He wished she'd meant that the way he wanted her to. He wished a lot of things when it came to Lark Leclair. Even though he knew perfectly well where wishing got you.

Wish in one hand and spit in the other, boy. See which fills up first.

Zeb had, he knew, cleaned the old saying up for him, which in itself had made him feel...he wasn't sure what. It had simply pounded home the thought that if the old man knew the truth, he wouldn't be talking to him at all.

With a grimace he yanked open the drawer again to put the sketch pad away. Yanked it hard enough that something slid and hit the back of the drawer, something hard and solid. Almost automatically he reached in, felt a hard edge, and started to pull it forward. Stopped as the message from his fingers registered.

That weird combination of chill and heat ripped through him, more powerful in this instant than it had been since the day he'd seen that news story. The hard object was a picture frame. And in that instant, without needing to look, he knew what it was. That the photograph it held had featured in his worst nightmares. A grinning seven-year-old boy at a birthday gathering. And the man whose birthday it was. The man who had caught the boy in his arms when he flung himself at him to sing "Happy Birthday." The man who was grimacing as he looked at the boy with dislike. Even hatred. He'd seen it in those dreams a thousand times.

Something harsh and ugly rose up from his gut, cutting off his breath and threatening to strangle him. He grabbed the frame out of the drawer and without even glancing at it flung the picture away from him, heard the glass in the frame shatter as it hit the wall.

Just like that day. Destroy. It's who you are.

He'd been a fool to come back here. He'd known it and done it anyway. But there was no putting back together what he'd irrevocably reduced to rubble that long-ago day. He should have known that all along.

He spun on his heel and ran for the bedroom. If he was smart, he'd try to get some sleep first. But if he was smart, he wouldn't be here at all. Or he wouldn't have left in the first place.

If he was smart, he wouldn't have done what had made it impossible for him to come back.

His thoughts were so jumbled now they weren't making sense even to him. He just knew he had to keep moving. It was a familiar drive, one he didn't question out of long habit. So he focused on grabbing his backpack from under the bed, grateful for the hard-learned lesson of keeping everything in it at all times. He barely had the presence of mind to check the kitchenette, grabbing anything edible and portable. He yanked on his jacket because it would be easier than trying to pack it, even though he knew the coolest night temperature in Texas in June would be warmer than the average midday in Ketchikan.

He went through the outside door carefully, but only because he was afraid if he rushed they'd hear him. But once he was far enough from the house, he did what he was best at.

He ran.

He'd head for the highway. He'd picked up a ride within less than an hour out on 290 before. At this point he didn't even care which way it was headed. Would they expect him to go west again, because he had thirteen years ago? Or would they figure east, or north this time? Maybe he should confound them all and head for Mexico. If his Spanish wasn't so rusty, he might try it. That'd be a switch.

The closer he got to town the faster his thoughts swirled. He knew he had to go through town to get to the highway. Unless he wanted to add a couple more hours and trespassing to his flight plan. He didn't want that. He wanted to be gone. Well away by daylight. After that, he'd just go where chance took him. Wherever the first person who'd pick up a hitchhiker was going would do.

Belatedly it occurred to him that here it was entirely possible he'd be recognized. He'd been seen, and he was sure the Last Stand grapevine was still fast, and at least a quarter accurate. So his best hope might be a trucker, although rules had gotten stricter about picking people up. Maybe he needed to just keep walking. Get himself out in the country more. People tended to have more sympathy if they saw you in the middle of nowhere, walking. He felt a bit sorry himself; his muscles weren't used to being on horseback, and that had been a long ride with Sage.

Sage.

How would his little sister—not really his sister, and not little anymore, but he ever and always thought of her that way because he couldn't seem to stop—feel when she realized he'd taken off? Would she be heartbroken again, or just angry? He hoped for angry; anger got you through, heartbreak just drowned you.

He'd write her, as soon as he could. He'd find a library or something with computer access and send her an email; he'd noticed her address on the paperwork on the land sale Slater had given him. The account statement he'd left on the desk. He almost laughed at himself; he'd killed their father, but was refusing money because he didn't think he had the right?

Interesting code you've got there.

If he'd planned this, he would have grabbed more food and water. But he'd been in a rush to escape, so had only grabbed what had been in the room, a handful of snack bars and a bottle and a half of soda. Warm Dr Pepper ought to be great about noonish.

By the time his chaotic thoughts slowed down he was at the Hickory Creek Spur. And his feet and legs were telling him they weren't eager for a return to the days when he'd walked for hours on end.

Hickory Creek.

Suddenly all he could think of was the time he'd spent there with Lark, who as she did with everything, seemed to have sensed he needed a break after their visit to Last Stand.

Lark.

He was going to remember her forever, however long that was for him. He knew that by the churning of his gut and the painful knot in his chest. She'd tried so hard to help him, made him see so much, face so much, but always gently, always as if she truly cared.

And sometimes, when she'd looked at him in that certain way, he'd thought there was something else there, something deeper, richer, more personal than just a good person's willingness to help.

Right. As if a woman like her would want anything to do with a disaster like you.

Still, he wished he could thank her for trying.

I care about you. More than I would have ever expected.

He told himself not to read into that what he wished was there. That she hadn't meant the kind of caring he wanted from her.

The kind of caring he had no right to expect from anyone.

Chapter Twenty-Nine

"He's gone. Really gone, this time. Backpack and all."

Lark stared at Sage across the dining table. She'd found her sitting there, alone, when she'd arrived this morning. "You mean…he just took off?" Her stomach turned over. He'd promised her he wouldn't. Of course, technically he'd only promised that first night. And he'd kept that. "He didn't say anything? Leave a note?"

"What he left," Sage said bitterly, "was this."

She slid a picture frame across the table to her. The first thing she noticed was the shattered glass that spiderwebbed across the photograph. But then she saw the two people in the image, a clearly delighted little boy, and the man who held him, the man who looked at the child with such delight in turn. And joy. And love.

She hadn't really had any doubts, but if she had this image would have erased them. Steven Highwater had loved this child as if he were his own.

She took a breath to steady herself. "I'm so sorry, Sage. But don't give up on him yet. Maybe he just needed some space."

"He took his stuff."

"That...could be just habit. He told me he never assumed he'd be in one place for long." It was a very scant possibility and she knew it, but the look on her friend's face was breaking her heart. "He didn't maybe go for another ride? To see more of the ranch again?"

Sage shook her head. "All horses in the barn, and all the vehicles are accounted for."

"What do your brothers think?"

Sage lowered her gaze and shook her head. "I haven't told them. I didn't check until after everybody went to work and he still hadn't come out."

"Maybe you should. They could look for him. We all could."

Sage's head came up then, and some of the Highwater fire flashed in her eyes then. "Maybe we shouldn't. If he hates us so much he'd take off again, when all we ever did was love him and search for him, then that's his choice to make."

"It is," Lark said, trying hard to find the right thing to say. "And the problem is his, too. You've spent the last thirteen years loving and missing him, he's spent them thinking you all must hate him. Believing you all blame him for what happened. Blaming himself for what happened."

"So what do we do?"

Lark wished she had an answer to that. Wished there was something she could do to ease her friend's pain. But the only thing she could think of was to lift some of the burden.

"Why don't I go tell Shane?" *So you don't have to.*

Sage sighed. "He'll want to mobilize everyone, including the department. And then he won't, because he's already broken rules he'd normally never break for Kane."

"That doesn't mean he and Sean can't look, does it?"

"They've spent thirteen years of their lives doing that."

Lark reached out and put her hands over Sage's. "Have you told Scott?"

Sage shook her head. "He'd leave the range and come barreling back here, and there's nothing he can do."

"Except be here for you," Lark said quietly. "Think about it, Sage. He's always said you were there for him, when no one else was. Let him give some of that back. You know that's important to a man like him. Let him be here for you."

For a moment Sage just looked at her. Then she turned her hands over and gripped Lark's fingers with her own. "You are a good, wise friend, Lark. I just wish you hadn't gained that wisdom the hard way."

"My life was a walk in the park, compared to Kane's."

"I think all of us can say that," Sage said quietly.

"I'm glad to hear you say that. I would hate, truly hate for you to become bitter over this, no matter what happens in the end."

Hope flared in her friend's eyes, those bluebonnet eyes Kane had sung about in that amazing, seductive voice, riding through the dark on the way home. "You don't think this is the end?"

"No. I don't."

Don't you dare make a liar out of me, Kane Highwater.

THERE WAS NO moon tonight, and the only way Kane knew the creek was there was the sound of it and the faintest of glints from what light there was.

He didn't know why he was back here. He'd caught a ride at first light yesterday, the carload of kids heady with the freedom of summer break had been headed to Fredericksburg, and while it wasn't even fifteen miles, they were miles he didn't have to walk. But he'd ended up walking them anyway, in reverse. In a direction he'd never expected to go of his own free will. And he didn't understand it.

He was back here beside Hickory Creek again, working on his second night in a row of little to no sleep, and he didn't know why. He didn't know why the hell he wasn't hitchhiking back out of town. Or just plain hiking, if that's what it took; he'd once gotten to where he could walk twenty-five miles in a day if he put his mind to it. He wasn't in that kind of shape now, but he could get back there.

He sat there, figuring. Three hundred and fifty miles or so to Pecos and then up into New Mexico again. At sixteen, that had taken him a month and then some. If he headed east, three fifty would put him in Louisiana. Retracing back to Oklahoma City would put him out of Texas at two seventy-five-ish. Or hey, he could just head north to the panhandle and be out of the state in a mere five hundred miles...

Texas was too damned big. Maybe his best bet would be to head for the Gulf. Two hundred miles or so. And when he hit the Gulf he could just keep walking. Might be the best thing all around.

Whoa.

His mind hadn't strayed down that dark path in quite a while. But this time it was different. He found himself thinking not about ending his own pain and confusion, but about what he'd leave behind. The Highwaters, who had never stopped looking for him. Especially Sage, who had honestly seemed so damned glad to see him.

And Lark.

That quickly he was back on that merry-go-round. The same thoughts he'd fought off before hammered at him anew. Lark, who had sat here with him in this very spot just yesterday. Lark, who had appeared out of nowhere and blown up his life, in more ways than one. Lark who had found him, who had seemed to know exactly what to say to ease the chaos in his heart and mind so many times. Lark who had understood how he felt, who had somehow always sensed when he was on the verge of cracking, and who always seemed to find the best way to fix it. Lark who had awakened parts of him that had been dormant for so long he'd begun to wonder now and then if they were permanently deadened.

Lark, who with her kind, caring heart, would feel as if she'd utterly failed if he ran, let alone if he took that walk out into the warm gulf waters.

You really want to do that to her?

He nearly laughed at himself. He didn't even want to leave without saying goodbye, without seeing her one more time. As if he needed that to have her image, her smile, her laugh, God help him her touch, seared into his brain forever.

And then the hottest, basest thought he carried, down deep, broke through all the clutter, all the denial. The thought that was truer than anything at this moment.

You really want to die without even the smallest taste of her?

No. No, he didn't. And if he was so out of practice that he was reading her wrong, if it had been only the kindness and caring of a gentle soul that he'd misinterpreted as a very female-to-male kind of interest...well, then he'd take that long hike. And maybe he'd be able to figure out where the hell to go next once he was clear of this damned town that so messed up his mind.

INDECISIVENESS WASN'T USUALLY one of Lark's problems, but tonight it had kept her awake until after midnight. She'd finally gotten out of bed, pulled on her UT sweatshirt even as she laughed at herself for finding sixty-degree temperatures a bit chill. Texas girl, she chided herself. You'd never make it in Alaska.

Alaska. Funny how that was the place that popped into her head.

So there she was, fruitlessly trying to at least doze on the couch in her living room, her mind spinning back to the source of her problem. Was he really gone? For good?

She told herself it was merely a logistics thing. She had to decide whether to call her boss back in the morning and tell her she was back.

She told herself she'd done her best, she'd truly tried, she just hadn't been able to find the key to Kane Highwater. Travis, she corrected, since obviously he'd decided to cut that cord for good.

Face it, he's gone, without even a goodbye.

Not that she expected him to say goodbye to her. But his family. Sage at the very least. He didn't owe her anything.

But you're always going to wonder, aren't you?

The little voice in her head wouldn't shut up, that voice that seemed connected to the crazy reaction she'd had to him from the first instant she'd ever seen him.

What breathing woman wouldn't wonder what it would be like to have that beautiful man want you?

That was where she'd really blown it. She'd let that…that response to him cloud things. She'd let the way he made her pulse kick up and her breath get stuck in her throat derail her emotions. And it hadn't just cost her. It had cost the Highwaters.

She groaned aloud, sat up and stared into the darkness of the room. She yawned, twice, then grimaced. If she was that darned tired why couldn't she sleep? Determinedly she put her head back down on the pillow propped against the arm of the couch. Counting sheep had never worked for her. Maybe something more Texan. Longhorns? Armadillos? That one made her smile at least, so she went with that.

She was at fifty-two armadillos and wondering why they were crossing the road when the knock came on her door. She jolted upright, only aware then that she'd actually been asleep and dreaming.

She waved a hand over her phone on the end table. Three a.m. Who the heck would be...

She leapt to her feet and ran to the door. She had to stretch upward to get to the peephole, all the while dreading the possibility that it would be Shane, or Sean, with awful news. Or worse, some other police officer she didn't know, a stranger bearing that news. She shook off the shiver that gripped her, telling herself that she knew almost every officer on the department anyway.

There was only dim light from the low-wattage fixture outside the door, and the fish-eye effect of the peephole distorted what she saw, but there was still no doubt. Only then did she realize how thoroughly he'd been etched into her mind, how much of her consciousness had been taken up by him.

Kane.

Later she might think about the fact that the way she reacted to the mere sight of him hadn't changed a bit since that first instant she'd seen him at the arena in Oklahoma. Or back in high school, for that matter. He still took her breath away.

But right now all she could think was *he's here, he's here, he's here.*

She yanked open the door and flipped on her entry light at the same time. He was turning away even as she did it. She was seized with the need to get him inside and keep him here, for so many reasons. She moved quickly, hoping she could surprise him enough that he wouldn't resist. She grabbed his arm and pulled him into the apartment. The movement brought her up against him as she pushed the door shut behind him.

He was staring at her now. Probably stunned that she'd had the gall. She was a little stunned she'd had the nerve. So stunned she forgot to let go of him.

"Kane," she whispered, and then her usually agile brain failed her and she couldn't think of another thing to say. She just stood there, looking up at him, even knowing that at this moment she was incapable of hiding what she was feeling. He looked exactly as he had the first time she'd seen him, even had on that same dark green shirt, now with the sleeves shoved up on his muscled forearms. And every nerve in her body reacted as it had in that moment, sparking to life as one.

She saw something shift in his gaze, in his expression.

And then he moved, his head lowering. Before she consciously realized what was happening her body made its own decision, and she tilted her head back. And then his mouth was on hers and she couldn't think at all. There was no room for logic or reason in the maelstrom of sensation, the swirling of heat and deliciousness that swamped her with the first touch of his lips.

She felt his hands cupping her face, and it seemed impossible that just that could sear her so. But then his tongue swept lightly over her lower lip and she had a whole new definition of searing. She barely realized she was leaning into him, that her hands had gone to his shoulders. Her fingers clenched, as if some part of her still feared he would vanish.

She couldn't resist the need for more and deepened the

kiss, probing past his lips and stroking her tongue along the even ridge of his teeth. She heard him make a low, rough sound, a sound that sent heat rippling through her. It raced along her nerves, pooling somewhere low and deep, and she moaned at the power of it.

And then it was gone. He wrenched away and stepped back, and the only thing that stopped her from crying out a protest was the look on his face. Because he looked like she felt, like someone who had had their perception of…everything changed in the space of a moment.

Chapter Thirty

"I SHOULDN'T HAVE—"

Lark stopped him with a finger to his lips. "No," she said softly. "Don't apologize, not for that. Don't make it another regret to carry."

How did she always know? Kane had to suppress a shiver.

"I've wanted that for so long," he admitted, even as he fought to control a reawakened body that wanted more, much more than a kiss. "But things are such a mess…"

"So have I." The admission sent another shiver through him. "I understand things are…complicated. But they don't have to stay that way."

That sounded like she was back in protective mode. He hated that. Maybe that was why the urge had overpowered him. Maybe he'd just wanted to scorch that idea, that he was someone she had to help, right out of her mind. Problem was, it had scorched a few other things in the process. Most of them his.

That kiss knocked you on your ass, admit it.

And just because she didn't want to hear him say he shouldn't have done it didn't change the truth of that. But damn...

He didn't know which was worse, regret that he'd done it, that he'd taken such a sweet, sweet taste of something forever out of his reach, or that it had been so much more than he'd even imagined. He'd thought about what he'd do if he ever worked up the nerve to kiss her and it wasn't what he hoped, because that's how his life had gone.

He'd never thought about what he'd do if it was even more than he'd hoped.

He was so stunned that he didn't really know how he'd ended up sitting on her couch. He was sluggishly realizing from the pillow beside him and the knitted throw tossed to one side that she'd been sleeping here. Which explained why she'd been at the door in an instant, when he'd already changed his mind and was turning to go.

"Just so you know," she said as she sat down beside him—too damned close beside him, making him want to grab her and kiss her again, kiss her and so much more—"I was glad you were here even before you kissed me. So glad I won't even ask why."

He had no idea what to say to that. But something else hit him when she said that about why he was here. He leaned forward and pulled the folded sheet of paper out of his back pocket. He thought it a little silly, he always did, but other people seemed to like the little sketches, so he gave it to her.

She gave him a curious glance as she unfolded the sketch. And he was watching her closely enough that he knew her reaction of pure delight was real.

"Yes! Kane this is perfect!" She looked up at him then,

and those spring-green eyes of hers were fairly glowing. "Have you ever done one in color? Or added color? This will make the perfect cover image."

"I...no. They're just little sketches, so I never bothered."

"Well now you must. I want this for the cover. It's exactly right. What shall we name him?"

He blinked. We? "Name...?"

"Our raccoon. We need a catchy, kid-friendly name." He couldn't describe the warm feeling that was creeping up on him with all this "we" and "our" she was saying, with such ease and naturalness. "Or no, maybe something funny because it's not a kid name, something very formal or ornate, the opposite of his cute raccoon-ness."

"Rutherford Raccoon." He said the first thing that popped into his head.

Lark's eyes widened, and she laughed with obvious delight. "Yes!"

And that warmth became an explosion of something he had no name for either, unless it was joy, something so foreign to him he couldn't quite accept it. He had to swallow before he could go on.

"Maybe an unusual middle initial. Like X or Q."

"Rutherford Q. Raccoon. I love it. Oh, he's going to be so much fun."

He figured he was smiling rather inanely, but he couldn't seem to help it. She put the drawing down on the coffee table, then sat back, studying him for a moment.

"What was it?" She asked it gently, as she always did.

"What?"

"What made it impossible for you to stay?"

He blinked, caught off guard by the sudden shift. But how like her to put it that way, taking the blame off of him and putting it on some external thing. He wouldn't have said what came out next if she hadn't startled him so. Or if he wasn't so damned tired. "What makes you think I'm not just a coward who always runs?"

She held his gaze steadily. The exact opposite of coward. "Is that how you feel?"

"Do you always have to dive headfirst into feelings?" he said, realizing even as he said it—snappishly—that given how this encounter had started that was a pretty stupid question. But he was a little boggled at how quickly things had changed from what he'd been feeling about her reaction to his sketch.

"Do you always dodge a question with a question?" That too-sweet tone again. And he wondered if she'd forgotten already, put out of her mind that hot, incredible kiss.

Maybe it wasn't so hot or incredible for her, idiot.

"Apparently," he muttered, closing his eyes wearily for a moment.

"Tell me what it was about that picture that set you off." His eyes snapped open. How the hell—? "Sage found it, the glass broken, when she went looking for you." He winced. Just that quickly they were back in the morass again. "She's terrified she's lost you for good this time," Lark added softly.

He had to close his eyes again, this time against a wave of pain. He sucked in a breath. "Hurting her seems to be what I do best."

"Was it seeing in that photo how much he loved you?"

And again his eyes snapped open. "What? He's looking at me like what I was, a kid who wasn't his, but that he was stuck with."

Lark drew back sharply. "That, *that's* what you see in that picture?"

"I've seen it practically every night for years."

She looked thoughtful then. "You mean you dream about it."

He shrugged. "I don't blame him for it anymore. He did more than most would. And he deserved better, much better than what I did to him."

He was startled when she grabbed up her phone from the coffee table in front of them. More startled when she apparently sent a text. Was she calling for Shane to come get him?

"Who are you texting at—what time is it?" he asked warily.

"Sage. She won't care what time it is." She gave him a sideways look. "And she's probably awake anyway—" Before she could even finish the sentence her phone chimed an answer. "Like I said."

He glanced toward the phone, but couldn't read the screen at the angle she was holding it. Intentional?

"Look, I know you're trying to help—"

"Hush. I'm waiting for something."

"I knew I shouldn't have come here," he muttered.

"And yet here you are. Eventually we'll talk about why." *Like hell. You don't want to know why I keep leaning on you.* "But right now I want you to do something."

"Spill my guts some more?" he asked with a grimace.

"No talking required," she said almost airily, her tone putting him off-balance yet again.

"Then what—" He stopped as her phone chimed again.

She glanced at it, then looked at him again. "Just close your eyes."

That, he could manage. He did so. "And?"

"I know it won't be fun, but I want you to think about those dreams. I want you to focus on your memory of that photograph. Put it front and center in your mind's eye."

"What—"

"Please, Kane. Just do it. Focus on it. Notice every aspect. What you're wearing, your expression, the background, his expression, what position you're both in, what every little detail looks like."

He couldn't seem to say no to her, so he did as she asked. He didn't have to work hard at it, not as often as it had haunted his nights. The image formed easily, and he tried to hold on to it even as his mind wanted to skitter away like a rat from a trap.

"Do you have it?" she asked.

"Yeah."

"Keep your eyes closed. Stare at it, in your head. Memorize it."

"I have it memorized already or I wouldn't be dreaming it," he pointed out rather sourly.

"Just do it. Keep it there." He thought he heard her take in a breath. "Now...open your eyes."

He did. She had her phone right in front of his face, and

there was a photograph showing on the screen. He blinked. It was like the one in his dreams, like it had been taken at nearly the same moment, but it was very different. In this picture the boy and the man were smiling, widely. At each other. The love fairly radiated from the image. From both of them.

"What do you see?" she asked, her voice more gentle than ever.

"I...what is this?"

"The truth."

His brow furrowed. He was feeling sluggish again, slow on the uptake.

"This is the real picture, Kane. Not the nightmare image your mind created. The way he's looking at you, the love...that's what was real."

His gaze shifted to her, disbelieving. "But...this isn't the same picture."

"It is. That's what the text was. I had Sage take it out of the broken frame and take a photo of it."

He shook his head, unable to even process what she was saying. And yet again she seemed to understand, because she tapped the phone's screen a couple of times, then held it out to him again, this time with the text exchange.

He's here.

Thank God. Please, please make him stay. I'll come right now.

Wait. Please trust me again and do something. Take a photo of the picture you showed me and text it.

Hang on.

The next bubble was the photo she'd enlarged to full screen and put in front of him. He sat staring at the messages, then at the picture again.

"The mind does strange, and sometimes horrible things when we're in pain," Lark said softly. "In your case, it twisted what was really in this photograph—the pure, beautiful love of a father and son—into what you were feeling about yourself and what happened that day."

He couldn't speak. He could barely breathe through the impossibly tight knot in his throat. He could only shake his head.

"What else has that pain done to you, Kane? What else has it twisted, changed? Did it convince you your family—and they are that—couldn't possibly want you anymore? Did it tell you it was all your fault? Did it make you believe, really believe that you were a killer? That you meant for what happened to happen?"

Her words poured down on him like hammer blows. If she kept on there was going to be nothing left of him. Which might be the best resolution he could hope for.

Finally, he looked at her. And what he saw in her face, in those amazing eyes, was the final blow. He felt himself break inside, felt all his defenses crumble. And as always, Lark seemed to know it. She reached for him, pulled him into her arms.

He didn't even try to resist. He just let her hold him, feeling like her embrace was the only thing keeping him from turning to dust right here.

Chapter Thirty-One

THIS WAS A strange sensation, Lark thought as she woke up in the morning light. Feeling jammed into a tiny space and yet not wanting to change anything.

They were lying on her couch, together, covered with the throw. And Kane was asleep in her arms, sound asleep, she suspected perhaps for the first time in far too long. The truth of that picture, the knowledge of how his mind and guilt had twisted things, had shattered him. She'd seen it happen as clearly as she'd ever seen anything happen to anyone in her life.

There would be much to do, now. Now he had to pick up the pieces and rebuild what he could of a life. But now, for the first time, she thought he would do it. Because she no longer sensed that hyper-alertness in him, that wire-strung tension that she knew was connected to that urge to run.

...things are complicated. But they don't have to stay that way.

Her own words came back to her. And as she lay there with her arms around him, savoring the heat of him pressed against her, and the unexpected pleasure at the simple fact that he trusted her enough to sleep, she felt an overwhelming urge to have all of those complicated things resolved. And selfishly, not just for his sake, or the Highwaters', but for her own. Because only when they were resolved could they pursue what leapt to life between them.

But how did you resolve the problems of nearly half a lifetime? Kane had been haunted by this for thirteen years. Would it take another thirteen for him to get past it? She didn't want to think it would. If only he hadn't run back then, if he'd been here for the inquiry Sean had given her the details about—including Judge Morales's conclusions—it would have been over. Sad, heartbreaking, yes, but not what he'd been through. Because he would have had his family beside him, would have seen how his true parentage didn't matter to them, just as hers hadn't mattered to her family. But how—

Judge Morales. Elena's mother's cousin. He wasn't a juvenile court judge so it wouldn't have been his case if Kane had stayed. The case certainly hadn't met the criteria for a shift to adult court. But because Kane was gone and Last Stand was his jurisdiction, he had conducted the inquiry, assigned at his own request because of who Steven Highwater had been.

But Kane was an adult now. Even if he'd been as guilty as he thought himself, he'd be dealing with the adult court now.

Thoughts began to tumble through her mind. And soon there were so many she had to act. She eased herself up from the couch, managing to do it without waking him, probably because he was so exhausted. For a moment she just stood there, looking at him, wondering if she should do this, if she wasn't asking for a lot of personal pain.

But the thought only lasted for a split second, because she knew it was too late for second thoughts. And that no matter the potential cost to herself, she had to do this. After that kiss, she was more certain than ever. She didn't want to be in this position any longer. She didn't want to be with him only because he needed her experience, her help.

She picked up her phone and walked back to her bedroom. And began to make some calls.

"WHAT?"

Kane knew he was staring at her blankly. This was the last thing he'd expected. Well, after waking up on her couch after having had the best sleep he'd had in years, in her arms.

"Simple question," Lark said. "Do you want this behind you once and for all?"

"I don't—"

"Do you want to be free? Want it dealt with, faced, over and done?"

He drew back at the ferocity in her tone. "Maybe," he said warily, "you'd better define 'it' for me."

"The death of Steven Highwater." She held his gaze. "Your father in all but DNA."

He started the denial that had become almost reflex. But the memory of that photograph stayed the words. He was still having trouble processing that his mind, his imagination, had so distorted that reality. That the image he had dreamed, night after night, of the man he'd spent sixteen years thinking of as his father looking at him with distaste and dislike, had been a lie.

And wondering about the answer to Lark's most insistent, most important question.

What else has that pain done to you, Kane?

Was it possible? Had the same inner force—his own feelings of guilt—that had so twisted his dreams twisted other realities? Was his whole idea of what had happened that day wrong?

"Take your life back, Kane," she said softly. "The man in that photo would never want you to live in the hell you've condemned yourself to."

He swallowed tightly. "I..."

"You can build a new life, but not until you clear away the debris."

He had to unclench his jaw to get the word out. "How?"

"A meeting. With all concerned. To have it all out. The hearing you never had, the judgment rendered by someone whose job it is, not your own conscience. Because you know now, from that picture, how things can get distorted in our heads."

Yes, he knew. He'd never forget that moment when he'd realized what his mind had done to warp that loving image.

"Where?"

"On neutral ground."

"Neutral? In Last Stand?"

"Neutral to all of us," she amended with a smile. And

that "us," and the look she gave him, had his mind rocketing back to that kiss. Not that it took much to do that. He'd relived it countless times in his mind already. Imagined what would have followed, if she hadn't called a halt.

What gleamed in her eyes then made him want to make that imagining a reality now. Right now. He moved toward her. But her next words were like ice water tossed on the fierce need.

"Kane…you can't be sure of anything right now."

"So you don't want someone with all this hanging over him?"

She jerked away from him, and he wished he could call back the sour words, wished he could beat back these seemingly instinctive and instant reactions of his. But at the same time, something about the glint of ferocity that came into those green eyes made him want her even more.

"I'm the one who thinks you don't have anything hanging over you that you haven't put there yourself," she said sharply. He winced inwardly, but said nothing, afraid to make things worse. "But I need an answer. Do you want this done once and for all, or not?"

A meeting. With all concerned. To have it all out.

He studied her for a moment, trying to figure out just how angry he'd made her. But all he could think of was what she'd said about him having nothing hanging over him that he hadn't put there himself.

Just like the picture?

Something stirred, down deep.

Do you want to be free?

He didn't know what it was.

Take your life back, Kane.

It grew, as if it were unfurling inside him.

You can build a new life.

A new life?

In the same instant he knew two things. That any life he'd want had to have her in it. And what that thing expanding inside him was.

Hope.

And no amount of telling himself that hope was for fools seemed to be able to quash it.

So maybe he was a fool. Maybe somewhere in the hell of the last thirteen years some small bit of foolish hope had survived.

"All right," he said, his voice grim with the effort to hide that hope. "Let's get it over with." *One way or the other.*

He had nothing to say as they got into her car. His mind wanted to plan ahead, to be ready for the inevitable, the need to leave again. But that damned bit of hope wouldn't let him alone.

They went past the road that led to the high school on the other side of the creek, and continued south. Past where they'd sat and talked, and where he'd spent those sleepless hours. She eventually slowed, clearly ready to make a turn onto a long driveway that wound through the trees on the bank of the creek. He saw a carved wooden sign that said "Hickory Creek Inn, Bed and Breakfast." This was new, but hardly surprising after all this time. And it was a beautiful spot, along the creek—

It hit him then. This was the Buckley place. Frank Buckley's place.

A cascade of thoughts tumbled through his mind, and when they hit bottom the only one that made sense to his rattled mind—and heart—was that Shane didn't want to arrest him. So they'd arranged for someone else to do it.

Frank Buckley, Texas Ranger.

Chapter Thirty-Two

LARK FELT THE change as if it had been a physical slap. Felt the sudden tension as he went rigid. It wasn't hard to guess that he'd remembered who lived here. She kept her voice tour-guide casual as she navigated the turn. "They opened the B&B about four years ago. After Ranger Buckley had to retire."

It was a moment before he said, his voice as stiff as his posture at the moment, "Had to?"

"Well, as much as Rangers ever retire, which as Scott says is as much as Marines do. But he was injured on duty. His shooting hand, unfortunately. But he's still got that knowledge. I know Shane's come to him more than once for advice, and Sean, too, on a tough case now and then."

"Like today?" He sounded like he was fighting suspicions. That he was being set up? Could he really think that of her?

"Do you really think I would do that, Kane?"

He didn't even look surprised, so she knew she'd been right about what had come into his head. He let out a long breath. "No. No, you wouldn't. It was just...gut reaction."

"I know," she said softly.

Trust. Many people had trusted her over the years, but it had never meant more to her than coming from this man.

She could see the big, white house now, with its distinctive observation tower dead center, and expansive wraparound porches. It was shaded by trees amid a swath of well-kept lawn and garden.

Lark went on in that same casual tone as she drove. "Anyway, there's a nice, big room where they serve breakfast to the guests. It's overlooking the creek, and they also rent it out for meetings. Or in this case, simply loan."

He drew back, and turned slightly in the passenger seat to look at her. "Who arranged all this?"

"Everybody did their part. I just made some calls."

"And just when did you do that?"

"This morning."

He blinked. "You put this all together in a day?"

"I didn't. Everyone did. Everyone who wants to see you get past this."

"Me? They're the ones who—"

He stopped as they came into a parking area. She saw him glance around. There were several cars. Among them was Shane's official SUV, and a too-plain car she guessed was Sean's. And other cars. Joey's, and Elena's, and the ranch truck Scott sometimes drove; Sage had said he hadn't settled on a personal vehicle yet.

Kane was looking from car to car, as if counting them.

"They're almost all here," Lark said as she stopped and put the car in park.

He grimaced wryly. "I was just looking for Poke tied up

somewhere. But she probably came with Scott, huh?"

She smiled when he mentioned the horse; that would be very Sage. "Probably. But I'm sure she'd have preferred to ride Poke over."

"So, what, everybody's taking the afternoon off for this?" He didn't want to go in. She could feel the tension building.

"Without hesitation." She reached across the seat, putting her hand first on his arm, then sliding down to take his hand, which was clenched into a fist as he stared out the windshield at the big, white house. He looked at her then. She saw him take a deep breath. Slowly his fist uncurled. His fingers wrapped around hers. And she sat there for a moment, moisture welling in her eyes as she thought about what it had taken for him to make just that little gesture. His eyes widened. And just as a single tear spilled over, he reached out and caught it with his thumb, so gently she probably would have barely registered the touch if not for the electric little jolt that shot through her.

They got out of the car and came together at the bottom of the wide, stone steps. He looked up, glancing from the American flag hanging from the porch post on one side to the Lone Star flag on the other side. She was just thinking she couldn't imagine how he was feeling when he reached out and took her hand. She gave him a squeeze, and they went up the five steps to the porch.

There was a man in the doorway, and Kane stopped dead.

She hadn't seen Frank Buckley in a while, but he looked much the same to her. Tall, strong, perhaps a bit more gray in his dark hair, a few more lines around his eyes, but those eyes were as clear and piercing as ever. And right now they were fastened on Kane.

"Finally home, huh?" The former ranger's voice was a deep rumble.

"That remains to be seen." Kane's voice was different, neutral but steady. He was decided now, to see this through—she could almost feel it.

"Hmm." The man looked at her and smiled. "Well, you've got one of the best on your side, I see." Lark smiled, pleased. She liked and respected this man, and it meant a great deal to her to have his approval. He looked back at Kane. "And it took some sand to come here and hash this out." He held out his hand to Kane. The injured hand, with the surgery scars and the permanently bent index finger.

Kane took it, they shook, but then Kane looked at that damaged hand for a moment. "That must have hurt."

"It did."

Kane looked up then, and met the older man's gaze steadily. "But not as much as what it took away from you?"

She saw surprise flicker in the man's dark eyes. And she imagined not much surprised Frank Buckley anymore.

"No," he agreed. "Not nearly as much." Something happened then between the two men. She wasn't sure what. But the Ranger's next words seemed pointed. "When I started out, I was a letter-of-the-law kind of guy. But the years have taught me that it's not always that simple or clear-cut."

Then he stepped to the side and gestured them inside what had been his family's home for generations but was now a business that had gone from risky to flourishing in the relatively short time it had been open.

It was always Karina's dream, to run a place like this. I had my turn, now it's hers.

She remembered his explanation for the unlikely move, and it made her smile again at him as they passed. His gaze flicked from her to Kane and back, and then he gave her a slight nod. For the smile, or was that in approval? She didn't know, but she hoped. The man was legendary for his quick and accurate assessments of situations and people. If Kane passed muster with him…

But he wasn't the final arbiter. Even the people gathered in the room they were headed for weren't. No, the final arbiter in the case of Kane Travis Highwater was the man beside her, Kane himself.

He was the only one who could put this to rest for good.

KANE SUPPOSED IT was a nice room. Spacious, with big windows that looked out over Hickory Creek and three sets of French doors that opened out onto a deck beside the flowing water. Despite its size it had a homey, welcoming feel. Unfortunately for him, there was too much tension in the room already for it to feel particularly welcoming to him.

But then, he hadn't expected a welcome anywhere in Last Stand, yet he'd gotten one. And maybe, just maybe, the chance at something he never would have dreamed of, in the woman beside him.

But this had to be done first. He had to, as Lark had said, put this behind him once and for all. Because he couldn't face her honestly, as a man, until he did.

They had all turned to look at him as he and Lark came in. He had to work to keep his expression even, but the feel of her hand in his helped. His gaze flicked around the room. They were all here. And each couple jabbed at him in a different way. Slater with Joey, who smiled at him, and in that moment looked like the girl he'd shared a lab table with. Scott with Sage, with hope glowing in her bluebonnet eyes. Sean with Elena, who he now knew had been there that day, had held Steven Highwater as he'd died, apparently absolving Kane with his last breath. And Lily with Shane, who had so ably stepped into his father's sizeable boots.

Then, to his surprise, the newest members of what was clearly a united front separated from their partners and walked toward him. They stopped in front of him. He didn't know what to do, what to say, but it didn't matter, because they had clearly planned this. It was his to simply endure. And it was only the beginning.

Joey began it, and sent him back to those days, when she, like his brother, had had a quote for every occasion. "Charles Williams, a British writer, once said 'Many promising reconciliations have broken down because while both parties come prepared to forgive, neither party come prepared to be forgiven.' Don't let that happen here, my old friend."

Then Shane's Lily stepped up. "Believe that thirteen years of searching, of never giving up, was done out of love, Kane. There have been many days when Shane was dead on his feet but kept going because some new possibility had popped up. Because it was you, and he loves you."

He swallowed tightly, hoped they weren't expecting answers because he had none, and he couldn't get any words out anyway.

When he was face-to-face with Sage's Scott, he remembered what he'd said that night on the road. *If I can stomach coming back to Last Stand, you can too.* Something glinted in the man's eyes, and he also remembered what this guy had been in the military, and had no doubt he could take him out in an instant.

"Bottom line," he said gruffly. "Don't leave and hurt her again." He started to turn, leaving it at that, but then looked back. "Oh, and trust Morales. He did right by me."

Lark had told him Morales had been the judge who had given him the military option when Scott had gotten into trouble. And that he'd overseen the inquiry into Steven Highwater's death. The inquiry he'd figured would have happened, but had expected would have ended with the issuance of that warrant he'd been looking for, for thirteen years. And ruled by that blind instinct, he hadn't really thought enough about what it meant that it hadn't been.

He hadn't thought enough, period. And it was time, past time, to end that. He was through running, no matter what got thrown at him today.

He barely had time to think that before Sean's Elena was there. He expected her to say something about how long and hard Sean had searched for him as well. But instead she reached up and touched his cheek.

"He loved you. It was in his eyes, in his voice, in those final moments. It did not matter that you were not his blood, you were in his heart. He did not blame you. And that is what you must live up to. You must be as he was, big enough to understand it was not your fault, Kane Highwater."

A violent shiver of emotion rippled through him. If he'd not been so determined, and if he'd not had Lark beside him, he might have gone to his knees.

The four of them began to walk away, clearly intending to leave the room. Kane looked at Lark. "Do they—" he nodded at the ones staying "—feel like I do, when you're here for me? Like I can't do this if you're not?"

Something flared, bright and warm and sweet in her eyes. "Thank you," she whispered. "And yes."

He lifted his head, looked at the quartet that was at the door now. "Wait." They stopped. Looked back. "Stay." That got him some surprised looks. "I need Lark. They need you." He grimaced, nodded toward Shane and the others. "Besides, it'll save them having to tell you everything later."

That got him a couple of wide smiles and even a laugh. And as they came back the atmosphere in the room suddenly changed, lightened, and he felt a strange sense of accomplishment at that. And he had the thought that he just might get through this after all. Whatever happened, it would be, as Lark had said, behind him. Over and done and dealt with, once and for all. And for the first time he was truly getting a sense of what that might feel like.

He looked back at her, putting as much as he could into

a whispered, "Thank you."

She didn't answer, but the smile she gave him then compounded that feeling of being on the verge of a freedom he hadn't known for thirteen years. And he smiled back at her, for the first time letting that hope show.

Scott and Shane gathered chairs from the other tables in the room. They didn't add them to the ones at the big table but arranged them close by.

The door behind them opened. A man came in. Average height, dark hair with gray at the temples. Dark eyes, with a calm, wise look to them. Hispanic maybe. Fifties, Kane guessed. And…Someone. With a capital S. He had an air about him. And even if he hadn't already guessed, the way Shane instantly started toward him would have done it.

The newcomer looked at Lark. Smiled. "Ms. Leclair."

"Hello, Judge Morales. Thank you for coming."

"Your Honor," said Shane as he got there, reaching out to shake his hand. "Yes, thank you."

Trust Morales. He did right by me.

But Scott had been…a victim of circumstance.

And then a thought he'd never allowed himself before crept into his mind. That in a way, so was he.

People sometimes can't avoid being a victim. But they can avoid staying one.

Steven Highwater's words, spoken so long ago Kane couldn't even remember the context, rang in his ears as if the man were here saying them now.

The man who had raised him, loved him as if he were his own, even though he knew. The man he'd loved and respected and wanted to be like for the first sixteen years of his life. He'd failed there.

But that didn't mean he had to keep failing.

He sucked in a deeper breath and slowly let it out. And belatedly realized the newcomer standing beside them, the judge, was watching intently. He met the man's steady gaze, held it.

"Thank you for coming, Your Honor," he said.

Chapter Thirty-Three

THE JUDGE HAD gestured him toward the long table set up by the windows. Lark wondered what he was thinking, the scenario his imagination was building, but the way he had greeted the judge gave her hope, that he would get this behind him instead of having it looming over his every step, his every breath.

Looming over them, making him hold back from what they could have, making him not trust the fire that sparked to life between them. And that was the selfish element of what she'd pushed them to here; her brain knew that he couldn't fully let go until this was done, and her heart was not willing to settle for less.

Could he let it go? Could he, who'd had so little reason for hope and trust, regain it here, among those who loved him regardless of what his faithless mother had done?

And as her emotions swirled and roiled, tangling with a brain that seemed to have stopped functioning, she wondered if this kind of chaos was what he'd been living with since…probably since he'd decided to come to the competition. God, had it really been only five days ago? It seemed impossible to her, so she could only imagine what it felt like to him.

This had been her idea, yet she'd been the one worrying since he'd agreed to it.

"This is not my courtroom, Mr. Highwater," Judge Morales said. Lark was watching Kane's face as he looked at the judge and saw only the faintest of flickers in his eyes at the name. "Nor is this an unresolved case. I'm here because your brother, Chief Highwater, requested it, and I have great respect for him and for your family."

Lark's gaze flicked to John Morales's face, wondering if he had any idea that he jabbed Kane three times in those few words, by denying there was anything to be resolved, asserting Shane was his brother, and the Highwaters his family. There was a wealth of wisdom in his dark eyes, and she suspected he knew exactly what he was doing.

"I conducted the inquiry into your father's death," the judge went on.

Oh, yes, the judge knew what he was doing.

Kane opened his mouth as if to speak. To deny the parentage? But he stopped himself. Some of that Highwater cool, whether he laid claim to it or not.

"The facts were simple. There was a verbal argument that took place on the sidewalk in front of Valencia's restaurant, involving Kane Travis Highwater and Steven Bowie Highwater." Kane winced this time, but still didn't speak. "There were witnesses to the argument," the judge continued, "but none to the actual incident."

"Except me," Kane said, his voice taut.

"Yes," Judge Morales agreed. "But since you were not

here to give a statement, I had to proceed without benefit of that."

"You want it now?" Kane looked up at the man then, and his voice was stronger. And she saw a steadiness in his gaze that told her yet again he was going to see this through. Like a Highwater. But she also knew he was about to condemn himself. "We argued. I lost my temper. I pushed him. Into the street. He was hit. And died. Because of me."

"I see." Judge Morales studied him for a long moment. "There are three problems with your statement, Mr. Highwater." Kane didn't react, apparently resigned for the moment to the use of the name he'd abandoned—or felt unworthy of?—all those years ago. "One, there has been a valid reinterpretation of some evidence."

Kane glanced at her, for a split second, and she knew he remembered what she'd told him about the scrape on the new boots.

"Two," Judge Morales continued, "the eyewitnesses to the actual argument all agreed on one thing. Which is rare enough to be noted, I might add. Eyewitness testimony is notoriously inconsistent between witnesses."

Kane looked puzzled now, and Lark wondered if anyone had actually told him what the results of the inquiry had been. Even if they had, he would still blame himself, because he had indeed pushed Steven Highwater. But she knew what Sean had been doing with that one new piece of information she'd given him, knew what he'd proven. She would have told Kane herself, except it was Sean's right; he'd worked so hard for this for so long.

"The witnesses consistently state you left the scene immediately, in fact were out of sight before the incident in the street occurred. Therefore, given the time elapsed, the certainty of your claim that you pushed him into the street is questionable."

Kane frowned, but Lark's breath caught. She hadn't realized there had been that much delay between the argument and the accident. Even a few seconds lent credence to the theory that it hadn't been solely Kane's shove that had sent Steven Highwater into the path of that truck.

"The third item…" Judge Morales nodded at Shane, who leaned forward, elbows on the table across from Kane as he spoke.

"This was the part we didn't have, bro," he said. Kane winced again at the appellation. "The witnesses said you were in front of Valencia's. But Lark told us you said you were actually in the doorway alcove to Valencia's."

Again Kane frowned. "That's where we were." Then he grimaced. "I was yelling my head off at him, and he was worried about blocking the sidewalk."

Shane shifted back in his chair, taking in a deep, audible breath. Then he looked at Sean, seated beside him and nodded. Sean leaned forward in turn.

"Do you still trust my freaky brain?" he asked.

Kane looked at him warily. "Yeah."

"I've spent hours since Lark told us what actually happened, working the logistics. I took measurements, I've diagrammed it from every angle, and run computer simulations of every scenario."

Despite everything, Kane almost smiled. "That sounds like you."

"Yeah. And I'm good at it. So believe me when I tell you this. From where you were standing, that far from the street, there is no way the kid you were could have pushed a man that size hard enough that he would have been unable to recover before he reached the curb. Unless something else happened."

Kane stared at Sean, his lips parted as if he were having trouble getting enough air.

"Like his ankle giving way, and him losing his balance," Slater put in from the other end of the table.

Lark saw him swallow as he shifted his gaze, and heard his quick intake of breath.

"A freakish, unexpected event no one could help," Sage said urgently from Lark's right. "No one, bro."

He didn't look at Sage. And Lark had the definite feeling it was because he thought if he did, he'd crumble before their eyes. Because the foundation of his life for thirteen years was crumbling. And again Judge Morales studied him for a moment before he spoke.

"Thirteen years ago, I proceeded on the assumption that if you had been there your plea would have been not guilty, or at the most *nolo contendere*."

"No contest at all," Kane muttered, sounding a little shell-shocked. Lark wondered if during some of those times hiding out in the shelter of libraries he'd been reading up on legal matters.

"These three things confirm to me my conclusion thirteen years ago was correct. If the facts laid out here had come before me in a trial situation—although it's unlikely you would have been brought before an adult court given your age and the circumstances at the time—for a decision, you likely would have received assignment to a course of anger management, perhaps a probationary period. Even the hardest-ass judge I know would have recommended deferred adjudication."

There were some smiles around the table as Judge Morales proved this definitely was not his courtroom. But Kane was looking a bit bewildered, so the judge explained.

"In Texas, this is the preferred option for a first-time offender because it gives you the chance to avoid a criminal record. You obey the terms of the agreement for the set period, and the charge is deemed dismissed. Of course if you blow it, the penalty is stiffer than if you'd been convicted in the first place." The judge smiled. "We're forgiving, but we Texans won't be taken for fools."

There were some answering smiles, but they were accompanied by knowing nods. There were no fools seated at this table, or in this room, Lark knew.

Kane still looked stunned. And then, very quietly, the judge spoke again.

"But what I would have done or not done then doesn't matter, does it, Kane? Because you've been guilty for so long in your own mind, of so much worse than a boy's temper in understandable circumstances, that you've convicted—and punished—yourself more than the state ever would have punished the boy you were."

Lark heard Kane suck in an audible breath. He was staring at the judge, as if he couldn't believe what he was hearing. As if he didn't dare believe.

Lark could have hugged the man, because in that moment she saw in Kane's eyes a renewed glimmer of what she'd seen when she'd convinced him to do this.

Hope.

Chapter Thirty-Four

"Now," Judge Morales said briskly, "were we in my courtroom, and were this an official proceeding, my ruling would include an assessment by an anger management expert, to determine if such a course is even necessary at this point. I suspect it is not."

Kane stared at the man, still reeling inwardly, still trying to process what was happening, what he was saying. The judge looked at Lark.

"Ms. Leclair, do you concur?"

"I do, Your Honor. He's developed a...very effective device for that."

Jasper, he thought a little numbly. She meant Jasper. He'd told her about the advice Zeb had given about using an image of the stubborn beast digging in his heels and refusing to give in to the snap of temper, and how it had worked for him.

"In that case," Judge Morales said, looking back at Kane, "my recommendation is some counseling, individual and family, to be certain all issues are dealt with. This would, of course, require you to remain in Last Stand, for monitoring purposes. I would think a year would do it."

For the first time he sensed Lark falter. Wondered what in those words had unsettled her. Did she not want him to stay? Did she think of what happened between them as some temporary thing, brought on by circumstances, by proximity? Suddenly that, even more than what was happening here, was the most urgent question in his mind. So urgent he threw caution to the winds and turned to look at her. And it took three Jaspers to rein in his voice to a normal tone.

"You don't like that idea?"

She looked at him, and he thought he would never see another spring that didn't remind him of the light green of her eyes. "I don't want you to stay because you're forced to."

A relief so fierce it left him numb for a moment flooded him. And with his normal caution in tatters, he made the most humbling admission of his life. "I was afraid you didn't want me to stay at all."

Warmth flooded her expression, and beneath the table she once more took his hand. "I think that's a discussion for later?"

He came back to the situation with a snap he could feel. Realized Judge Morales was looking at him. At them. Not with interest, but with…understanding. And when he spoke again, Kane could have sworn he was fighting a smile.

"Now, you understand of course, that since this is not my courtroom, and I am not here in my official capacity, that these are recommendations only." He glanced at Lark, then went back to Kane. "If you stay, it will be by your choice."

He felt the change in Lark, felt her relief, through the

connection of their hands, and he had the thought that it was very odd that he could tell so much without words. But then, hadn't she been doing the same to him from the moment they'd met? Maybe it had always gone both ways, but he'd just been too distracted by the chaos to realize it.

"It will be up to you, what happens now," the judge said. "I have no enforcement authority here."

"But I do," Shane said, so cheerfully Kane's gaze shot to him, and he nearly gaped. "And you're staying, bro. We want that year. After that, we'll...renegotiate."

A year. Month after month after month. No moving on after a few days or weeks. A year in one place.

This place.

He looked around the table, at the men who still called themselves his brothers, and the woman who had ever been his sister in his heart.

"It wasn't your fault," Sean said quietly.

"But even if it had been, we would still love you," Sage whispered.

"She's right," Slater agreed. "'We pardon as long as we love,' La Rochefoucauld said."

"So do we have your promise to stay, at least for that year, bro?" Shane asked.

He stared at the man who had become the patriarch of the Highwater clan, who had done it with all the steadiness and courage and kindness and fairness of his father.

"You'd trust a promise from me?"

"I would." No hesitation.

"We all would," Sean said.

Slater only smiled, in that wise way Kane remembered he'd always had.

He had the sudden thought that he had the answer now to what Lark had once asked him, why he'd cut his brothers off when he hadn't done the same with Sage. It was because living up to them, to the example they set, to the men they were, would be a monumental task.

Lark.

He turned to her again. And the moment he looked into her eyes he knew he had to have an answer from her before he decided whether to take on what he knew would be the biggest challenge of his life.

"I...will you step outside and talk with me for a minute?"

"Of course," she said, rising even before he did. "Out by the creek, perhaps?" She glanced at Sage. "I hear it's a good place to go."

His brow furrowed as he stood up, but it was Shane he looked at. "I said we'd trust you," was all the police chief of Last Stand said. "We'll be here when you get back."

They stepped through the closest set of French doors, and he felt the pressure ease a little. She seemed to know where she wanted to go, so he merely walked with her. They followed the path indicated with an arrow and a small sign labeled "Creek Overlook." He grabbed her hand, something he'd wanted to do since they'd stepped outside.

"What was that about, with Sage?" he finally asked.

"This is where she and Scott came to work out their relationship." Lark gave him a smile, a sweet but almost teasing one. "It's also where they used to meet in high school, after you told him he should talk to her."

He blinked; he hadn't expected that.

"It wasn't the B&B then, of course. So technically they were trespassing. And they thought they were sneaking that past Ranger Buckley."

He let out a rough laugh at that. "I could have told them that was impossible." Then, curious, he asked, "So he knew, but he didn't stop them?"

"Underneath that tough, Ranger exterior Frank Buckley is, I suspect, a romantic at heart."

His laugh was better this time. "Coming from anyone else, I'd blow that off."

Her smile was wide and pleased then. "Don't think I don't know the faith that implies."

They'd reached the overlook, where a ledge of limestone projected out over the creek, near one of the spots where, when the water was high, it was possible to swim, or at least cool off. Something he seemed to need every time he was with her.

He reached out and grasped her shoulders, turned her to face him. He opened his mouth to speak, but her lips parted at the same moment and he simply had to have another taste of her. He lowered his head. She didn't protest but rather stretched up to meet him.

And it was as sweet, as hot, as necessary as it had been the first time. Only the power of this thing that leapt to life between them could keep his roiling thoughts at bay, could give him the balance he needed to face down the rest of his life. He tasted her long and deep, and welcomed with fierce pleasure her eager response.

When he finally had to break the kiss to breathe, he tightened his arms around her. Hers tightened in turn around him, and he barely suppressed a shudder of violent response to the pleasure of simply that.

It was a long time before he could find the power of speech again. "I don't know if I can do this," he finally got out.

She pulled back slightly, and looked up at him. "You've done so many things, things I never would have imagined trying. You can do this, too. You can put it behind you. Never to be forgotten, but not running your life any longer." She reached up, cupped his face in her hands. "It's there, waiting, Kane. All you have to do is grab it."

"I..."

"I know it's hard to trust, after all you've been through. But you've got your family back—" she gestured back toward the inn "—bigger and better than ever. Every one of them will help you, in their own special ways."

"And you?" he asked, his voice rough with emotion.

"I'll always be there, if you need me."

"And what if I said I'll always need you?"

He heard her breath catch. "So much is happening, Kane, so much has changed, you can't be sure of that now."

"I can," he said stubbornly.

"Give it—give us—some time. Find your balance, and then we'll figure everything else out."

"I like the 'we' part," he said rather gruffly. "But I don't want you to…be there if you're only feeling sorry for me."

She pulled back. And her chin came up in that way he'd come to know. "I only feel pity for people who won't even try. Is that what you're saying, you're not even going to try?"

"No, I'm not saying that." Even though the idea scared the hell out of him, the thought of running again was worse. And the thought of leaving her was beyond bearing. "But damn, Lark, you deserve better. More. I've got nothing and—" He broke off as she laughed at him.

"You're a Highwater, as far as your family is concerned. That's a lot more than nothing." She reached up and tapped the end of his nose. "Not to mention a fifth of the Highwater ranch, plus that healthy investment account. Who's to say I'm not after that, hmmm?"

He blinked. He hadn't quite believed that Steven Highwater had really left him a fifth of the ranch. And he'd completely forgotten that two hundred grand sitting in an account with his name on it.

"I…you wouldn't. You'd never do that, never even think that way," he finally said.

"No, I wouldn't. I'm glad you know that."

"What I don't know is why he would…do that."

"He loved you," Lark said quietly, but firmly. "Whenever, however he found out, or if he always knew because of the timing, it made no difference to his feelings for you. He was that kind of man."

He hadn't really thought about that, either. Had the senior Highwater always known? Or had the woman who'd birthed him thrown it at him sometime later, in one of her drunken rages? He'd only been four when she'd died, but he still remembered those, all too well. And yet Steven Highwater, a man hardly lacking in courage, had stayed. For them.

Your father in all but DNA...

"You have so much to think about, Kane. You need to find your place with them again, settle in, get your feet under you."

"In a cliché mood?" he asked, not quite sourly.

"Things become cliché for a reason, often because they're the best way to sum something up."

"So is this how you wound up your cases? Some good clichéd advice to the little kid and send him off?"

He knew the words were a mistake, but he was too afraid he was losing her to stop them. She backed up sharply, breaking their embrace.

"If you're angling for a slap to go with the advice you're on the right track," she said, in that too-sweet tone. "And if you still harbor the thought that I think of you as one of my cases, then you really do need that counseling."

He had that coming. That knowledge didn't ameliorate the jab of panic he felt when she turned to walk away. But then she looked back at him.

"Go back in there and make that promise, Kane. Or run again. Those are your only options. With one, I'll be here when you're solid again, and we can try to build something together. The other, I'll worry about you, probably forever, but I'll move on. Because you will have left me no choice."

And then she was gone and he was left there in the shade of a big pecan tree, wondering if he had the sand to do this, to remake his life.

Wondering if he had the nerve to reach out and take what the most amazing woman he'd ever met was offering.

Wondering if he had half the courage of the man who truly had been his father in the only sense that counted.

Chapter Thirty-Five

LARK WATCHED THE Ainsworths walk out of the courtroom with a smile. They were going to be great parents. She'd known that from the beginning. And that baby was going to have a good, safe life and be loved. Just as she had been.

"They're going to make it," the woman beside her said. "At our first meeting they'd thought ahead, already had a plan in place for when they inevitably disagreed on some aspect of parenting their new daughter."

She turned to look at Patricia Cruz, the founder of *Building Families*. "Yes, they are." She smiled. "I've liked them from the moment I did the home study. When they told me they didn't clean up any more than usual because they thought it important for the child that I see how they actually live, I knew they'd make it."

And they had. The finalization hearing just completed made little April theirs, and Lark couldn't be happier.

Well, she couldn't be happier for them. She could be a lot happier for herself.

When she'd walked away from Kane that day, she'd dared to hang on to the hope that it wouldn't be long. That he'd take the chance offered him to rejoin his family. That he'd make peace with what had been, in essence, a cruel accident of fate. That with the comfort and unwavering support of the Highwaters, he'd take back the name he'd been gifted with, whether it was biologically true or not.

And that when he'd done all that, he would come to her, so they could explore what happened between them and—her most foolish hope, perhaps—build a life around it.

The first three days without a word hadn't bothered her a lot; she was concerned, but more about him than the lack of contact. But she knew he had an incredible amount of stuff to work through, so forged on with her work, prepping for this hearing and another after that.

But when the weekend passed the same way, she began to feel a twinge. Maybe she had misjudged. Maybe now that he knew he had a place in his family that was enough. Maybe he didn't need her support anymore.

Maybe he didn't need her anymore.

And worst of all, maybe...maybe that kiss hadn't been as incredibly spectacular for him. While for her, it had been life changing.

She thought again about going to him. She wanted to. But deep down she knew she couldn't. It had to be his decision. He was the one who'd had so much to deal with; he was the one who had to know he could do it on his own.

It was ironic, she supposed, that the man who'd lived such a crazy life, who'd been forced to deal with things most people would never face, would end up having trouble adjusting to a normal reality.

And the best thing she could do for him now was wait. Wait to see if she was going to be part of that reality.

"Thanks for the muscle loan, bro."

Kane gave his sister—for she had ever been that—a crooked smile as they stepped back to look at the new water trough they'd set in place. "I'm still stunned you admitted you needed it."

"This ain't Hollywood, and I'm no female superhero."

"I think Scott would argue that point," he said mildly.

That earned him the best smile yet, and it warmed places that had been chilled for so long they'd almost forgotten what it was like to feel like this.

"You two are getting along," she said.

"We've got something in common," he said. "Although he handled it a hell of a lot better than I did."

"Just differently," Sage said, yet pride glowed in her bluebonnet eyes. "But he did it well, didn't he?"

He hugged her, simply because at long last he could. "I'm so happy for you, little sis. He's a good, good man and he's obviously crazy about you."

"And I about him. Even though it took him a while to deal with everything." She leaned back and looked up at him. "Speaking of men crazy about their women, have you seen Lark yet?"

He went still. He wanted to dodge the question, but he'd sworn that off, especially with Sage. "No."

"It's been too long, bro. You know what she's going to be thinking."

"That she dodged a bullet?" he suggested.

"If I wasn't so darned happy you're home I'd clobber you for that. Stop thinking that way."

He sighed. "She deserves better than somebody who's—"

"Life is fixed? Settled? Problems resolved? Or who happens to be too pretty for his own good? Or how about a rich property owner, does she deserve that?"

He laughed—he couldn't help it. He'd been laughing a lot lately, now that the initial shock of the radical changes had worn off a bit.

"She loves you, you know. And if you tell me it's too soon I may clobber you anyway."

"I won't. I think we spent a lifetime together just on that ride home from Oklahoma City."

"She's one of the best people I know, Kane," Sage said, her tone serious now. "You'd be a fool to let her slip away."

"Believe me, I know that."

"Then don't let it slide too long. You're not the only one who knows how special she is."

His gaze narrowed sharply as something sharp and vicious sliced deep in his gut. "Are you saying there's somebody else?"

"Ha! Got you, bro. If how you felt just at the thought doesn't wake you up, nothing will."

He stared at this amazing woman that fourteen-year-old girl he remembered had become, and gave a rueful shake of his head. "Scott," he said dryly, "has his work cut out for him."

"Fortunately for him," she said airily, "he's more than up to the task. In every way."

"Whoa. That slid right into TMI."

"Question is, are you?"

That the sexual innuendo of her joking comment had kicked heated memories to life in his brain didn't stop him from realizing his sister was dead serious now. Every night since she'd walked away he'd lain in the dark aching for Lark, but not feeling like he could go to her. Not yet.

I'll be here when you're solid again, and we can try to build something together.

Was he solid again? It was true, he felt better than he'd ever expected to, this soon. He'd made his peace with Steven Highwater, as much as he ever could. It had taken a while, to find the right way. A trip to the cemetery hadn't done it, although it had reawakened the ache he'd carried with him for thirteen years. He'd spent some time staring at the portrait on the living room wall, but what he'd needed hadn't come then, either.

It had only come when Shane, catching him staring at that image, had somehow understood and told him what he had always done when he needed to feel Dad was close. So he'd ridden out to the ledge, and it was there, looking out over the Hill Country he hadn't realized he'd missed so much, that he'd finally felt a sort of calm steal over him. The same kind of steady calm that the man himself had always exuded.

The water trough had been heavy work in the summer

evening heat, and he'd already put in a full day of work, so he went back to his wing and took a quick shower. When he was done and pulling out clean, non-ragged clothes—the novelty of which had still not quite worn off—his gaze landed on the set of keys lying on the dresser. The keys to one of the ranch trucks Scott had given him last week when he'd started his new job, unexpectedly working for Ranger Buckley at the inn.

Finally bought my own, so you might as well take over these wheels. Warning, though, having the truck means you get to run errands and pick up stuff half the time. The man had given him a look of understanding before going on. *That's not necessarily a bad thing, though, when you're trying to find your way in Last Stand again.*

Kane knew he hadn't meant find his way logistically.

He headed back into the main house, thinking he'd grab a Coke to finish cooling off, and putting a stop at the market in town to stock his own small fridge on his mental list for tomorrow. But his steps slowed and then halted when he saw Sean and Shane there, and their conversation ended so abruptly he knew it had to have been about him. And something about the way they had looked—like two cops, not two cowboys—made him nervous.

"Didn't mean to interrupt," he muttered, turning to grab the can from the door rack, intending to go back the way he'd come.

"You didn't. We were waiting for you," Shane said.

Uh-oh. "Why?"

"Easy, bro, it's not an ambush," Sean said with a grin.

"Just a question."

They were learning to read him all too well. He managed not to grimace as he popped the can open. "What?"

Sean deferred to Shane—or maybe his boss—on that one. And Shane asked rather bluntly, "Do you want to find your biological father?"

Kane froze, the can of soda halfway to his mouth. "What?" he repeated, in an entirely different tone.

"We got used to looking for you," Sean said. "We can just as easily switch that over to looking for him, if you want. You'd have to do some DNA testing, and it might come to nothing if he's not in records anywhere, but...we could try."

He'd lost track of how many times they'd stunned him, but this had to be the topper. He stared at them, utterly speechless. They waited. Patiently. Until he was finally able to get out the one thing that seemed most important.

"I thought...I expected y'all to hate me, and now you're offering...this?"

"Glad to hear that Texas creeping back in," Shane said with a smile. "But yes. It's up to you."

I don't know who either of my biological parents are. Never have.

Lark's words on that midnight ride that seemed an eon ago now, rang in his head.

You say that like...

Like it doesn't matter? That's because it doesn't.

He sucked in a long, deep breath. And went with his gut, with the searing, impossible truth.

"It means more to me than I can say that you'd do that.

But it doesn't matter. Not anymore."

The smiles he got from both of them then broke down the last, small barrier in his mind. And when Shane reached out to put a hand on his shoulder, and said quietly, "Glad to hear it, Kane Highwater. Glad to hear it," he accepted it at last.

Kane Highwater. It was his name, a damned good name, and he'd carry it with pride.

"So," Shane said in an entirely different tone, "let me explain about Sunday dinner around here."

He blinked. And for the third time said, "What?"

Shane laughed. "Go get her. You've waited long enough. Kept her waiting long enough."

"But..." Was he ready? Not himself, he'd found his place, dealt with his demons, and felt like he had the strength now to handle any that dared to reappear. He'd found that strength here, with the family who had never abandoned him.

"She's perfect for you," Shane said. "She's perfect for us. The last missing piece to make the Highwater clan complete."

Kane stared at him. That was something his father would have said. And it set up an ache inside him he didn't think he could bear. She was the missing piece for him, too, the piece that would finally make him whole again. But she deserved the best man he could possibly be, and—

"If I can manage it with the Queen of Last Stand," Sean said with a grin, "you can do it with Lark."

The phrase triggered an old memory, of teenaged Sean

calling Elena that. He hadn't understood what he'd meant then. He did now.

"Sunday dinner with the family is a serious thing," Shane said.

Sean's grin widened. "And Monday morning after is a declaration of intent."

Shane lifted a brow at him. "You do have intentions, don't you?"

It welled up inside him like a gusher, like Spindletop gone wild.

"Yes. Yes, I do."

He yanked out the keys he'd stuffed in his pocket and headed for the door.

Chapter Thirty-Six

LARK HEARD THE running steps on the stairs as she finished tidying up her desk after finishing the final reports on the Ainsworth adoption. Jimmy again, she supposed. Although it sounded like someone bigger. Maybe it was—

The knock on her door was urgent, and her pulse kicked up. She ran over, barely remembering to take the precaution of checking the peephole first. When she did, her pulse went into overdrive. Kane.

She pulled the door open swiftly. Before she could say a word he had pulled her into his arms and his mouth came down on hers fiercely. She vaguely heard a slam, realized he'd kicked the door closed. Considering what had happened the last time he'd done this, it was probably just as well.

His hands were on her hungrily, his mouth became more demanding, and she put everything she'd been longing for in the time he'd been gone into kissing him back.

She felt a shiver ripple through him. He broke the kiss and then, unsteadily, he gripped her shoulders. "Did you mean it?" He sounded as breathless as she felt. Or as edgy.

"I meant everything I ever said to you," she answered,

not certain what exactly he was referring to.

He pulled back his hands, and she saw his fingers curl into fists as he stared at her and said in a rush, "I'm home. I'm staying. I've got a job. I've got access to that money now. I've got the papers on my part of the ranch. Is that solid enough?"

She got it then. "That wasn't at all what I meant by 'solid.' But let me ask you one thing."

"Anything."

"What's your name?"

He blinked. But then she saw understanding dawn in eyes that were more gold than anything right now. "Kane Travis Highwater," he said, and his voice was steady now. Steady enough to tell her he meant it, and understood why she'd asked.

"That's all I really needed to know," she said softly.

And this time it was she who grabbed him, kissed him with all the need that had built up since she'd kissed him last.

WHEN HIS HANDS slid over sleek, bare skin Kane realized he'd slipped them under her shirt. It hadn't been his intention, but once he felt the incredible, silken softness of her he knew he was lost. He'd never felt anything like this in his life, and he knew he just wasn't strong enough to resist. And the fact that she was pushing and pulling at his clothes as fast as he was hers only added to the urgency.

It took everything he had in him, every bit of hard-won determination to stop for even a moment.

"Lark?"

It was all he could get out. He just had to hope she understood the question he couldn't find the breath to ask. He understood, finally, why she'd called a halt before. He'd understood it since the day he'd gone to bed in his wing and realized just as he was falling asleep that he hadn't thought once about leaving, that he'd slipped into a role here so easily and completely, that he now thought of the ranch as what he'd just called it. Home.

But she had to be sure. To be sure that he didn't need her anymore, not in the way he had at first.

But he sure as hell needed her.

"Yes," she said, her own hands still moving over him as if she felt the same hunger. "Yes, yes."

Her eagerness gave him back the breath to ask, "You're sure?"

"If you're prepared."

It took him a second, it had been so long. But he remembered the condom the crew lead aboard the *Kenai King* had jokingly stuffed in his pocket, saying he needed to go out and use it. He'd had no interest then.

He hadn't known Lark, then.

And he'd put it back in his pocket this morning.

"Never thought I'd thank that jerk," he muttered as he dug out the packet. She laughed, cupped his face with her hands, and kissed him. Heat flared at the first touch of her lips, and he pulled her hard against him. Then she was tasting him as if she couldn't get enough, and the heat became an inferno.

He'd never set foot in her bedroom, but he still knew it was too far away. They went down to the couch where they'd spent that night, when she'd held him like the broken soul he'd been, and then given him the chance to retake his life.

He didn't even care how awkward it was, or that he'd knocked something over kicking free of his jeans and getting her out of her clothes, all he cared about was the feel of her, the sight of her, naked now in his arms. He cupped her breasts. They rounded soft and warm into his hands, the peaks already tight and ready. He flicked his tongue over them, and when she moaned in response he nearly lost it right then.

He tried to hold back, because he wanted to kiss every inch of her until she was as hot, as needy as he was feeling right now. But then she arched against him, capturing aching, rigid flesh between them, and he knew he wouldn't hold out that long. He tried to explain, to tell her how long it had been for him, to apologize for what he knew was going to be way too fast.

"It's been—" She cut off his words abruptly when she reached between them to curl her fingers around him.

"Inevitable," she finished for him, the touch combined with the husky note in her voice nearly sending him over the edge right then.

He snapped. "Imperative," he said, and it came out almost a growl.

And then he was sliding into her slick, welcoming heat,

feeling her flesh clasping his, and nothing else mattered except the rising, driving need. He clenched his jaw with the effort to slow himself down, to make it last. But when he heard her gasp out his name, when he felt her clench around him, and realized she'd been as close to the edge as he had, he let go with a guttural groan that echoed the explosion of his body.

And it hit him with all the wonder of the Northern Lights or anything else he'd seen on that list, that Lark, only Lark, was the real answer to the question he'd never dared ask, where and what he was meant to be.

―

"THIS IS…"

"Luscious? Decadent? Heart attack inducing?" Lark suggested.

He grinned. "Probably all three. I've never had—or even thought of—French toast with cinnamon rolls before."

"And you should probably keep it that way for at least a year, considering the calories."

"Okay." He got out his phone, called up the calendar app.

"What are you doing?"

"Marking this day next year, so we remember."

The smile she gave him then was brighter than the Texas sun. "I like the sound of that."

"I love you, Lark Leclair."

"And I you, Kane Highwater."

He smiled at the name he was getting used to again. The name he'd reclaimed.

The name that had one day made him ride up to that Hill Country ledge where Steven Highwater used to go, and fervently thank the man who had given it to him. And the peace that had filled him in that moment had been the turning point, the time when the Highwater ranch had once more felt utterly and completely like home.

As had become almost habit he called up an image on the phone, the picture of the picture that was once again framed on his desk. The picture that was so full of love it sometimes still scared him to remember how badly he'd distorted it in his mind. It was a lesson he would never forget.

Lark came over and leaned on his shoulder to see what he was looking at.

"I'm glad you have him back," she said softly.

"Me, too." He gave her a sideways glance.

"What was that look for?" she asked.

"Just wondering if that brain of mine distorted…something else."

"What?"

"Last night."

She held his gaze levelly. "If you're remembering it as the wildest, hottest sex in the history of sex, then I'd say no, no distortion there."

She said it with such heartfelt sincerity there suddenly wasn't enough air in the room. There might not be enough in the world. He was speechless. Not talking was not a rarity for him. In fact it was more the norm. But it was usually because he didn't want to talk, not because he couldn't think of anything to say. Not because every word had been blasted out of his head. Every word except one.

"Lark..."

"It was everything I imagined it would be, and more." Her voice was tinged with the same kind of wonder he was feeling, roiling around inside him at the memories of how explosive they were together.

He was still struggling with words. "You...imagined?"

"I've been imagining it since the first instant I saw you at the arena." She paused, looking at him in that way he'd learned meant her next words would be the point. "Before I even realized it was you."

He stared at her. Until this instant, the thought hadn't crystallized in his head, that he'd been afraid it had only happened because she felt...responsible somehow, for making him come back here. But if a spark had happened before she'd even known who he was—just as it had happened for him, with the first sight of her—that blasted that idea.

And the last doubt he had vanished. About her feelings, anyway. He'd known his from that first instant.

You wanted her in bed before you even knew her name.

When he didn't speak she lowered her gaze, and her voice had suddenly gone tiny when she said, "I guess I shouldn't have admitted that, huh?"

It was the first time he'd ever heard self-doubt in her tone, and it jabbed at him. And before he could stop himself he'd reached out and gently lifted her chin with fingers he was surprised weren't shaking. And he knew he had to give her the truth.

"Why not? I felt the same way. I was in the middle of what I thought was the biggest mistake I'd made in a decade, but all I could think when I first saw you was that...I didn't even know your name but you were making me feel things I hadn't let myself feel in even longer. Want things...want you."

This time they made it to her bed. And gave her overactive neighbor some competition. And later, sated and lazily wrapped around each other, Kane asked how she'd feel about leaving her overactive neighbor behind for a quieter, more private place, a certain wing of the house on the Highwater ranch.

A place that wouldn't truly be his home again unless she was in it.

"ARE YOU CRAZY?" Kane stared at his eldest brother. Shane had blown up his equilibrium completely with this suggestion that Kane be his best man at his wedding.

"Sometimes, I'm told," Shane said easily, as if it were just another Sunday afternoon.

Kane was sure that was true. He'd seen the videos now, not just the "hell or high water" one with the fools deciding to take down the chief as he escorts them to court, but the one where Shane had taken out a terrorist headed to a packed stadium wearing a suicide vest. The only reason he was still alive was that the dead man's switch malfunctioned. But he'd been willing to do that, to sacrifice himself to save thousands of others he didn't even know.

"But Slater—"

"Is all for it," that brother said from behind him.

"And he knew better than to ask me," Sean said cheerfully. "I mean, I would have done it, for him, but I would have hated being in the spotlight like that."

Kane turned to look at Slater. "But...his best man? It should be you. You're the next oldest, and you're not butting heads all the time now and you doing it...well, it symbolizes that."

Something shifted in Slater's distinctive, blue-green eyes. "Well, well. Emerson said 'Wisdom has its root in goodness, and not goodness its root in wisdom.' Remember that the next time you get to feeling you don't deserve your place here, brother mine."

"You doing it symbolizes to everyone that you have all of us behind you," Sage put in.

"And half the town's going to be there," Lily said, looking rather uneasy. "Apparently the chief getting married is a huge deal in Last Stand."

"But...it's only a couple of weeks away. You can't change it now." He was starting to feel a bit queasy. He'd only been back in Last Stand for a month, but he knew Lily was right. Half the town would be there in one way or another, including the mayor. And Judge Morales would be there—he'd mentioned it at their meeting last week. He was a little surprised they weren't throwing a parade.

"Could I make a suggestion?" Lark asked from beside him. Beside him, where she'd always been, even when he'd tried to push her away, telling himself it was for her own good. But Shane had been right, she'd been the missing piece that made the Highwater clan complete.

We did it...Dad.

"You," Shane said to Lark firmly, "can make suggestions like anyone else in this family."

Kane felt his throat tighten, saw color tinge Lark's cheeks at all the assumptions contained in that statement. Saw the warmth in her eyes when she turned her gaze on him. A warmth he'd work every day of the rest of his life to deserve.

"Sing for them," she said.

He blinked. "*What?*"

"It's what you can do for them that no one else can," she said.

"Yes!" Sage yelped, clearly excited at the idea.

Kane turned the idea over in his mind. Played with it for a moment. It would be a symbol, of sorts, but not one that would displace one of the brothers he'd just regained. He'd be nervous. He hadn't really sung in front of anyone—except Lark, that night on a dark road—since he'd been aboard the *Kenai King*, when they'd made that huge catch and were celebrating.

He looked at his brother, who was nodding, clearly liking the idea. "I'll do it," Kane said. "For you, I'll do it."

"Leave it to Lark to come up with the best ideas!" Joey exclaimed.

He smiled at his former lab partner, then turned to the woman who had so changed his life. "For the best ideas, I always leave it to Lark," he said, not even trying to hide the roughness emotion had put in his voice.

And for the first time in over a decade, he felt his eyes sting with tears. That they were the good kind, from a happiness he'd never expected to find, was just another of the gifts she'd given him.

Later, with relatively new rider Lark aboard their gentlest, calmest horse, Whiskers, and him riding the rangy buckskin he'd established a bond with in the past weeks, they headed out for a ride. She'd taken to riding, and the ranch, like someone who'd dreamed about the life for years. And only in the face of her delight was he able to admit, even to himself, just how much he'd missed both those things.

"How does it feel," she asked as they cleared the first rise, "to be riding over land you own?"

He gave a slow shake of his head. He was still having trouble wrapping his mind around that fact. "It's good just to be here," he said finally.

"I ran into Ranger Buckley this morning, coming out of the bakery." She'd brought a selection from Kolaches that had had them all satisfying their cravings this morning. "He said he was really glad he'd hired you."

One corner of his mouth quirked up. "He's a good guy. Intimidating as hell, but a good guy. And I like the work. It's always something different—one day in the garden, one day repairs, one day carpentry, one day something else."

"So all the skills you picked up on your journey are coming in handy."

"Yeah," he said with a rather sheepish smile.

"You know what I'd like to do, once the wedding is done and things settle down?"

"You mean until Slater and Joey tie the knot?" he said rather wryly.

"And then Sean and Elena?" she said, grinning. "And Scott and Sage?"

"Yeah, them too." *And us? Someday?* It was a thought that had been straying into his mind a lot lately. And on that someday—but not too distant—he hoped he'd feel enough like he deserved her to ask her. "But what do you want to do?" he asked now, thinking he'd do anything with her. Anything for her.

"I'd like to go to the Grand Canyon."

He blinked. "What?"

"I want to meet Zeb." The grin widened. "And Jasper."

His chest tightened almost unbearably at the thought that she'd want to do that. "I'd...like to do that. I never really thanked Zeb for everything he did for me."

"In fact, I'd like to meet everyone who helped you along the way. But this is a place to start. Maybe you could do a drawing for him, of him and Jasper."

He smiled widely at that. Joey was right, leave it to Lark to have the best ideas. "I could do that."

"Then let's go. Maybe after summer, when it's less crowded and it would be easier for the Buckleys to do without you." He laughed at that, and she gave him an arched brow. "Didn't I mention his wife was with him, and she said she didn't know how they'd gotten along without you?"

He gaped at her. "She did?"

"She did," Lark confirmed.

He had no idea what to say to that, so they rode on in silence for a while. It wasn't the height of summer yet, so there was still some green around. And then Lark practically blasted him out of the saddle with one simple question.

"Do you ever want kids?"

"I...what?"

"Simple question," she said. So casually he didn't know what to think.

"I...don't know. I've never thought about it."

"Never dared to?"

"Pretty much," he admitted. "Lark, are you asking if...what *are* you asking?"

She turned her head to look at him directly. "Easy, Highwater," she said, using the name easily. It still gave him a small jolt, but he was getting used to it again. "I didn't necessarily mean ours." She added with another one of those grins that leveled him, "Yet."

The thought that this woman would even consider children with him took his breath away, and it was a long moment before he could get out an echoing, "Yet."

Something flashed in those light green eyes and a sudden image formed in his mind, of the future, brighter than he ever could have hoped for. "You know staying for Sunday dinner tonight is a thing around here," he said abruptly.

"So I've heard. Even before you asked." She gave him a

sideways look. "Joey told me it was a big deal. And Elena told me it's practically a declaration. Sage just said 'About time.'"

He grimaced at the last one. It had taken him too damned long to get his balance again. "Did they tell you what staying over for Monday breakfast means?"

"No."

He'd asked her to stay over, but he hadn't explained. And now his voice was nearly hoarse as he said, "It means those kids might be closer than you thought."

Her cheeks pinkened again. He liked that, it made it easier for him to tell what she was feeling, and he needed every advantage he could get.

"Good to know we're on the same page. But actually, I was thinking you'd make a good foster dad."

He drew back sharply, and his horse's head came up at the sudden movement. "I...what? They'd never let me do that, with my history."

"I think you're exactly what they need," she declared. "Somebody who understands the desperation a kid can feel."

"Somebody who's weak enough to run instead of face it?" The old bitterness rose up for the first time in weeks, almost startling him.

"Weak? You call surviving on your own at sixteen weak? You think going hungry instead of selling yourself is weak? Or doing backbreaking physical labor to make enough to buy a sandwich weak? Don't you dare, Kane Highwater. If anybody's weak it's me. I couldn't handle the kids who needed help the most. I had to walk away because I wasn't strong enough to—"

"Stop it!" He reached out and grabbed her free wrist. "You're so far from weak it's ridiculous to even use the word."

She looked at him and smiled. "Back at you."

He stared at her. Then smiled wryly. "You set me up."

"Moi?" she asked innocently.

He was still smiling at her when they reached the spot he'd been headed for, that he wanted to show her. It had become a frequent destination for them all. They dismounted and he led her over to the limestone ledge that looked out over a huge expanse of the rolling Hill Country that, he knew now, had never been out of his heart.

They sat in the shade of a Shumard red oak that Shane had once said his father had planted here decades ago for just that reason.

"This was his place," he said, knowing he didn't have to explain who, not to Lark. "It's where he came to sit and think, to wrestle with a problem." He took in a deep breath. "He probably came here about me more than once."

"I can see why," Lark said, looking out into the distance. "There's a sort of peace here in this spot. A calming."

"I've been out here a lot, lately. Sometimes…it's like I can almost feel him here." He looked out over the hills. "I came here once to thank him. For loving me, for giving me his name."

She reached out and took his hand. "I'm glad. If his spirit lingers anywhere, it would be here," she said. "And if there's anyone he would linger for, it would be you."

He stared at her. "Why would you think that?"

She lifted one shoulder, as if the answer was obvious. And maybe it was, to her. "He knew the others would be okay, that Shane would see to them as he'd promised. And as Elena told us, it was you he was worried about in his last moments. It only makes sense."

It did, in a sort of way he still found hard to accept. "I used to wonder, when I heard people talking about...her, why he stayed. Why he kept trying with her."

"He stayed because he loved his children. All of them," she added pointedly. "And maybe..."

"What?" he asked when she hesitated, unlike her.

It was a moment before she met his gaze and answered. "I have the feeling that when a Highwater loves, they love true. And completely."

A slow smile curved his mouth, and he reached out and took both her hands in his. "This one does," he said wholeheartedly. "I love you, Lark."

The smile she gave him then was brighter than the sunrise he sometimes watched from this very spot. "I will never get tired of hearing that," she said. "Or saying it. I love you, Kane Highwater. And I love that you're finally home at last."

"This is my last stand," he promised.

Because she was right—as usual.

Epilogue

HE HELD THE book in his hands, smiling that it smelled so new. It was beyond amazing to see the cover, that quick, silly sketch he'd done of the raccoon, who was now in full color and looking very wise.

He ran a finger over her name under the title, *RUTHERFORD Q. RACCOON FINDS HIS WAY HOME.*

And below the drawing, the unexpected, the "Illustrated by Kane Highwater."

His eyes stung a little and he lifted his gaze to the room around him. The walls were decorated with a few of the sketches from the book now—minus any of the dark, shadowy figure they'd created, meant to warn children that sometimes you couldn't tell who the monster was, while at the same time impressing upon them that there were good people who want to help.

But it was the one that was awaiting framing that he liked best. It wasn't a caricature but an actual pencil drawing of her he'd done as she talked to the children who had come to the first reading of the new book at the library just today. That one was going to hang in their bedroom.

Their bedroom. His life had changed so much it was still

sometimes hard for him to believe. He had his family back, expanded by five very different people who still somehow managed to be a perfect fit. And he'd added two more after a trip to Austin to meet the parents who had raised this incredible woman, and who with their quiet, unshakable adoration for the daughter they'd chosen removed the final nail from that coffin he felt like he'd been in since that day, freeing him once and for all. What had happened was still horribly sad, but it no longer tortured him. Nor did the dreams, not when he had Lark in his arms every night.

His job had expanded as well, when Karina Buckley had overheard him singing while he was working one day and insisted he perform for the guests at the inn, which had ballooned into a regular occurrence and earned him a local following he'd never have expected.

But most of all he had Lark, who had made it all possible and kept him sane with her steady, unwavering love.

He heard her before she leaned down behind him and rested her arms on his shoulders as he sat on the couch in their living room. "It's beautiful," he said as he touched the cover again. The copies of the hardbound, children's sized book had been delivered barely in time, and this was the first time he'd had a chance to really look at it.

She reached past him and pulled open the cover. "This is what you really need to read," she said as she turned a couple of pages.

And this time he read the dedication through blurry eyes.

Again for Kane
Who faced the monsters, found his way home, and won.

With all my love.

He couldn't speak. She simply overwhelmed him with the power of that love. She didn't try to change him, or insist he get past everything that haunted him forever, she simply understood. And loved.

And now that he'd met her parents, who quite clearly adored her—and who had accepted him without question—he understood a little better why she was the woman she was.

It was a couple of minutes before he could get any words out at all. And when he did, they weren't what he wanted to say but all he could say.

"When I called, Zeb said he has new great-grandkids."

"Then we'd better pack a copy of both books," she said, and when he looked up at her he saw in those beloved green eyes that she'd understood once more. Everything.

"When we get back, maybe we can talk more about...the foster kid thing." It was the only thing he could think of right now that would show her just how much he loved her. And the way she looked at him, smiled at him, and the warmth in her voice when she answered told him she'd understood that, too.

"I think the ranch would be a great place for a kid to find the right path."

He gave her a crooked smile. "With you for a guide, anyway."

"I think the best guide is one who's already walked that path," she said, and leaned down to kiss him. "And, it'll give you practice."

"Practice?"

"For one of our own someday."

To his continued amazement he no longer panicked at the idea. In fact, he welcomed it. And even he had to acknowledge he'd come a very long way. That he had what he'd never dared hope for, and only because of this amazing, incredible woman.

She'd made it all possible, and now it had happened.

Kane Highwater had come home.

The End

Want more? Check out Shane and Liliana's story in *The Lone Star Lawman*!

Sign up for Tule's newsletter for more great reads and weekly deals!

If you enjoyed *Lone Star Homecoming,*
you'll love the other books in....

The Texas Justice series

Book 1: *Lone Star Lawman*

Book 2: *Lone Star Nights*

Book 3: *A Lone Star Christmas*

Book 4: *Lone Star Reunion*

Book 5: *Lone Star Homecoming*

Available now at your favorite online retailer!

More books by Justine Davis

The Whiskey River series

Book 1: *Whiskey River Rescue*

Book 2: *Whiskey River Runaway*

Book 3: *Whiskey River Rockstar*

Available now at your favorite online retailer!

About the Author

Author of more than 70 books, (she sold her first ten in less than two years) Justine Davis is a five time winner of the coveted RWA RITA Award, including for being inducted into the RWA Hall of Fame. A fifteen time nominee for RT Book Review awards, she has won four times, received three of their lifetime achievement awards, and had four titles on the magazine's 200 Best of all Time list. Her books have appeared on national best seller lists, including USA Today. She has been featured on CNN, taught at several national and international conferences, and at the UCLA writer's program.

After years of working in law enforcement, and more years doing both, Justine now writes full time. She lives near beautiful Puget Sound in Washington State, peacefully coexisting with deer, bears, a pair of bald eagles, a tailless raccoon, and her beloved '67 Corvette roadster. When she's not writing, taking photographs, or driving said roadster (and yes, it goes very fast) she tends to her knitting. Literally.

Visit Justine at her website JustineDavis.com